DEAD MAN'S HANDS

DAVID J. GATWARD

WEIRDSTONE PUBLISHING

Dead Man's Hands
by
David J. Gatward

Copyright © 2023 by David J. Gatward
All rights reserved.

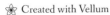 Created with Vellum

To Mandy, for being brave and crazy enough to host the first ever DCI Harry Grimm event at The Fountain Inn!

Grimm: nickname for a dour and forbidding individual, from Old High German grim [meaning] 'stern', 'severe'. From a Germanic personal name, Grima, [meaning] 'mask'. (*www.ancestory.co.uk*)

ONE

The only reason Lance Hamilton had decided to go to the meeting that Friday evening was because he hadn't been invited. Not that the meeting had been by invitation only; anyone who had wanted to go along could. But no one—not even his own supposed son, though that was hardly a surprise—had mentioned it to him, not even in passing, and that riled him.

Leaving his vehicle in the car park behind the primary school, the soft, bright light of the evening glinting off the deep red paintwork, Lance made his way down into Hawes and along to the Market Hall, to see what all the fuss was about. Not that he really needed to drive there at all, but leaving a vehicle standing for too long was never a good idea, certainly not one as old as his. And he rather enjoyed driving around in a classic.

The massive bonnet of the Jaguar 1982 XJS certainly made him smile, not least because he'd won the car in a card game a couple of months ago, much to the blatant irritation of the player, who had put it in the pot in a moment of mad, misplaced confidence. He'd won other things playing poker over the years, and a good amount of money, too, but the car, well, it was the best pot he'd ever taken home, that was for sure.

The excursion would also give him the chance to deliver the

note he had in his pocket, and that turned his smile into a smug grin. It had, after all, been a long time coming. And the thought of the look on the recipient's face when he eventually gave it to them, caused Lance's grin to break into a laugh.

The evening was warm, even for July, the Dales having baked under the sun for long enough that rain was almost a distant memory. And yet, as Lance gazed out beyond the houses that made up the small market town at the top of Wensleydale, the green hues of the valley, fells, and fields were not only lush but radiant. He had come to realise that green here was not a single colour, but a vast and constantly turning wheel of myriad shades, as though an artist's palette had been spilled.

Lance had the urge to pinch himself for being lucky enough to live here at all, and in many ways, luck had quite a lot to do with it. There was no doubt that he'd worked hard, invested wisely. Luck, though, had also held his hand, and not just metaphorically either. To Lance, life was one big poker game. He had gambled and won more times than he'd ever lost, but then he had always believed if you wanted to make money, you had to take risks. It was just a pity that some people were such poor losers.

Moving to the Dales in his mid-forties had been one of the easiest decisions Lance had ever made, and after sorting out his affairs, he'd transported himself and the family away from a brick-and-tarmac metropolis to Herriot Country.

Gone were the noise and the hustle and bustle, the constant need to rush everywhere, and a life fueled by high pressure, coffee shops, and a few too many croissants and bagels. In their place was a peace and quiet Lance had never really known he'd needed until he'd experienced it; clean, fresh air, a commute along ancient lanes threaded over centuries through field and fell, and a sense that he had somehow learned to not only breathe again, but sleep.

Wensleydale was a place of personal healing and professional success for Lance, and his business venture was built on that belief. The glossy marketing materials, his website, made that especially clear.

Now, ten years after that initial move, he had a large and ever-growing portfolio of high-end holiday cottages across the area, and each one promised a little oasis of calm, an escape from the greedy, drooling maw of modern life, a chance for those who worked hard in the city to take a deep dive into the embrace of the Dales and recharge.

It had worked for him; he wanted it to work for others, though at a price, obviously. Indeed, why should the locals be the only ones to benefit? A place like Wensleydale should be accessed by the many, not just kept for the few. Well, so long as they could afford what he was offering. Such a place was a vital resource for those who had given up so much by living in the city. And it was Lance who helped them access it and enjoy it.

Having arrived at the meeting a little early, Lance decided to go for a short walk, and took himself from the marketplace and up the thin, dark path between the church and the graveyard, the dead kept at bay by stern iron railings mottled with rust, and grass overgrown and spotted with purple and white clover. At the end of the path, he then tramped out onto the narrow flagstone path that connected Hawes and Gayle like an artery.

The walk along the path, where sheep starred at him from fields while grazing, and below him the scalloped limestone bed of Gayle beck gave song to the water's path, though little there was of it, allowed Lance to drink in the distant view of Wether Fell. Yes, the sight was utterly astonishing to behold, but it also reinforced just how strongly he believed that his business was not simply profitable—and it was, very much so—but also a worthwhile endeavor.

A while later, he left the footpath to head past the creamery and across the fields back down into Hawes. Lance knew he provided tourists with the best holiday homes in the area, perhaps even the country. He'd won awards that said as much. He was also bringing money into the Dales because tourists loved to buy things and visit cafés and restaurants and local attractions, and that, in turn, helped with local employment. This meeting then was perhaps a good opportunity to point these things out to those who saw him as the enemy. Some more than others, perhaps, though they had their reasons. The reason behind the letter in his pocket was a sure enough sign of that.

Slipping into the Market Hall, Lance found that although the large room wasn't exactly full, there were certainly enough people for him to keep a low profile and take a seat in the back row. Of course, someone would notice him soon enough, but he wasn't there to make a scene, not yet anyway, and not unless he felt either compelled to or was given little choice in the matter. He just wanted to know what all the fuss was about, and if his opinion was sought, then he would provide it.

The small room to the side was open to provide tea, coffee, and biscuits, but Lance avoided that, and leaned forward to keep his head down, as though busy with something hugely important on his phone.

At the front of the hall was a table, behind which were two seats facing all the others. Lance had a good idea who would soon occupy them.

A shadow fell across Lance, and someone sat down beside him, a little too close for comfort, he thought. Either that, or they were simply far too large for the chair they'd plonked themselves down on. Then a warm breath invaded his space with a heady scent of beer, tobacco, and just at the back of it all, cheese-and-onion crisps. He knew exactly who it was and sighed. Not a good start, but it was to be expected, all things considered.

'Come along to see what else you can get your grubby little hands on, is that it?'

Lance ignored the comment and kept staring at the game he was playing on his phone.

A finger prodded his shoulder.

'I'm talking to you, Hamilton.'

'Clearly.'

'You're not going to look at me, then?'

The voice did little to improve the smell, riddled as it was with the rattle of phlegm at the back of the throat.

Lance gave up on the game and turned to face his new neighbour.

'Hello, Mr Fothergill,' he said.

The man leaned in a little closer, his face a landscape carved out by a life lived outside. Lance couldn't help but stare at the valleys and cliffs where wrinkles had no doubt once been. This was a man who could have been any age between fifty and a hundred, and he didn't look all that good for either end of the spectrum. With large hands, broad shoulders, and what little hair he had scraped back with Brylcreem, there was an air of vintage threat to him, Lance thought, almost as though he had stepped right out of the 1940s to bother him now.

'Don't you Mr Fothergill me,' the man spat through gritted teeth, and leaned in even further to the point where Lance pushed himself back in his own seat.

'My apologies,' Lance replied. 'So, what brings you here this evening, Aldwin?'

Aldwin's eyes grew wide, his jaw clenched, amusing Lance with how sometimes simple politeness was the best defence, and that using the man's first name had only riled him further.

'You know bloody well what,' Aldwin said. 'You, and what you did, you greedy git.'

'I didn't do anything,' Lance said, and watched Aldwin's eyes almost pop out of his worn, haggard face.

'You bought their house, didn't you, you bastard? That's what you did. And I'm sitting here right now to tell you to give it back.'

Lance sighed, constantly amazed by people's lack of business acumen; it wasn't personal. Well, not all the time, anyway. This was a different case, but he wasn't about to let on. Not to Aldwin, anyway.

'First of all, it wasn't their house because it was only under offer,' he said. 'Contracts hadn't been signed or exchanged; it was entirely above board. And I can't exactly give something back to someone when it wasn't theirs in the first place, can I? All I did was make the seller a better offer. Simple business, nothing more.'

Aldwin laughed, the sound cold and twisted by disbelief.

'There's more to it, though, isn't there?' he said. 'I know there is, and I won't have you or anyone else telling me anything different.' He tapped the side of his nose. 'I've already got a sniff of what it is, too, like, so that's a warning to you, you hear?'

Lance asked, 'Are you threatening me, Aldwin? I've done nothing illegal.'

But Aldwin wasn't listening and was now on his feet.

'It was going to be their first house,' he spat, Lance now completely in his shadow. 'No, it was going to be more than that. It was going to be their first home, and whatever you did, you've ruined it all for them, haven't you?'

'At risk of repeating myself, *not illegal*,' said Lance, putting emphasis on the last two words.

'You've no shame, have you?' Aldwin said. 'Not a bit of it. And with her being pregnant and all?'

Aldwin's voice was reaching a loud enough volume to draw stares from across the room and Lance saw eyes fall on him, then narrow with obvious distaste.

'There's nothing I can do,' Lance said. 'A deal is a deal. I'm sure they'll find somewhere else.'

Without any warning, Aldwin lunged at Lance and grabbed his collar.

'You're a greedy little bastard, that's what you are!' he said, shaking Lance enough to make his chair move, his voice now raised to a bellowing shout. 'Do you know how difficult it is for anyone to buy a house round here, never mind trying to do it when you're young? Do you? No, of course you don't, because you just swan around with your fat wallet and fancy ways, don't you? Well, it shouldn't be allowed. Folk like you, coming up here, buying places that the locals need, making a bad situation worse. It's not right! It's not right at all!'

Lance did his best to ignore the clenched fist at his throat and stared up at the man who was glaring down at him with not just hatred, but genuine hurt; there were tears in his eyes. Then Lance saw a small, pale hand slip under Aldwin's arm and try to pull him away.

Aldwin resisted for a moment or two, but finally, his shoulders slumped, and he gave in.

'It shouldn't be allowed, it just shouldn't!' he muttered, as Aldwin's wife, Karen, led her husband off to another part of the hall. 'That man, he's done something, I know it. Bribed someone, I reckon. I'll prove it, too. I will, you just watch me.'

Karen's intervention didn't stop Aldwin from staring back at Lance, nor anyone else he noticed. As she forced him to sit down, he roared, 'You'll get yours, Hamilton, you mark my words! You've had it coming for years, you shite arse!'

Lance straightened his collar and ignored him.

Now that everyone knew he was there, he leaned back in his chair and folded his arms, trying his utmost to look relaxed. Hopefully, the meeting would be over quickly, and he could then nip to the pub for a swift one in a quiet corner, maybe even have a packet of crisps.

He was in the middle of enjoying a fantasy about cold beer, deciding then that he would leave his car and walk home, allowing him the chance to have a few beers, when someone stood up behind the table at the front of the hall and everyone gradually fell quiet.

Lance smiled knowingly; as he'd suspected, the man who was leading proceedings was that bloody annoying little accountant, Andrew Wilson. Yes, the man was certainly good at what he did, which was a relief, because it wasn't like local accountants were easy to come by, but that didn't mean Lance had to like him.

He was the kind of man Lance would describe as damp, insipid even. An over-used tea bag of a man. None of this was helped by how, when he wasn't at work in his accountant's get-up of grey suit, white shirt, and too much aftershave, Andrew was usually found wearing his other costume, that being a threadbare linen jacket, white shirt, cravat, and most ridiculous of all, a tweed baker boy hat turned backwards. Despite his age, which Lance put at probably around the same as his own—not that he had ever confirmed it—he sported a beard comprised mainly of stubble, neatly shaved, like he had at some point in his life wished to be a lookalike for George Michael in his post-Wham! days.

Andrew was someone to whom directing the local amateur dramatics group was clearly up there with being on the West End or Broadway. Following a sudden illness that had rendered the regular director out of action, he had stepped in to take over the production of the group's current show, and he managed to mix theatric fawning with such an astonishing lack of charm, that Lance wondered how the man didn't simply dissolve under the sun.

Beside Andrew sat a woman Lance easily recognised, though had he been blindfolded, he felt sure he could have sensed her regardless, and probably heard her sniffing out his wallet. The greedy little cow. Nice arse, though, he thought with a lewd grin. If he was honest, other than her truly fantastic rear end, he couldn't help wondering why he had married her in the first place. It had seemed like a good idea at the time, true enough, the kind of thing everyone did at least once. He'd never do it again, though. God, no.

Lance couldn't resist raising a hand to give her a little wave. She spotted him, stared back, her eyes cold as stone, then lifted her hand to rub her cheek. So, it's still hurting then, he thought. Good. She'd had it coming, much like the divorce, which he hoped wouldn't take too long to sort out. Her feckless son had been a little luckier, ducking out of the way in time to avoid receiving some of the same himself. He'd already been taught his lesson, though, so Lance wasn't too bothered.

It was at this point that his musings on his failed marriage and disappointing stepson were interrupted as Andrew drew himself up to his full height, such as it was, and spoke.

TWO

'Enough! Please, will everyone just calm down!'

Andrew's voice was surprisingly loud and clear, which was a good thing, as the meeting had only been going for fifteen minutes, and already the hall was echoing with the sound of angry people trying to make their point while others did the same. Lance thought the sound was like gulls and stray dogs fighting over fish scraps. He could easily imagine the small weasel of a man enjoying berating anyone foolish enough to tread the boards for him. That Lance's wife, Leslie, was happy to put up with it didn't surprise him; she'd had delusions of her own acting greatness for as long as he had known her.

Much like the alliteration of their names, the way she would trot off to various auditions for bit parts on adverts or the odd television show had been endearing. It had even been a bit of a turn-on, a little fantasy Lance could have all to himself, that she was a big television star, and he was her secret bit of rough away from the spotlight and camera flashes. Plus, she was a few years younger than him, and looked bloody good hanging off his arm, or she had, back in the early days when they'd liked each other.

Then they'd got married, and after an enjoyable honeymoon period of a few years, things had rolled steadily downhill, not exactly helped by the fact that Lance really wasn't cut out for being a stepdad, and certainly not for a stepson like the one he'd acquired. He'd tried, bought the lad things, but his generosity hadn't been reciprocated with what Lance regarded as reasonable expectations of quiet and being left to get on with things.

That this dulling of ardour had been acerbated by his moving them north, obviously occurred to Lance, but Leslie hadn't exactly been in a position to argue, had she? There was only so much dream chasing that Lance could support, and eventually he'd drawn a line under it, told Leslie and her son, Archie, that they were moving, and that was that.

She had protested, said how going to auditions would be impossible, that she hadn't gone to drama school so that she could just up sticks and move to the arse end of nowhere, that it wasn't fair to her son. What about his schooling, his friends?

Lance's answer had been quite simple, 'Get a proper job, then.' And she had, but only after they had moved; she now worked as Andrew's personal assistant.

The marriage had quickly turned from love and passion, to acceptance and convenience, and finally, to an emptiness so echoing and hollow that he'd filed for divorce.

'But he's half the problem, isn't he?' a tall, thin man said, standing and jabbing a finger in Lance's direction like a leafless tree caught in a sharp breeze, and pulling him from his thoughts. 'Well, not just him, but those like him. Cheats.'

Though he didn't know the man's name, Lance recognised him. He stayed quietly in his seat, though his hand unconsciously jangled his car keys, and couldn't help but smirk.

'No, he's all of it, if you ask me,' said another, though who it was, Lance couldn't quite see.

A woman's voice chipped in with, 'Oh, you don't know the half of what he's like,' and Lance caught sight of her, dressed as usual in clay-stained dungarees.

'We've not come here to throw stones, have we?' Andrew said, flapping his hands gently in front of him as though trying to calm down a naughty child. 'This is a discussion about local housing and what we can all do to improve it.'

'And I've just told you how we can improve it,' the man on his feet said.

Lance watched Andrew turn to Leslie, who handed him a sheet from the notes she had been taking.

'What you actually suggested, Mr Weatherill,' said Andrew, turning to read from the sheet, 'and this is the censored version, obviously, because we can't have the minutes filled with expletives, was that we should, "tar and feather Mr Hamilton, force him to sell all of his properties to locals, then run him out of town."'

'Well, it would work, wouldn't it?' Jeff replied, and Lance enjoyed how indignant the man sounded.

'No, it would not work,' Andrew replied. 'For a start, it would be illegal.'

'It's what he deserves, though; they all do, bloody incomers.'

They all do? thought Lance. What on earth did this Jeff mean by *all*? Who else was there? Did he really mean anyone and everyone who had bought a property locally but hadn't actually been born in the Dales and couldn't trace their family tree back generations?

'I'm an incomer, too, Jeff,' said Andrew. 'Remember that. In fact, quite a few people here are, all of whom have come along to try and help solve the problem.'

'Yes, but you're all different to that bastard sitting over there, aren't you?' Jeff replied. 'You're not trying to buy up half the dale! And anyway, he's a liar and a cheat, I can promise you that for nowt.'

'What do you mean, exactly?' Andrew asked.

Jeff looked like he was about to say something, but the words didn't come.

Lance smiled knowingly to himself about that.

'As I've said, this isn't about throwing stones or apportioning blame,' Andrew continued.

'Then what is it about?'

'Trying to find a solution, to work out a way to get new houses built, to look at planning in the area, to see if we can sit down with the local council and—'

'I still say a bit of tar and feathering would be a bloody sight more effective,' Jeff grumbled, and slumped back down into his chair.

Another man raised a hand, then stood up, his large frame dwarfing everyone in the room.

'Mr Calvert,' said Andrew. 'You wish to say something?'

'We can't just go blaming anyone and everyone,' the man said. 'It's not just folk from outside buying houses up; there's plenty of locals at it, too, like. Instead of all this shouting and blaming, what we need is a way to speak with the council, the national parks, anyone we can, to look at getting affordable housing, right? That's what the area needs, isn't it? Somewhere decent to rent or buy. It's not too much to ask, I don't think.'

'We've no chance,' came a reply.

Mr Calvert continued, 'The Dales can't just be preserved like a museum, can it? It needs people living in it to look after it, and the only way to do that is to provide somewhere for them to live. It's not rocket science.'

At last, Lance thought, someone speaking some sense. And, having allowed most of those gathered to direct their anger at him for what had been thirty minutes or thereabouts—as though he alone was responsible for high property prices and a shrinking market—he decided it was time for him to stand up and have his say as well.

'Ah, Mr Hamilton,' said Andrew, as Lance rose to his feet and raised his hand to get the man's attention. 'You have something you'd like to share?'

'I do,' Lance replied, noticing the eyes of his wife doing their level best to burn holes in his face.

'Well, we're not interested in any of your bollocks,' a voice called out.

'Sit your arse down before I park my boot up it,' added another.

Lance ignored them.

The large man stood up.

'Let him speak,' he said, his voice loud, commanding, and calm. 'We can't solve anything by shouting and pointing fingers.'

'If he points a finger at me, I'll bite it off,' someone grumbled.

'I really do understand how everyone must feel,' Lance said, his words drowned out immediately by a wave of gasps and muttered disbelief, and a generous sprinkling of cold laughter. 'The housing market is tough for anyone these days. You really do have my sympathy.'

'I'd rather have your bank balance,' said a woman's voice, garnering more laughter than it deserved, Lance thought, and all of it mean.

'Yes, you're right, I do own a good number of properties in the area and—'

'How many?'

'It wouldn't be appropriate for me to—'

A barrage of voices jostling for position cut Lance off.

'Oh, he doesn't think it would be appropriate to say, does he?'

'Bloody airs and graces ...'

'Come on, is it ten? Twenty? A hundred?'

'Rich bastard ...'

Lance was sorely tempted to tell them, just to shut them all up, but kept schtum on the facts.

Another voice cut in.

'I can tell them if you want.'

The voice belonged to a young man sitting next to a woman of the same age. Lance stared at him for a second or two, just long enough for it to get purposefully awkward, then turned away.

'All I want to do,' Lance continued, 'is point out how my business has actually benefited the local community, of which you are all a part.' He gestured towards the large man. 'And what our friend Mr Calvert here said just now makes a lot of sense. You should all listen to him. It is more than clear that you won't listen to me.'

More laughter, punctuated with calls for him to 'shut up' and 'bugger off'.

'I bring tourists to the area,' Lance explained, or at least tried to over the ever-increasing din. 'They spend their money here, do they not? They visit your pubs and shops and restaurants, your bed and breakfasts and hotels. I also provide employment, another fact which cannot be disputed.'

'Yes, it bloody well can!'

This voice was loud, gruff, and rose from the sea of faces in front of Lance as Neptune would from the waves of a storm.

'Jeff, you've had your say,' said Andrew, but Jeff ignored him.

Jeff, who Lance recalled, had already suggested he be tarred and feathered, was tall, slim, and had the look about him of a crow or a raven, a carrion creature happy to pick at the bones of the dead. Perhaps it was an unkind description, but right then, Lance didn't really give a damn.

'I can show you the wage slips if you want,' Lance said. 'I've a team of cleaners who look after my properties.'

'Hardly opening doors to bright new futures for the young, though, are you?' said the tall man. 'And what about tradesfolk like me? You don't employ us at all, do you? No. Instead, you bring people in from outside for maintenance and decorating and all the rest. And let's not forget the small issue of you being a cheat.'

'Have we met?' Lance said, knowing full well that they had.

'You know damned well who I am,' Jeff said through gritted teeth.

Lance smiled.

'Ah, yes, of course I do. I can't remember how, though; perhaps you could remind me?'

Lance knew he was baiting him, but it only seemed fair.

'I'm a sparky by trade,' Jeff said, not answering the question. No doubt on purpose, Lance thought. 'But our business covers all housework and repairs, decorating, even a bit of building work if it's needed.'

'And do you have a business card or a website perhaps that I can look at?'

Jeff let out such a sharp, raw laugh that it cut the atmosphere in two with all the tact and surgical accuracy of a chainsaw.

'Why the bloody hell would I have either of those?' he asked. 'People know who I am, they trust me, that's how it works round here.'

Lance gave a shrug.

'Not much I can say to that, really, is there?'

Jeff stared at Lance a moment or two longer, his face going gradually purple, before dropping himself forcefully into his chair, once again muttering the word '*Cheat*' under his breath.

Lance noticed then that Andrew was staring at him. He stared back.

'Is there anything else?' Andrew asked.

Yes, there is, Lance thought, but he knew there was no point saying any of it. Still, at least he knew now, didn't he? The locals didn't just not understand him, they didn't like him, and by all accounts, wanted him gone. Except for that large chap, but it didn't sound like they were interested in anything he was saying either. As for leaving? Well, he was very, very pleased to be able to disappoint them. Move house, yes, but leave the area? Not a chance of it.

'No, I think that's everything, Andrew,' Lance said. Then he stood up, and with a wave not only to his wife, but the young couple on the left who were both staring daggers at him, and a friendly nod to both Jeff and Aldwin, made his way out of the Market Hall with shouts and swearing, and a well-aimed flat cap, which caught him slap bang in the middle of his back, chasing him on his way.

Without a second's thought, Lance crossed the high street. He was tempted to pop into the Fountain Inn, but that looked a little busy, so he headed into The Board Inn instead. Pint ordered, he considered drinking it outside, but the evening was too warm, and at least it was cool inside the pub, so he took his pint to a dark corner and sat down. The drink lasted all of five minutes, so Lance took himself back to the bar for another. Yes, I will definitely be walking, he thought, so why not do it a little fuzzy around the edges?

As the pint was being poured, Lance sensed someone approach him and he turned to see a woman standing beside him. She was, as always, wearing faded blue denim dungarees, faint smudges of clay visible in the material. He recalled having spotted her in the Market Hall, then remembered what she had said.

'Evening, Sal.'

The woman didn't acknowledge him, and instead ordered a double vodka on the rocks.

Lance's pint arrived, and he paid for it with a tap of his phone.

'I didn't see you at the meeting,' he lied.

'I saw you,' the woman said, breaking her silence. 'Heard you, too. More's the pity.'

Lance had no response to that.

The woman's drink arrived.

Lance waited for a moment or two, aware that Sal was staring at him, her eyes narrow slits, her lips pursed. She was swirling her drink, the ice clinking loudly against the side of the glass.

'See you around, then,' Lance said.

He was about to head back to where he had been sitting when the door to the pub opened and, within moments, the area around the bar grew crowded. The faces staring at him were all from the meeting. Aldwin was there, right at the front, along with his wife. Behind him was Jeff, and the young couple Lance had waved to as he'd left the Market Hall.

Lance returned their stares, waited for someone to say something, anything at all to break the silence, then gave up, and lifted his pint to his mouth for a sip.

The slap across his left cheek came out of nowhere. One second, he was about to take a gulp, and the next he was seeing stars, his pint all down his front, and the glass smashed on the floor, the shards glinting up at him with mean intent.

Face stinging, shirt soaking wet, Lance was momentarily lost for words. When he found them, all he could think to say was, 'Well, I suppose I deserved that.'

'You deserve a hell of a lot more,' Sal said, 'and you'll get it, too, trust me.' She handed Lance the double vodka she had just ordered. 'Here, drink this instead,' she said. 'Should help numb the pain of being such a rotten bastard.'

Then she was gone, pushing through the others who had gathered around him, marching out of the pub and into the evening beyond.

Lance felt the eyes of every other punter in the pub fall on him. He had a choice, to either just walk out, taking the shame of what had just happened with him, or shrug it off.

He turned to the man behind the bar, lifting up the unwanted vodka.

'Think I'll be needing another,' he said, 'and a dustpan and brush for the glass.'

Waiting for his drink, he turned to those who had clearly followed him to the pub from the Market Hall meeting. Andrew was missing, he noted, and so was Leslie. Probably in a cupboard somewhere, busy doing other things, he thought, a wry smile briefly creasing his lips. It wasn't like he was entirely without sin either, though, and he rubbed his cheek where Sal had struck him.

'Nice of you to all join me,' he said. 'I do hope the meeting was useful.' Sal's vodka was still in his hand, so he lifted it in a silent toast. 'So, what's everyone drinking, then? This round's on me.'

'Always with the smarm and the charm, aren't you?' Aldwin said. 'Well, it won't work, not with us.'

'Suit yourself,' said Lance, placing the vodka back down on the bar. He noticed then that the barman had not yet started to pour him another pint. He tried to catch the man's eye, but Aldwin jabbed a finger into his shoulder hard enough to have him take a step back from the bar.

'You're not welcome,' he said. 'I thought we'd made that clear, like.'

'It's a free country,' Lance said. 'I know you don't like

what I do, how I make my living, but that's just how things are. And like I said, it's not as though I don't bring money into the area. I do, an awful lot of it, as I tried to explain, which you seem to consistently forget.' His words and tone shocked him a little. He wasn't usually so abrupt or confrontational, but Sal's slap and his beer-soaked shirt hadn't helped with his temperament. He just wanted a drink and to be left alone.

'Right now, I don't care about what you do; what I care about is what you did,' said Aldwin. 'You took our lass's house, and there was no need for that, was there? Not really. But you just waded in there, didn't you, with your big fat wallet and took it?'

There was a need, Lance thought, but he wasn't about to tell Aldwin what it was.

'I didn't take it,' he said, then added a little lie to spice things up. 'Actually, I didn't even know it was their house, not until it was too late, anyway.'

'Maybe you should talk to your son more, then,' a voice muttered, though Lance was unable to tell who had spoken.

'What I did was business,' he continued. 'It certainly wasn't personal. And, if I had known, then maybe—'

A cold laugh cut him off, and Lance's attention was drawn to the young couple. It was the young man who had laughed, a little too knowingly, he thought, and was about to reach into his pocket for that note he'd brought with him, when the pub door opened and in walked Andrew, and with him, Leslie.

'If this keeps on, I'm going to start feeling popular,' Lance said, though he was the only one who laughed.

Andrew said, 'I must say, it's good to see everyone getting along after the heated discussion in the hall.'

Jeff roared with laughter at that, but the sound had all the warmth of a frozen bag of peas.

'We'll get along just fine, once he's left,' he said.

'I'm not leaving, Jeff,' said Lance. 'I was here first.'

'It wasn't a request,' said Jeff, and Lance saw that the man wasn't simply staring at him, but edging closer, rage in his eyes, fists clenched.

Lance stood his ground. He wasn't a fighter, but neither had he ever been happy to be pushed around by the likes of Jeff.

Jeff reached out and grabbed Lance around the scruff of the neck, then Aldwin stepped in beside him and did the same.

Lance, not entirely happy that this had happened twice in one night, and to an expensive shirt, too, was then pinned to the bar. Pain shot through his spine and made him wonder if these two men were looking to snap him in two.

'Dad, don't!'

Lance looked over to see the young woman staring at him.

'He's not worth it,' she added, turning her narrowed eyes from Lance to Aldwin.

'He's not? You sure about that?' Aldwin replied.

'Please, Dad ... You know I'm right. We'll be fine.'

'But I want to,' Aldwin said, and Lance felt his shirt tighten further around his neck. 'I really, really want to. He deserves a good kicking, doesn't he? I don't think anyone here's going to disagree with me on it either, are they?'

A murmur of agreement rippled through the small crowd.

'See?' Aldwin said, half smiling, his eyes on Lance, and filled with murderous intent.

'There are plenty of other places to go for a drink,' the young woman said, stepping forward and resting a hand on her father's arm. 'Please? Dad? Let's just leave it, yeah? He's caused enough pain as it is, and if he can't see that, then there's no hope, is there?'

Aldwin released Lance from his grip, but Jeff only twisted his collar tighter.

'She may be able to tell you what to do, but not me,' he said, looking first at Aldwin, then turning his attention to Lance.

'If I were you,' he said, leaning in close, his voice a whisper at the back of the darkest of caves, 'I'd be keeping an eye over my shoulder, if you know what I mean.'

'Is that a threat?' asked Lance.

'There's no knowing what some of us might do. And by some of us, I mean me.'

'Yes, definitely a threat.'

'You're a cheat,' Jeff said. 'You cheated me out of what was rightfully mine, and I want it back.'

Lance said nothing.

Jeff let go, then gave him a wink, made all the colder by the lack of a smile to accompany it, and the gentle, almost affectionate tap he gave Lance's cheek with his rough hand.

Lance stared at the group in front of him, waiting for someone to say something, but none of them did. Instead, they all turned around and, one by one, exited the pub. The only one who spoke was Andrew, as he made to leave, with Leslie beside him.

'Best get on,' he said. 'Calamity Jane won't direct itself now, will it?'

Lance rolled his eyes.

'Doing some one-to-one with the star tonight, are you?' he asked.

Leslie's eyes grew wide, and Lance briefly imagined them popping out of her head in an explosion of blood and gore.

'We've the costumes to sort out,' Andrew said, maintaining that sickening level of politeness Lance could only take for so long, which was probably why their meetings were always so short. 'I can't exactly go playing a dashing army lieutenant with a rusty sabre and creased uniform now, can I?'

And with that, they were gone, leaving behind the young man and his wife. They stayed just long enough to fill the room with what Lance assumed was anger, though he sensed disappointment, too, and a lot of it, like it had been stored up for years and was now overflowing. Then, at last, and much to his relief, he was alone.

Lance turned to the barman.

'Well, that was fun, wasn't it?' he said. 'About that drink ...'

The barman shook his head.

'Probably best you get yourself home,' he said.

'Are you asking me to leave?'

'Just a suggestion. And maybe you should stay away for a while, too, eh?'

'Barred as well?'

There was no reply. Lance knew there didn't need to be one. He went to protest, but quickly thought better of it. He just didn't have the energy.

'You know, you're probably right,' he said.

Brushing himself down, as though doing so would make his sopping shirt look any better, Lance pushed away from the bar to leave the pub, then turned back and grabbed the vodka Sal had given him after the slap. He necked it. She'd bought it for him after all, so there was no point in wasting it.

Outside, Lance breathed in the warm evening air, then set off home just fast enough to make it look like he had important business to deal with, deciding at the last minute to take a little detour to the chippy on the way. He'd eat on the way back; the path home was a pleasant one, across fields and along a rough lane, and the food would only make it even more enjoyable. He had no doubt that Leslie wouldn't be home anyway, so an evening with a bottle of wine and his record collection awaited.

Outside the chippy, Lance reached into his pocket for his phone, and his fingers brushed against the note he'd taken with him, still undelivered. But that could wait until tomorrow.

And so, with a greasy bag of chips in his hand, and his face still smarting a little—perhaps even as much as Leslie's had earlier that evening he thought, laughing—Lance sauntered off into the evening as, behind him, quiet footsteps followed.

THREE

Police Constable Jadyn Okri had arrived at the school in Leyburn after driving through scenery that was quickly becoming his favourite. He had moved to the picturesque village of Reeth in Swaledale a few months ago to put an end to the rather long commute he'd had from Catterick, and to be a little closer to another member of the team whom he was growing rather fond of: Detective Constable Jenny Blades.

It was still early days for them, but he had to admit that she was on his mind more often than not. He hadn't really thought too much about the location itself, and knew little about Swaledale, but already he was finding himself increasingly smitten by the place. There was a different kind of beauty to it, and sometimes he had the distinct impression that he was driving not just through the countryside, but time itself, rolling along lanes and through villages gently haunted by their younger days.

Wensleydale was a wide and sweeping valley lined with dramatic fells and cut through by broad rivers and tumbling streams. Swaledale, Jadyn had come to notice, was just as dramatic, but in a different way. The valley was smaller, narrower, darker, and yet in places so bright that every corner seemed to promise a new and secret world bathed in sunshine. It seemed older, too, though Jadyn knew that was impossible, because the Dales were all ancient places, and had long watched people come and go. And yet every time he returned home, driving into Reeth to cut across its green, or when he headed out in the late evening for a pint in the Black Bull, he couldn't shift the strange sensation that somehow he was walking in another time entirely. One evening, the sound of someone riding a horse through the village had been so evocative that he had half expected to look up and see a cart rolling through, piled high with golden hay, held down by nothing more than a couple of pitchforks.

Right then, though, he was very much in the present, and trying to help advise the school on a problem that was getting out of hand enough for the headteacher to ask them to do an assembly about it, then meet with them after for a chat. And that issue was vaping.

Having been fully prepared for a few hundred bored faces, phones going off, inappropriate laughter, and heckling, the assembly had gone considerably better than Jadyn had expected, and at the end, he had even managed to have a chat with a few kids who had stayed behind for a natter. No doubt it was just a delay tactic to avoid going to lessons, but he had taken advantage of it, and made sure they all had his contact details should they need to contact him about anything he and Police Community Support Officer Liz Coates had mentioned in their chat.

Assembly done, Jadyn and Liz were sitting in the headteacher's office, along with the headteacher, Mrs Brooke, and Mr Bansal, a young Asian teacher and the head of year nine.

'I just don't understand the attraction,' said Mr Bansal. 'I mean, why would you? Why would anyone?'

'It's hard to say,' Jadyn said, but the teacher continued to talk over him.

'Social media, that's the problem,' he said, warming to his subject, with lots of arm waving and gesticulating, like a preacher racing towards the punchline of a sermon. 'That's where the kids find out about all kinds of stuff, isn't it? Influencers or whatever they're called, earning a living from being vacuous, shallow husks of humanity; those are the people kids look up to nowadays! It makes me spit! I tell you, if I had my way, I'd take the lot of them and—'

Jadyn decided it was best to cut off Mr Bansal's tirade before it went too far.

'I understand that you had an argument with a shopkeeper,' he said, flipping open his notebook.

This, after all, was the actual reason he and Liz were at the school; the call had come in from the shopkeeper himself, a Mr Lofthouse, who ran the shop with his son, Nathan, and Jadyn and Liz had popped around for a visit. Mr Lofthouse and his son had been understanding about the vaping issue the school was facing, but were worried that if teachers started attacking shop owners at random, it might not end so well.

Mr Lofthouse had also wanted to point out that if Mr Bansal ever did the same again, there was a good chance he'd have no choice but to '*punch the daft sod in the mouth because I can't have that kind of stupid going on in my shop, can I? I've a business to run!*'

On contacting the school, the headteacher, Mrs Brooke, had sounded almost relieved, and had soon persuaded them to speak at an assembly, not just about vaping as such, but about various other aspects of police work.

'Yes, about that,' Mr Bansal explained. 'I was doing a little bit of investigating myself, asked around, took samples of what we've found in school with me to check as well, you see, that kind of thing. And things maybe got a little out of hand.'

'Taking the law into your own hands is never a good idea,' Jadyn said, again remembering the shopkeeper's verbalized threat, which he'd had to, in turn, warn him about not actually following through on, should Mr Bansal turn up again. 'The police strongly advise against it.'

'I wasn't taking the law into my own hands,' the teacher

replied. 'I'm not some kind of vigilante, not by a long shot! I mean, just look at me; do I look like Dirty Harry?'

That's an old-school reference, Jadyn thought. Most people now would probably mention The Punisher.

'I'd just had enough, that's all,' continued Mr Bansal. 'And I've been doing a lot of research, and I saw these bloody things at the counter when I went in, and I think I just lost the plot a bit. I wasn't violent, and if that's what the shopkeeper said, he's lying. I'm not a violent man! I'm just angry and I've had enough.'

Jadyn said, 'Apparently you got out your credit card and said how you wanted to buy all of the disposable vapes in the shop, because if that was the only way to stop them getting into the hands of kids, then that's what you were willing to do.'

'Well, I didn't know what else to do. That seemed like the best course of action.'

'And then, after presenting your credit card, you tried to pull the display off the counter.'

'Ah, yes ...'

'The shopkeeper had to slap your hands with a rolled-up newspaper just to get you to let go.'

'He shouldn't have done that. I didn't do it for long.'

'Long enough for us to end up being called by the shopkeeper and to now be sat here with you having this chat,' Jadyn said, and saw the teacher's shoulders slump. 'So, how long has vaping been a problem?'

'You mean you're not here to arrest me?'

Jadyn shook his head.

'The shopkeeper was concerned about you, and about what's happening with vapes at the school. We've had a chat with them and they're vigilant when it comes to who they sell to, checking IDs, that kind of thing, plus they have an excellent knowledge of the community they serve. They know you have a problem, and they want to help. They just don't think that you going out and trying to buy up all the vapes in Wensleydale is the best way to go about it.'

Mr Bansal smiled.

'You were asking how long it's been a problem, the vaping I mean,' he said, and glanced at the headteacher as though asking for permission to share confidential information. 'A couple of years, maybe? We knew it was going on before that, obviously, but it was only a few pupils back then. Now? Well, now it seems like they're all at it. Thanks for the assembly, by the way. Not sure it will have done any good, but it is appreciated.'

'Thanks,' said Jadyn.

'It's true, though, what he's just said,' said Mrs Brooke. 'Vaping is completely out of hand. We find those bloody awful disposables all over the place, but that's not the real problem, I'm afraid. Well, it is, but it leads to a bigger one.'

'How do you mean?' Liz asked.

Mr Bansal said, 'It's the kids themselves, you see? Energy drinks used to be a problem, because we'd have pupils bouncing off the walls after having a couple of cans for breakfast. Now it's vapes; all that nicotine and God knows what else rushing around their system. You can't teach them; it's impossible! Lessons are little more than an exercise in crowd control sometimes. It's not fair to them, it's not fair to the rest of the kids, and it's not fair to their families, either. They should be banned! It's ridiculous!'

'Reminds me of alcopops,' Mrs Brooke added. 'The stink that whole thing caused, but it blew over eventually. I'm not sure if this will. That's how worried we are.'

Jadyn wasn't surprised. He knew kids liked to experiment, not least because he'd been much the same, and not all that long ago either, but to hear that vaping was actually causing a problem in the classroom? He hadn't expected that, or if he had, not to this extent.

'They even have vaping competitions,' said the headteacher. 'And by they, I don't mean the kids, I mean adults, posting this nonsense all over the internet. It's ridiculous! So, of course the kids copy, don't they? They get together to try and outdo each other with these vast plumes they can expel. The world, it's gone mad, I'm sure of it.'

'Do you have any idea where they're buying them from?' Liz asked.

'Well, not that shop that reported me, so that's something,' said Mr Bansal. 'Though I'm sure there are plenty that do.'

'A lot of shops sell disposables, but by law, only to those over eighteen,' said Jadyn.

'Because that law makes so much difference, doesn't it?' the headteacher laughed. 'All the kids need to do is send in an older brother or sister, an older friend. Not different from getting hold of normal cigarettes or booze. Not so much a loophole as a huge, gaping maw.'

'I don't think that's the main route though,' said Mr Bansal, shaking his head. 'Obviously, some of the vapes are bought from shops, but I've not seen anything like the ones we've found behind the counter.'

'Which means someone is bringing them in by other means,' said Liz.

Mr Bansal placed a bag on the coffee table in front of them and tipped it up.

'Here you go,' he said.

Dozens of vapes spilled out. Jadyn reeled from the sudden stench that thrust its way into the room. The stink was a sweet, cloying mix of candy and fruit, as though someone had just thrown a grenade into a sweet shop.

'Reeks a bit, doesn't it?' the headteacher said, looking over at Jadyn. 'You touch one of those things and the smell's on your hands for hours.'

'As you can see, they look like pens,' said Mr Bansal. 'Highlighters, that kind of thing. You wouldn't spot them in a pencil case, would you? And we can't just go around searching kids because that's ridiculous and also illegal. The situation, it's a complete bloody nightmare.'

Liz reached out and picked up a vape the colour and shape of, as Mr Bansal had just pointed out, a bright yellow highlighter pen. He's right, Jadyn thought, you just wouldn't know.

'Honestly, sometimes, I actually find myself wishing that they were all smoking cigarettes instead,' Mrs Brooke said. 'Sounds flippant, I know, but back then, back in the days when kids tried cigarettes, they were few and far between, really. Yes, a good number tried it, but few kept at it. You could smell them a mile off as well. Plus, it was and is expensive. These things? They're pocket money, that's all, and they taste and smell like sweets, so of course kids are going to give it a go, aren't they? This stuff, it's marketed directly at them, and it's making someone somewhere a hideous amount of money.'

'It makes me so angry!' said Mr Bansal. 'And I know I shouldn't have done what I did, but I was just out researching, trying to find out where the kids were getting them, and then one thing led to another. I saw red, I know I did, and I shouldn't have.'

Jadyn caught Liz's eye and could tell she was thinking the same, that they needed to discourage any such activity before something got out of hand.

'Our advice right now is that you leave the investigations to us,' he said. 'Although we understand why you took action, we would definitely suggest that you don't do anymore. Things can go very bad, very quickly, and an argument that becomes a fight can soon see someone injured, in hospital even. It's not a good scenario from any angle.'

'We know that,' said Mrs Brooke, 'but we can't just sit back and let this continue, can we? Surely you can understand that. Yes, we should've called you in earlier, but it'll need more than a couple of police officers to sort this out, I'm sure.'

A call came in on Jadyn's radio. He glanced at Liz, then stood up and left the room to answer it outside.

'We need to go,' he said, stepping back into the room and looking at Liz. Then he turned his attention to the two teachers. 'I'm afraid we've another call to attend to,' he said, making sure what he said was bland enough to give nothing away. 'But we will be looking into this immediately and will let you know as soon as we have anything.'

The two teachers stood up. Mr Bansal held out the bag of vapes.

'You may as well have these,' he said. 'Evidence or something, right? I don't really want them hanging around in school anyway.'

Liz took the bag and smiled a thank you.

Once they were out of earshot, Liz asked, 'What is it? What's happened?'

'A body's been found over in Hawes,' Jadyn said, the words odd and uncomfortable in his mouth. 'Jim's in the office and took the call. Jen and Gordy are off today.'

'Jen on another race?'

'She is,' said Jadyn with a smile. 'Matt's meeting us there, but he'll be awhile yet. He's up in Kirkby Stephen, sorting out a domestic disturbance involving someone taking a chainsaw to a motorbike or something.'

'Why on earth would anyone do that?'

'I know,' Jadyn said, shaking his head. 'Chainsaws are seriously dangerous.'

'No, not that,' said Liz. 'I mean, ruin a motorbike.' Then she added, 'We'll be first on-scene, then.'

'Jim's heading there now to chat with the woman who found the body and make sure she's okay,' said Jadyn, 'and to ensure the place is shut down until we get there.'

Outside the school, Liz climbed onto her motorbike, and Jadyn opened the door to his car.

'Just so we're clear, this isn't a race,' he said, climbing into the driver's seat.

Liz winked, pulled on her helmet, and keyed the ignition. Then, with a loud rev of the engine, she sped up the drive from the school and headed off down into Leyburn and on to Hawes. Jadyn laughed, pulled his door shut, and headed off after her.

. . .

ARRIVING IN HAWES, Jadyn drove to the address Jim had given him and slowed down to park up outside a small industrial unit on the outskirts of town, not too far along from Mike's garage. Liz was already there and was climbing off her bike. He saw Jim further down the road and gave the PCSO a wave, then joined Liz as they walked over to speak with him.

'What have we got, then, Jim?' Liz asked. 'Jadyn said a body's been found.'

'It has,' Jim said. 'Sally Dent called it in. She's a potter, makes lots of mugs and plates and stuff. Supplies souvenirs to shops up and down the dale. Nice stuff, too, if you're into that kind of thing. This is her studio.'

'Do we know who it is?' asked Jadyn.

'Sally thinks it's Lance Hamilton. I can't say that I can confirm that; I've only had a quick look through the door, like.'

'Is he local?' Jadyn asked. 'You said that you know him.'

'He is,' said Jim, 'but I've never spoken to him, and I'd be hard-pressed to recognise him. I know Hawes is small, and that people think everyone in the Dales knows everyone else, but some folk still manage to stay under the radar, don't they? What I do know is that he owns a fair number of holiday properties around and about. We don't exactly mix in the same circles, really, what with mine being about police work and farming, and his being about, well, I've no idea actually. What do people with lots of property and money do?'

'I'm going to go with drink champagne and drive fast cars,' said Liz. 'Anything else?'

'Well, I can say that he's definitely dead,' said Jim.

'Drawing on your extensive medical background there, then?' Jadyn smiled.

'Ha ha,' said Jim. 'What I mean is, I know I'm not the district surgeon or a doctor or anything, but it's pretty obvious, even to me.'

'That doesn't sound good,' said Jadyn.

'It isn't,' agreed Jim, shaking his head. 'There's blood for a start. Not loads, but enough to make you think that losing it wouldn't be good if you wanted to stay alive.'

'For a start?' said Liz, her eyes widening. 'What else is there, then?'

'Well,' said Jim, 'about that ...'

Jadyn waited, but Jim said no more.

'About what?' he said. 'You can't leave it at that. How bad can it be?'

'I don't know, really,' said Jim. 'Are there gradients of bad when it comes to this stuff? It's not Texas Chainsaw Massacre bad, if that's anything to go by.'

'It isn't,' said Liz. 'And that hasn't really helped at all with what I'm now imagining is in there.'

Still, Jim said no more.

'Come on,' Jadyn said. 'Tell us.'

Jim lifted up his hands.

'Why are you waving?' Jadyn asked.

'I'm not waving,' Jim said. 'I'm telling you; it's his hands.'

Jadyn wasn't sure he'd heard correctly.

'The hands?'

'Yes.' Jim lifted his hands to chest height and wiggled his fingers.

'What about them?' Liz asked.

For a moment, Jim was silent, but when he eventually spoke, his voice was almost a whisper, as though the weight of what he had to say had forced all the air out of his lungs.

'They're not there,' he said.

FOUR

'For someone who has shot more than his fair share of guns in his time, you're not exactly a natural, are you, lad?'

Harry was standing in a field out the back of West Burton. Around him, the rising slopes of the fells were hidden beneath a shimmering sea of trees, and from deep beneath the sleepy bows, a cuckoo called. He was standing next to Arthur, Grace's dad, and still-not-retired gamekeeper, much to Grace's chagrin. Her lead secured to a metal loop corkscrewed into the ground, Smudge was bathing in the midday sun next to Jess. Arthur had left his old dog back home to snooze the day away on the sofa.

'They weren't generally shotguns,' Harry said. 'They were semi-automatic rifles.'

Harry heard Grace let out a short laugh but kept his attention on the old man, who was staring at him intently, challenging him almost.

'That makes a difference, does it?' Arthur asked.

'Yes.'

'How's that, then?'

Harry wasn't exactly sure, but he was desperately looking for some way to explain why, of the two dozen or so clay pigeons he'd just tried to blast out of the sky, he'd missed twenty and only nicked the others. Or, as Arthur had said, 'Nowt but given the little buggers a scare.'

'And it wasn't just rifles,' he said. 'I've shot pistols, grenade launchers—'

'But not shotguns,' said Arthur.

'No, that's not what I said. Yes, I've used shotguns,' Harry explained, 'but only to take off door hinges.' He caught sight of Grace's shoulders shaking as she stifled a laugh at that little detail, though the memory wasn't one that held all that much humour, not when he thought of the things he'd found on the other sides of those doors. 'And that's a bit different than trying to hit a small black disc flying at a thousand miles an hour.'

'Sounds to me like you're making excuses.'

'They're not excuses.'

'Then hit something, lad!' Arthur said, slapping Harry hard on his shoulder, his strength and power in no way diminished by his advancing years. 'Which, if you don't mind me saying so, begins with you listening to what I'm saying, and doing what you're told, and not you just constantly doing what you've always done. That make sense?'

'I am listening and doing what I'm told.'

Arthur shook his head and tutted.

'You're not a natural learner, are you? A little thick-eared if you ask me, like.'

Harry heaved in a deep breath through his nose, held it, breathed out.

'He's right, you know.'

Harry glanced over his shoulder to find Grace looking up at him through a half smile, eyebrows raised enough to let him know she thought he was being a bit of an idiot. She was sitting on a weatherworn clay trap that Arthur had brought down in the back of his old Land Rover. The trap was a metal contraption that looked both deeply uncomfortable and highly dangerous. It comprised an uncomfortable seat, which was nothing more than a triangular slab of metal, a metal arm on which a clay pigeon was rested, and a spring clearly powerful enough on release to snap a telegraph pole in half.

'Is he now?' Harry replied, his eyes firmly on Grace's own.

'You're still closing one eye, aren't you?'

'Yes.'

'Then stop.'

'I'm trying to.'

'You ready then, Grace?' Arthur called over to his daughter.

Harry watched Grace pull back the arm of the clay trap and slip in another clay pigeon.

'Sure am.'

'Now remember,' Arthur said, 'both eyes open, and stay just ahead of the clay as you fire. They're racing away from you in a straight line. Honestly, these couldn't be easier, which is why we've started with them. You can't miss.'

'So, you keep saying,' Harry muttered.

'And when you get your eye in and you've dusted a few, we'll move things around and have you trying them coming in from the left. How's that sound? Honestly, you'll get the hang of it soon enough. Just do as I've said and bloody well hit something!'

Harry had the shotgun in his shoulder and bellowed, 'Pull!' his voice loud enough to crack the sky.

Grace released the arm of the clay trap and it swung out with a violent, metallic clang. The clay pigeon soared into the sky. Harry focused on keeping both eyes open, saw the clay, made sure he was just ahead of it, and fired.

The clay continued on its merry way, utterly undisturbed by Harry's attempt to smash it to pieces.

'Bollocks!'

He would've gone for another shot, but the clay had already disappeared.

'You were just a bit ahead of it,' said Arthur.

'Yep, you were,' agreed Grace. 'Close though. Much better.'

Harry broke the shotgun, and the spent cartridge ejected past his ear close enough to make him flinch.

'How can you even tell?' he asked. 'You can't actually see the shot, can you?'

'Yes, we can,' said Arthur, stooping down to pick up Harry's dead cartridge. 'And you were just ahead of the clay, like we said.'

'Well, you said to shoot just ahead of the clay, so that's what I did.'

'Not that far, though. And you didn't keep the gun moving, did you? You went ahead, stopped, fired.' Arthur lifted an invisible shotgun to his cheek. 'You need to find the clay, move the gun just in front of it, and keep it moving as you fire. Otherwise, by the time you've pulled the trigger, that little clay has already buggered off, hasn't it?'

Harry went to say something, thought better of it, and kept his mouth shut.

'How about we have a break?' Grace suggested.

Harry glanced at his watch. It was almost lunchtime, and he was definitely getting peckish. He knew they had plenty of food with them because he'd helped pack it into Grace's vehicle. Plus, Grace was never one for under-catering.

Harry handed the shotgun to Arthur, then followed Grace.

A few minutes later, they were all munching on a small Cockett's pork pie each and drinking a glass of fresh, ice-cold apple juice.

'Hard to believe it's been a year,' Grace said. 'Well, just over, if we want to be picky, but seeing as neither of us is any good at dates, this one will do well enough, won't it?'

Harry wasn't only terrible at dates, he wasn't exactly brilliant with anniversaries, either. But when Grace had suggested a go at shooting clays as a way to celebrate the fact they had been seeing each other for just over a year now, he'd been a little concerned at first that shooting things was her idea of a celebration, then happy to go along with it.

Now, though, he wasn't so sure because he'd been so completely bloody useless at it. How could he have missed so many? Also, he hadn't expected to be sharing the day with Arthur.

Not that he didn't like the old man; quite the opposite actually. Harry was just hoping that he wasn't going to stay around for the whole day, and certainly not the evening, at any rate. Shooting was one way to celebrate an anniversary, but there were others, and Harry was certainly looking forward to those, too.

'It will more than do,' he said, and finished off the pork pie. 'And I'll hit something eventually, I'm sure. How's Tom doing?'

'He's young, he's keen. What else could I possibly wish for in an apprentice?' Grace said.

Tom was a young lad Harry had met during a previous investigation. He lived over in Marsett, a hamlet just above Semerwater. He didn't exactly get on with his parents—well, his father anyway —and had run away. Once he'd been found, one thing had led to another, and Grace had ended up deciding to take him on as an apprentice gamekeeper. He was still at school, so had that to finish, but by all accounts, working for Grace had only improved things there. He was a hard worker, too, never shying away from being out in all weathers and getting his hands dirty.

'What's he up to today?'

'He's with a fishing party,' said Arthur. 'A group from somewhere Manchester way, I think, booked themselves a day on the river, so he's managing that, providing a bit of tuition too, no doubt.'

Harry was impressed.

'And he's no issue with teaching adults?'

Grace shook her head.

'He's a natural,' she said. 'Knows what he's on about, doesn't take any lip, and in minutes has most people casting flies better than they've ever done before.'

'It's quite something to watch,' added Arthur. 'He's young, but he's got an old head on him, if that makes sense.' He then leaned over and tapped Harry on the head. 'And he listens, Harry, he listens!'

Grace said, 'You should take up fly-fishing.'

Harry shook his head, laughed.

'One hobby at a time, I think,' he said. 'And if I'm no good at this, I'm not sure I want a teenager shouting at me about how bad I am at something else.'

'Hobby?' Arthur's voice was all shock and disbelief. 'Shooting and fishing aren't hobbies, lad, they're life skills! Now, shall we be getting on?'

They packed away the picnic, then headed back over to the clay trap. As Arthur handed the shotgun back to Harry, a car horn cut through the air, sending birds scattering from trees. From another field, the lonely baa of a sheep called out as though in reply.

Harry turned around to see the top half of a nondescript four-by-four parked on the other side of the wall, near the gate.

'Who's that, then?' he asked.

'Not a clue,' said Grace.

Arthur just shrugged.

A figure emerged from the vehicle, opened the gate, and marched towards them. As they drew closer, Harry saw that it was a man dressed in sandals, canvas shorts, and a loose linen shirt unbuttoned a little further than was entirely necessary, the last few buttons straining against what they were preventing from bursting into view. Harry wasn't sure they were really up to the job, either.

'Is it you doing all of that shooting?' the man bellowed as he walked up to them. He came to an abrupt stop in front of Harry, Grace, and Arthur, his voice cut short by Harry's face.

Harry was used to it, but sometimes it riled him more than others. And for whatever reason, this was one of those times.

'Can we help you, sir?' he asked.

The man's face was a contorted mix of writhing horror and liquid fascination, a clear picture of someone who knew they really shouldn't stare, but just couldn't help themselves.

'You've left the gate open,' Arthur said.

The man, Harry saw, was a little taken aback by this statement.

'I'm sorry, I've done what with the gate?'

'The gate,' Arthur repeated, this time jabbing a thick finger behind the man and directly at the gate. 'It was closed, wasn't it, when you arrived? You opened it to get into the field, and you've gone and left it open.'

'So?'

'So, animals can get out, can't they? That's usually what they do when a gate is left open, which is why we close them.'

The man frowned, then made a dramatic show of taking in the field they were standing in, looking left and right and left again, before giving a slow, deliberate shrug, his hands squished into his hips like they were resting on shelves of putty.

'Not exactly a stampede, is it?' he said. 'Probably because there are no animals in the field at all. You know, I would even go so far as to say that the field is absolutely empty of animals, wouldn't you?'

'I would, but that doesn't matter,' said Arthur. 'So, what you'll be doing right now is turning around and taking yourself back over there to shut it, regardless of whether there are animals in this particular field or not. Though there are, as you can see, two dogs.'

'Two dogs that are tied up.'

Harry watched as Arthur stepped in close to the man.

'You've heard of the Countryside Code, no doubt. Well, you see, the whole point of it is that we all follow it regardless. Because if you forget now, when there's nowt in the field, who's to say you won't forget when there is?'

'Me, that's who.'

'And I don't know you from Adam, do I?' said Arthur. 'Forgive me if I'm not entirely confident in taking you at your word.'

'Who's Adam?'

'My point exactly. So, if you wouldn't mind?'

Arthur once again gestured over towards the gate.

The man didn't move.

'Just out of interest,' said Harry, interrupting, 'you mind if I ask why you're here in the first place?'

'I'm here because I'm on holiday and you've gone and disturbed my Saturday morning with all that god-awful noisy shooting,' the man said.

'What about it?'

'It's loud and I want you to stop. It's illegal, I'm sure of it.'

Grace laughed.

'It's not funny.'

'No, you're right, it's not,' she said. 'You are though, whether or not you're meaning to be.'

'You were saying?' said Harry.

'I was saying that all of this shooting is loud and I want it to stop,' the man repeated. 'I've come here on holiday, to get away from noise and to relax, and you're out here banging away, aren't you? It's off-putting, to say the least.'

Harry caught a wide-eyed look from Grace.

'Banging away?' she said. 'Well, if we were, then you're absolutely right, because it would be off-putting, wouldn't it? But I don't think we were, and I'm fairly sure we would know. I'm also sure I wouldn't want my dad watching.'

Harry watched the man try to work out what Grace was getting at, then give up.

'Do you even have a licence?' the man continued, now oblivious to what Grace had just said. 'Is any of this legal? This is the countryside, you know; people like me, we expect it to be quiet and peaceful, don't we? That's why we come here. We do not want it to be like this, not at all!'

Harry wanted to calm the situation, but wasn't entirely sure how. Realising he was still holding the shotgun, he went to hand it back to Arthur. Arthur ignored the gun and stepped in front of the man.

'First of all, yes, I have a licence,' he said. 'As does my daughter here. Harry here doesn't need one, as he's with us and we're trying our best to help him hit something out of the sky. Not easy, I have to say, but there we go.'

The man rolled his eyes, and Harry wasn't sure that was such a good idea, really, considering the look Arthur then gave him.

'Now, about any of this being illegal ...'

'Like I'm going to believe anything you tell me,' the man said.

Arthur ignored him.

'First off, we called 101 to let the police know what we're doing.'

Harry glanced at Grace on hearing this, only to see her return it with a look that said yes, that's what we're supposed to do, but no, we didn't.

'Now, I'd like to draw your attention to the Highways Act 1980,' Arthur continued. 'It's one I'm well aware of, you might say, what with my being a gamekeeper and all. Anyway, if you have a look at section 161, you'll find under the bit that explains penalties for certain kinds of danger and annoyance, that should discharges of any firearm or firework within fifty feet of the centre of a highway, cause a user of said highway to be injured, interrupted or endangered, then the person responsible is guilty of an offence and liable to a fine.'

The man laughed.

'See? I was right! This is wholly illegal.'

Arthur pointed over the man's shoulder to the gate.

'How far do you think that is from where we are now?' he asked.

The man shrugged.

'Fifty metres?'

'A hundred,' said Arthur. 'And that's a little different to fifty feet, isn't it?'

'So?'

'So, what we're doing is legal, very much so, actually. And fun though this conversation's been, can I suggest that you hurry back to wherever you're staying and mind your own business?'

Harry saw another vehicle pull up at the gate.

The man looked over, and on seeing the vehicle smiled the smile of someone not only smug but used to getting his own way.

'Good,' he said, clapping his hands together and giving them a good rub. 'They're here. I called them, you see, to tell them about all of this, and to say that I was coming down to have a word.'

Harry watched a familiar figure climb out of the vehicle and walk through the gate, closing it behind him.

'You called the police?' Arthur said, scratching his head. 'About this?'

'Of course I did,' said the man. 'It was the right thing to do.'

'Wouldn't be so sure about that, if I were you,' replied Arthur, looking up at Harry with a wry smile. 'But I do admire your confidence, no matter how misplaced, like.'

The man turned to face the approaching police officer.

'Thank you for coming,' he said. 'I assume you'll be confiscating the weapons and taking them all in for questioning? In fact, I fully expect you to; I don't want to see my taxes wasted on little more than a polite telling off.'

'It's not a weapon, it's a shotgun,' Arthur muttered. Then added, 'Bloody idiot.'

The police officer ignored the man and looked at Harry.

'Now then, Boss,' he said. 'Everything okay?'

'Officer Okri,' said Harry, aware of the confusion now beginning to write itself into the man's expression.

'Sorry about this,' said Jadyn. 'I know it's your day off and all, but we've had something come up.'

'That doesn't sound good,' he said, seeing the worry in Jadyn's eyes. 'What's happened?'

At first, Harry had been pleased to see the young constable walking across the field, happy for an interruption to the man's complaints. Now though, just a few words later, and he was anything but; whatever Jadyn was here for, Harry was damned sure it wasn't to bring him good news.

'You're needed,' Jadyn said. 'There's been an incident up in Hawes.'

Before Harry could say anything, the man butted in.

'Excuse me, Officer, but do you know him?' he asked, looking at Jadyn and stepping in between Harry and the constable. 'Then why haven't you arrested him?'

'Who is this?' Jadyn asked.

Harry shrugged.

'I'm the person who called you,' the man said.

It was Jadyn who shrugged this time.

'Sorry, you must've spoken to someone else.'

'And they didn't pass on the message? What is this country coming to?'

Harry gave Jadyn just enough of a look to let him know he needed to say something, then turned to face the man.

'I'm Detective Chief Inspector Harry Grimm,' said Harry. 'And right now, sir, I feel it is my duty to tell you that you're currently at risk of facing charges relating to trespass and to criminal damage. Oh, and I might add driving without due care and attention to that as well, though that all depends on how keen you are to delay me in my duties. I'm going to advise you that it's probably best you keep it to as little as possible or, even better, not at all.'

'What? Criminal damage? Trespass? You can't be serious!'

Harry pointed at his own face.

'Does this look like the face of a man who is anything other than serious?' he asked.

Jadyn leaned in close to the man and added quietly, 'He does angry as well, but you really don't want to see that, trust me.'

'But I've not damaged anything! And all I've done is walk across a sodding field!'

'The gate,' said Arthur. 'You left it open, remember? Naughty.'

'That's not criminal damage.'

'It would be if you'd let animals out onto the road, like, remember?'

'But there are no animals!'

'There could be, and then where would you be?'

'And there is nothing at all wrong with my driving!'

Harry stared down at the man's feet, gave his chin a thoughtful rub.

'You're wearing sandals.'

'How the hell is that relevant?'

'Sandals, flip flops, high-heeled shoes, they're not advisable to wear while driving because you can't react quickly enough to a potential issue on the road,' Harry explained. 'Now, they're not exactly illegal, true, but right now, I can't say it's looking good for you.'

Harry glanced at Jadyn, who got the hint and took out his notebook.

'Can I take your name, sir?' he asked.

The man's jaw fell open, but no words came out.

'Sir? Your name?' Jadyn repeated.

The man tried to say something, but all he did was splutter on his flagrant indignation.

'My advice,' Harry said, 'is that you turn yourself around and head home, have a think about what you've learned today, and maybe see if you can go so far as to never do any of it ever again.'

'But the gun! The noise!'

Harry growled.

At last, the man backed away, then turned and marched off. At the gate, he looked back at Harry.

'You've not heard the last of this!' he shouted, even raising a fist to shake at them. 'You've not!'

'No, I'm quite sure I haven't,' Harry muttered.

At last, the man drove off, wheels spinning and sending a pathetic little cloud of dust into the air.

'That was fun!' Arthur laughed, and slapped Harry on the shoulder.

Harry looked back at Jadyn, then led him far enough away from Grace and her dad for them to speak in private.

'This incident, then ...'

'We've a body, Boss,' Jadyn said.

'What was that?' asked Harry, not so much because he'd not heard correctly, but more that he just hadn't wanted to.

'A body,' Jadyn repeated.

Harry felt his shoulders slump.

'Bollocks.'

'Yeah,' said Jadyn. 'Thought you might say that.'

FIVE

Harry glanced over at Grace and Arthur, who were busy chatting and making a fuss of the dogs. He wanted to go over and join them, and he wanted whatever Jadyn had brought him to disappear and leave him alone. Days off, he had come to realise over his years in the police, weren't simply there to allow you to recharge so that you could then go back in and crack on with the day job. They existed to ensure you developed a life outside of the police. Unfortunately, the job had a habit of interrupting those days, just like right now.

That's what life had once been like back in Bristol, back when his existence had been a car crash of dark days survived only by refusing to let the criminals he hunted win. Some still had, and those investigations haunted him, but less and less as time went on, the Dales almost a cure to a disease he had never even realised he'd had.

Now, everything was different, so much so that a simple comparison was not possible. Night and day, that's what it is, Harry thought, but even on sun-blessed days such as this, darkness still liked to intrude, wiping its grubby hands all over it, leaving a stain he just couldn't ignore. Sometimes, that stain seemed all the more obvious on the brighter days, as though all the sun wanted to do was to shine a light on the bad things.

He turned to Jadyn.

'What about the rest of the team? Where are they and who's doing what?'

'Jim and Liz, they're at the crime scene,' Jadyn began, 'and—'

Harry held up a hand to shush Jadyn.

The constable looked confused.

'What is it, Boss?'

'You mean,' said Harry, 'that right now, we've a body with two PCSOs looking after it and no one else?'

Jadyn shook his head.

'No, that's not what I said; Matt's there now. He arrived as I was leaving. He's spent the morning dealing with someone who took a chainsaw to a motorbike. Rather him than me.'

Harry sighed.

'But you were going to leave them there alone without a police officer, weren't you? To come fetch me?'

Harry saw a look of confusion creep across Jadyn's face.

'Jim and Liz are fine with what they were doing, and Matt was on his way, and—'

'And what?'

Harry knew he was being grumpier than usual, and that was making him jump on Jadyn a little too harshly, but sometimes things had to be said.

'They know what they're doing, don't they?' continued Jadyn, and Harry guessed now that the young constable knew what he was getting at. 'I mean, I know they're PCSOs, so they're not badged like the rest of us, but they're—'

'Exactly,' Harry said, cutting Jadyn off mid-flow. 'They're PCSOs. We all know they're both bloody good at their jobs, and often do a hell of a lot more than they're expected or even trained to do. But this isn't about them. We all blur the lines and bend the rules here, I know, because we have to. That's all part of the job and living where we do, but something like what you've just told me?' Harry paused to make sure he had Jadyn's full attention. 'I would expect you to know that what you should've done is send one of them to fetch me, instead of heading over here yourself. Is that understood?'

Harry watched Jadyn's well-muscled shoulders sag a little. It had needed saying, though, so he would leave it at that. Jadyn was a good police officer, but sometimes the closeness of the team could make them all a little complacent. And that went for himself as much as any of them, and Harry wondered then if the bollocking he'd just metered out was as much for him as it was Jadyn.

'Sorry, Boss. I wasn't thinking. Well, I was, just not enough. Knew I had to get you over to the crime scene, and I'd tried your phone and couldn't get through.'

'What?'

Harry pulled out his phone. No signal.

'This isn't about me needing apologies,' he said, softening his voice as he put his phone away. 'I'm just pointing it out to make sure it doesn't happen again. Clear?'

'Crystal,' Jadyn nodded.

'Good. Now, you said Matt's there now, right?'

'He's the scene guard until we get there,' said Jadyn. 'Jim and Liz, they've cordoned the area off and will deal with any nosy types. Not that there will be many; the crime scene is out of the way really, just down past Mike's place. It isn't somewhere people will be walking past and having a look-see.'

'You mean Mike's garage?' Well, that's something, Harry thought. 'Take me through what we know so far.'

Jadyn took out his notebook. 'The body of Mr Lance Hamilton, age fifty-five, was found this morning by Sally Dent at approximately ten forty-five AM in her studio.'

'She was able to ID him, then?'

'She was,' Jadyn said. 'Very positively, too.'

'How do you mean? Are they friends?'

'We've not been able to question her yet; she was still in shock when we arrived. Not sure how she is now, though. Liz is looking after her until we get back.'

'You said studio,' said Harry.

'She's a potter,' Jadyn explained. 'You know, someone who makes pots and mugs and stuff, that kind of thing. Uses a wheel.'

'I do know what a potter is, Constable.'

'Can't see the attraction myself,' Jadyn added. 'Don't think I'd have the patience for anything like that. Art was never a strong point. Never enjoyed it at school.'

'You and me both.' Harry smiled. 'But then, I've never really been good with hobbies.'

'You should take up knitting,' Jadyn suggested.

'No, I don't think I should,' Harry replied, forcing himself to avoid examining why it was he didn't have a hobby or an interest, because he had a feeling looking too deeply there would uncover more than he was prepared to deal with.

'My dad's giving that a go. Seems to enjoy it,' Jadyn continued. 'Constantly making scarves. So, you might be getting one for Christmas.'

'I don't want a scarf for Christmas, or for any other reason, actually.'

'Well, I'm going to have to do something with them, aren't I? He's already given me three.'

Moving on from any further talk about scarves, Harry asked, 'So, what can you tell me about the body?'

'Jim was on the scene first,' Jadyn said. 'Ms Dent has confirmed she didn't enter the studio or touch the body or anything else. She was in shock when we arrived, and Liz went to fetch a blanket from my vehicle. Once she was comfortable, Jim popped back to the office and made up a flask of sweet tea, and that seemed to help a bit, too.'

'And what about you?' Harry asked. 'Yes, Jim was there first, but you were the first police officer, so what did you do?'

'I was able to confirm what both Ms Dent and Jim told me, that there was a body and that he, I mean the victim, Lance Hamilton, was definitely dead.'

'Definitely,' Harry repeated.

'Absolutely. I'd put money on it.'

'I'd prefer it if you didn't,' said Harry. 'However, I am going to assume that the cause of death was obvious?'

'You could say that, yes.'

Harry waited for Jadyn to elaborate, but the constable wasn't forthcoming.

'And ...?' he prompted.

'Blood, I saw that first,' said Jadyn. 'Jim mentioned it and he was right, there's plenty of it, which is never a good sign, is it?'

'Not generally, no,' Harry agreed. Hoping there was a little more to it than that, he added, 'Blood on its own isn't enough, though.'

'I know,' agreed Jadyn. 'But ...' He paused for a little too long. 'You see, both hands, they're missing.'

Harry rubbed his forehead in a pointless attempt to help him take in what Jadyn had just said, as though he could somehow push the information into his head and not only keep it there, but have it make some sort of sense. Had he really heard the constable correctly?

'Both hands?'

'Yes.'

'Missing?'

'Very much so. Not there at all, as far as I could tell.'

'In what way? I mean, you're sure this Mr Hamilton wasn't just sitting funny or wearing very long cuffs? You're absolutely sure the hands aren't there? Hands don't just go crawling off.'

'I'm sure, Boss,' said Jadyn. 'The hands are definitely not there; cut off at the wrists, by the looks of things. My guess is that he bled out. The body was sitting in a chair, clearly visible from the door. I couldn't see the hands near the body, or on the floor either.'

'And he's sitting in a chair? Without his hands?'

'Yes.'

'Could you see any signs of a struggle?'

Jadyn was quiet for a moment.

'No, I couldn't,' he said at last. 'Though we only looked in from the door. The room looked undisturbed. There are shelves with pots on them, drying, I guess, not that I'd know, but it didn't look to me like there had been a fight or anything. And a struggle would've definitely made a mess, I think. It looked like he'd just sat down and died. Just, you know, without his hands.'

'Then where the hell are they?' Harry demanded, neither looking for nor expecting an answer.

Jadyn said nothing.

'And we can't go making assumptions or jumping to conclusions,' Harry said. 'There's no way anyone can be sure that he bled out or that there wasn't a struggle, not until we've had the scene of crime team on it.' Then he added, 'So all we have is this Mr Hamilton, sitting in a chair, his hands have been cut off, there's blood, no signs of a struggle, and that's it?'

'Doesn't make much sense right now, does it?' said Jadyn. 'Less so now that I've said it out loud to you. Anyway, I've called the district surgeon, and she's on her way over to verify the death. We have his address and next of kin—he's married—so we can get over there and have a look around, see if there's anything there that can give us an idea what actually happened to him, and why.'

Harry scratched his chin, the phantom itch of his scars bothering him, but also to hide his smile at Jadyn, not only sounding like a competent police officer, but like a detective, too. Earlier in the year, he'd been responsible for investigating and arresting a gang of hare coursers, and Harry wondered if that had done his confidence some good. Also, and as he had said himself just a few minutes ago, they blurred the lines in the team, so it was no surprise that Jadyn was picking up things and maybe pushing faster than he would have had he been stationed elsewhere. Harry would encourage it from now on, that was for sure.

'Scene of crime team?'

'Done,' said Jadyn, then looked at his watch. 'I reckon if we set off now, we should still get back to Hawes before they turn up.'

'It's probably best we just head over there. We can talk as you're driving. And it sounds like you've got everything in hand.'

He dropped a hand onto Jadyn's shoulder. 'Well done, Constable Okri. Good work.'

The slightly deflated Jadyn perked up again.

'Thanks, Boss,' he smiled.

Harry said, 'I'll be with you in a minute.'

Jadyn headed back to his vehicle. Harry walked over to Arthur, Grace, and the dogs. Smudge sidled on over to nuzzle against his legs and Harry dropped down to give her ears a rub. She let out a soft, almost cat-like purr, then flopped down on the ground and showed Harry her belly. Harry obliged and gave it a rub.

'That all looked rather serious,' said Grace.

'It is,' said Harry, giving no further details about what had happened, his eyes on Smudge, who was using her front paws to reach up and hold his arm as he stroked her tummy. 'And I'm afraid I need to go.'

Harry noticed a definite pause before Grace spoke again.

'Duty calls then, does it?' she said at last.

Harry looked up and nodded, quite sure he had heard Grace add a quiet *again*.

'It's been a lovely morning,' he said, smiling. 'Really, I mean that. I'd rather stay here, that's for sure.'

'Can Gordy or Matt not look after things?' Grace asked. 'You don't have to go to every incident, do you? If you did, you'd be working twenty-four seven, and sometimes, it seems like you are, like you enjoy it.'

Harry shook his head.

'No, I don't,' he said, 'but Gordy's got the day off, and Matt—'

'So have you,' interrupted Grace. 'That's what today is, isn't it? A day off? You need them as much as anyone else.'

There wasn't much Harry could say to that because Grace was absolutely right, so he finished what he had been trying to say.

'Matt's already there, and Gordy is away for a day or two with Anna. For something like this, I really do need to be there. I'll call you later when I know what time I'll be done.'

'Well, it won't be in time to continue with any of this, will it?'

said Grace, the edge in her voice growing keener with every word. 'May as well just pack up and head home, eh, Dad?'

'You don't have to …'

'Well, there's not much point in staying, is there?'

'You get off, lad,' said Arthur, and Harry saw the old man turn his eyes on his daughter. 'We'll be fine, won't we, Grace?'

Grace smiled, though Harry wasn't so sure that her eyes had joined in with as much enthusiasm as usual. He felt sure that he should say something, that he wanted to say something, but whatever it was, it was stuck so far down his throat that when he opened his mouth, no words came. He looked at Grace, managed a faint smile, then with a nod to Arthur, turned on his heels and jogged after Jadyn.

SIX

The journey over to Hawes was swift thanks to Jadyn's blues and twos and the surprisingly empty roads. The only traffic they encountered was a bit of a queue to get into the ice cream parlour just a mile or so out of Aysgarth, on the road heading towards Bainbridge. Harry hadn't yet managed to stop by to try it out, but judging by Jadyn's enthusiasm for the place, and what he'd heard plenty of other people say about it, he'd have to do so soon, if only to stop him from talking about it.

'There's a bloke on the mountain rescue team who won't shut up about it,' Jadyn pointed out as they raced past the entrance to the parlour's small car park. 'Apparently, he has this little notebook filled with all his favourite places to get ice cream, and not just in the Dales either; all over the country. They've got loads of flavours, even liquorice.'

'As an ice cream?'

'It's brilliant!' Jadyn said. 'My favourite though, is black cherries and cream.'

Jadyn eventually stopped talking about ice cream, and soon enough, they turned onto the road to head along to the crime scene. Harry spotted his brother, Ben, busy at work in the yard of Mike's garage, and gave a wave. Ben returned it with a grease-stained hand and a broad, relaxed grin.

Harry shook his head, smiling to himself, once again amazed at the change in his younger brother. In every way possible, he was unrecognizable from what he had been before coming to Wensleydale; the Dales had changed him in so many ways, that was true, and the job had clearly done him a world of good, but it was PCSO Liz Coates who had really made the difference. She hadn't changed him, Harry thought, just given him the space to be himself, and to breathe. They were good together, and he could not be happier for them.

'Here we go,' Jadyn said, slowing the vehicle to a stop by the pavement.

Harry looked ahead to see cordon tape around a small, low building, Matt front and centre. He couldn't see Liz yet but knew she would be close by with the woman who had found the body. Jim was nowhere in sight.

Climbing out of Jadyn's vehicle, Harry gave a nod to Matt, who was making his way over to meet them, when a voice called out from behind. He turned around to see Jim approaching, a carrier bag over one arm, and his hands clutching two cardboard trays of disposable cups.

'Coffees,' Jim said, coming over to meet them. 'Figured you'd want one anyway, Boss, so I just went ahead and got them for everyone.'

Harry reached out and took a coffee, lifting the scalding liquid to his lips, enjoying the rich, earthy aroma as he took a burning sip.

'Good work, Jim,' he said. 'What's in the bag?'

'Just a few bits and bobs,' said Jim, placing the rest of the coffees on the bonnet of Jadyn's car and unhooking the bag from his arm to hand it to Harry. 'Here you go.'

Harry opened the bag to find it was filled with lots of smaller white paper bags.

'Grabbed a load of sandwiches from the Penny Garth at the top of Hawes,' Jim explained, 'then couldn't resist popping into Cockett's for jam tarts and some shortbread biscuits. Help yourself.'

Harry did exactly that as Matt came to a stop in front of him and took a coffee.

'Now then, Boss,' said the detective sergeant, looking at Harry as he dipped a hand into the bag to remove a sandwich. 'How are you doing, then?'

'Oh, just grand,' Harry said with a little more huff than he meant to express. 'Where's Liz?'

'She's over in the Land Rover,' Matt said, gesturing behind him with a dip of his head. Harry glanced up the road, seeing the old truck parked up. 'Looking after Sally Dent.'

Jadyn and Jim headed off to stand over by the cordon tape, coffees and sandwiches in hand.

Harry bit into his sandwich, which he immediately discovered was not only filled with a considerable amount of roast beef, but enough horseradish to burn the back of his eyes with every bite.

'Rough to be called away from your day with Grace,' said Matt. Seeing that Harry's eyes were watering, he added, 'You alright there?'

Harry wiped his eyes and took another bite, enjoying the pain of what he was eating as much as the taste.

'Don't forget Arthur. Oh, and the dogs,' he said.

'What?'

'Arthur; he was there, too.'

Harry saw confusion on Matt's face.

'Arthur? But I thought it was a special day, an anniversary, or something,' said Matt, a mischievous grin creeping onto his face. 'Just the two of you, like.'

Then he winked, though Harry ignored it.

'He was there to teach me to shoot,' Harry explained. 'Grace couldn't do it on her own, as they needed one of them on the clay trap, so she was on that, while Arthur gave me the benefit of his wisdom on all things shotguns. And believe you me, he knows an awful lot about the subject, that's for sure.'

'But you were in the Paras, so I'm going to assume you can shoot. At least I hope you can; don't really like the idea of our crack troops not being able to do the very thing they've actually been trained to do.'

'You assume incorrectly,' said Harry. 'Not about the Paras, or me being able to shoot, because I can, or at least I used to be able to. Today, though? Couldn't hit a bloody thing.'

Matt laughed, and the sound was so jovial that Harry couldn't help but join in.

'It's not funny,' he said, still laughing.

'Oh, I think it is,' said Matt.

Harry said, 'Well, it's a bit different to handling an SA80,' and saw confusion flicker on Matt's face. 'That's the rifle used by the British Army,' he explained. 'I'm pretty good with one of those, just not so good with a shotgun trying to hit tiny clay plates flying through the air at a thousand miles an hour.'

'Between you and me, neither am I,' said Matt. 'It's a bit of fun though, isn't it? And I do love the smell after you've fired a few.'

'I quickly developed the undeniable urge to snap the gun in half and throw it into a tree,' grumbled Harry.

'Patience isn't a strong point with you, is it? Grace isn't too disappointed, I hope. About the day, I mean, and you being called away. Not you being a shite shot.'

Harry gave Matt a moment to quell his laughing.

'No, she's fine,' he said. Though remembering how they'd parted, he wasn't so sure. He took another bite of the sandwich, the burn of the horseradish refusing to diminish.

'Are you sure you're alright, there?' Matt asked.

Harry wiped his eyes again.

'Fine,' he said. 'Jadyn's given me a rundown of what we've got.'

'No doubt you'll be wanting a look around before the SOC team turns up,' said Matt, then glanced at his watch. 'Margaret should be arriving any moment now.'

Margaret Shaw was the district surgeon who would come out to confirm death. It was a formality, but a vital one. It also gave

Harry the chance to have a natter with one of his favourite people in the Dales.

'Do we know when the SOC team will arrive?'

'Actually, Sowerby called just before you arrived to say they'll be another half hour,' Matt said. 'So, we've plenty of time.'

Harry finished his sandwich, drained his coffee.

'Best we go have a look then.'

A car horn stopped Harry before he had made his first step away from Jadyn's vehicle. Turning around, he saw a shiny, dark blue Range Rover thump into the kerb at the side of the road, before bumping up onto the pavement and coming to a sudden stop, one wheel firmly off the road. The engine was given a blisteringly loud rev, then turned off.

'Margaret?' Harry said, as much to himself as to Matt.

'Not seen her drive that thing before, have you?' said Matt.

The driver's door opened and out stepped a woman wearing Wellington boots and a waxed jacket covered in patches and holes. Harry watched as she slammed the door, swore loudly at the vehicle, gave it a stern kick, then turned to walk towards them.

'Hello, Margaret,' he said, as she came to stand in front of him. 'New wheels there, I see?'

'Yes, and they're too bloody big!' Margaret said, not exactly answering the question. 'The whole thing is just one enormous lump of stupidity; it's like trying to drive a barge! No idea why I bought it. What the hell was I thinking? Well, shall I tell you? I wasn't thinking at all, was I? No, not in the slightest, that's more than clear. I got whisked along by all this guff and nonsense from the delightful sales team at the garage. Only went along for a test drive because I got a leaflet through the letterbox about it and I was bored. And next thing I know, I'm driving home in that! I'm a fool, Harry, a damned fool!'

Harry was having to work hard not to laugh.

'It's very nice, though,' he said. 'I'm sure you'll get used to it.'

'I don't want to get used to it!' Margaret replied. 'I want shot of the thing; that's what I want. You should've seen the look on Rebecca's face when she saw it.'

'I can imagine.'

'I'm an idiot, Harry, that's what I am, an absolute bloody idiot! I'm too old to be doing anything like this.'

'Don't be so hard on yourself,' said Matt. 'Give it time, and you'll be fine.'

For a moment or two, Harry watched as Margaret simply stood there, staring at her new vehicle, huffing and puffing loudly as though to do so enough would make the thing disappear or perhaps just drive away of its own accord never to be seen again.

'Anyway, enough of all that,' she said at last, turning around to face Harry directly. She clapped her hands together. 'Let's go and have a look at what we've got then, shall we?'

'Lead the way,' Harry said, turning to Matt, who handed them all disposable facemasks, gloves, and covers for their shoes.

Matt walked over to the cordon tape, where it was lifted by Jadyn, who was now the scene guard, with Jim standing beside him. They'd both finished their sandwiches.

'Morning, Margaret,' Jim said.

'And you can shut up as well,' Margaret replied, storming past. Harry smiled as he chased after her, hearing Jim laughing quietly behind them as he followed.

Coming up to the building, Matt stopped.

'Right, now then,' he said, holding his hands out as if to ward Harry and Margaret away from what they were about to see, 'just to warn you, it's not pretty, if you know what I mean.'

Margaret sucked in a long, slow breath, then exhaled just as slowly.

'My dear detective,' she said, reaching out to rest a gentle hand on Matt's arm, 'I've seen things so awful I should by rights be an absolute wreck of a human, someone who never sleeps and finds solace in the bottom of a bottle. You will notice I am none of those. Well, on Tuesdays maybe, and so long as the bottle is a decent red, but anyway, let's not dilly-dally, eh?'

Matt led the way, followed by Margaret. Harry was bringing up the rear when he paused as he heard footsteps behind him. He turned around to see a figure in a white boilersuit jogging over; it was Rebecca Sowerby, the pathologist, and Margaret's only daughter. Parked up in front of Jadyn's vehicle were two large, white transit vans, their contents already being disgorged by the SOC team. He could hear the engines popping and clinking as they cooled.

'Thought you weren't going to be here for another half an hour,' Harry said.

'Sorry to disappoint you,' Rebecca replied.

Harry noticed an edge to the pathologist's voice.

'That's not what I meant.'

'If you must know, a jackknifed tractor-trailer blocked the road. Farmer cleared it rather more quickly than anyone expected.'

'You're just in time to join us, then.'

'Well, I wouldn't want to miss anything.'

'Your mum's leading the way.'

'Of course she is. No change there, then. You've seen her new vehicle?'

Harry laughed.

'Couldn't miss it.'

Sowerby shook her head and rolled her eyes.

'What the hell was she thinking? Such a waste of money, and at her age, too! Sometimes, she's just got no sense at all.'

'To be honest, I think it kind of suits her,' said Harry, noticing a weary and irritated edge to the pathologist's voice, 'though judging by the look in your eyes right now, I'm going to assume you don't exactly agree.'

'She's an absolute bloody liability in it,' Sowerby said. 'If she doesn't drive into a field or through a house or off a cliff, I'll be amazed.' She then leaned around Harry and called over to her mother. 'Nice bit of parking there, Mum. Next time, see if you can't take up even more of the pavement.'

'That's not helpful, Rebecca,' Margaret replied, without turning to look at her daughter. 'Not helpful at all.'

'She's got a point,' whispered Harry.

Sowerby turned narrowed eyes on Harry.

'Has she, now? Really? And what point would that be? More to the point, what's it got to do with you?'

Harry stared at the pathologist for a moment, a little taken aback. The edge in her voice seemed to be getting sharper by the second. It reminded him of how things used to be between them, in his early days in the Dales, when they really hadn't got on at all. But gradually they'd learned to work together, and eventually developed a relationship that he not only respected but valued. And perhaps, if pushed, Harry thought he might even go so far as to describe Rebecca as a friend. So, what had her so on edge this morning?

'You okay?' he asked.

'I'm fine.'

'Of course you are.'

'Can we just get on?'

Seeing that he wasn't going to get anything more from Sowerby, Harry gave a nod to Matt up front, and they all headed towards the open door of the studio.

SEVEN

'I've already seen what we're dealing with,' Matt said, standing aside to let the others pass. 'And it's not exactly spacious in there either; if I come in with you, odds are that most of those shelves will quickly become acquainted with my shoulder, and in the excitement, lose all those pots they're supporting.'

'You make it sound like you're the clumsiest man on the planet,' said Margaret.

'I am,' Matt replied. 'Though Harry gives me a run for my money.'

Harry ignored the comment and followed Margaret into the studio, with the pathologist coming along behind.

The studio was small, though Harry wasn't sure how large a pottery studio was supposed to be. He saw the shelves Matt was so afraid of attached to the opposite wall, next to a sink. To the right of the open door were two potter's wheels, and to the left, a glass display cabinet filled with objects so complex in design that Harry was baffled as to how they could be made only from clay. Hanging on the walls were hooks with aprons, two speakers wired to an old music system covered in dust and clay, and various shelves of books. Another set of shelves was straining under the weight of numerous white tubs. In the wall to the right sat another door. Harry pointed at it.

'That leads to the kiln,' Matt said, leaning in through the open door.

'You've had a look?' Harry asked.

'No,' Matt replied. 'Wasn't about to risk disturbing the crime scene. Sally, the lass who owns the place, she told me. That's why she was down here today, you see; she'd had stuff in the kiln and needed to see how it was doing, I think. Don't quote me on that, though; probably best to ask her. She said something about having to clear the kiln out to fill it again with all the new stuff she's been making. And looking at those shelves over there, she's been busy.'

'Well, I can absolutely confirm that he's dead,' Margaret said, standing just inside the door. 'And I can, hand on heart, say that it's moments like these that make me happy to have spent so long at university and in numerous hospitals honing my trade. Otherwise, how would I have known?'

'It's procedure, Mum,' Sowerby said, shaking her head, her voice sharp.

'Well, my dear, sometimes procedure is an ass.'

Harry laughed at that, but as he moved closer to the body, to stand next to Sowerby, his smile soon died.

'I don't think I've ever seen anything like this,' he said.

'You say that with a modicum of surprise,' said Margaret.

'Like you, like all of us, I've seen some of the worst things imaginable,' Harry replied. 'This, though? It kind of looks like a little bit of torture, doesn't it? But I don't think it is.'

Harry could tell that the others were all staring at him.

'What?' he said.

'A little bit of torture?' said Sowerby. 'And what's that supposed to mean?'

Yeah, something is definitely niggling at her, Harry thought, but decided it was probably best to ignore it for now.

'Well, it wasn't an accident, was it?' he said. 'That's more than obvious.'

'Nothing at a crime scene is ever obvious.'

'I'm going to take a risk here and suggest, fairly confidently, that he didn't cut his hands off while messing around with clay.'

Sowerby asked, 'How can you be flippant when faced with something like this? Sometimes, no, a lot of the time, I just don't understand you at all.'

'I'm not being flippant,' Harry replied.

'Anyway, there's no such thing as a little bit of torture, is there?' Sowerby said. 'Any torture is a lot of torture, because it's torture.'

Harry shook his head.

'Trust me, there are scales of awful when it comes to this stuff,' he said. 'People can be pretty imaginative when it comes to inflicting pain.'

'There's no one in this room who hasn't seen evidence of that,' said Margaret.

Harry continued.

'You'll have gangs kidnapping members of other gangs, sometimes to extort information or money, other times out of revenge. Then there are those individuals who just love doing awful things to others because they can, because it gives them a thrill, makes them feel powerful, sometimes even because the other party actually wants them to.'

'Spare us the details,' said Sowerby, holding a hand up to shush Harry. 'I don't need them, and I don't think anyone else here does, either.'

'The worst, though,' Harry said, continuing anyway, and probably because the pathologist's bad mood was rubbing off on him, 'was a bloke who called himself an enforcer.'

Matt asked, 'What did he enforce?'

'In simple terms, terror and pain if you missed a payment on a loan or ignored his messages.'

'A loan shark?'

'He enjoyed it,' Harry said. 'He hoped people would miss payments because that gave him a chance to indulge himself. He dressed in a suit, looked respectable, carried a briefcase. When we finally pinned something on him and had a look inside, we found not only a very professional range of instruments that Margaret here would know more about than any of us, but also a collection of souvenirs.'

'You don't have to tell us what they were,' said Matt.

'Let's just say he was a firm believer in the notion of having his pound of flesh,' said Harry. 'The suitcase contained various fingers and ears and toes, even a nose, all preserved in tightly sealed jars, but what we found when we searched his property?' Harry shook his head. 'It still haunts me. Sometimes, there are things that can never be unseen.'

'Back to what you were saying then,' said Matt, 'and the quicker the better I think; so how is this not torture, then?'

Harry moved further into the room, careful to disturb nothing, touch nothing.

'For a start, look at his wrists.'

'What about them?' asked Sowerby. 'We can all see his hands have been cut off, can't we?'

'Yes, but our victim isn't tied to the chair he's in,' said Harry. 'He's just sitting there, with both of his hands missing. And like you've just said, we can all see that they've been cut or hacked off in some way.'

'What's your point?' Sowerby asked.

'My point is that the only way to do that to anyone, to cut their hands off, is to have the wrists tied tightly to something, and to have the rest of the victim incapacitated somehow. Either that, or you drug them to make sure they're unconscious, or at the very least, unable to do anything about what's happening to them.'

'You're right, it is a bit odd, isn't it?' said Margaret.

'There's no sign of a struggle either,' Harry said, gesturing to the rest of the room with a wave of his hand. 'Matt, you said it yourself, that if you came in, you'd knock into something, break a few pots, right? So, how did our friend end up here, not only dead but minus his hands, without kicking up a bit of a fuss about it?'

'On that point,' Sowerby said, crouching down to have a look at the wounds on the wrists, and at the blood, which had stained the victim's trousers, and pooled on the floor. 'Is it me, or does there not seem to be all that much blood?'

Harry wasn't sure. His eyes were focused on the wrists and the questions racing around his mind.

'Why take the hands in the first place?' he asked. 'If this was a gang thing—and I'm going to go out on a limb here and guess that it isn't, because this area isn't exactly awash with them—then I'd be thinking that there was some symbolism here, like the hands had touched something they shouldn't have, or he was a thief, that kind of thing. But this? It doesn't add up. I know nothing about who or what Mr Hamilton was, so maybe when I do, it'll all make a lot more sense. But at first glance, it's a little strange.'

'And where are the hands, anyway?' asked Matt, looking around the studio. 'You think whoever did this took them? And if they did, why?'

'Souvenirs, like Harry just said, maybe,' said Margaret.

'Why would they do any of this?' Harry asked.

A shadow appeared behind Matt. It was the photographer, a man whose misplaced sense of humour was not found amusing by anyone Harry knew, and especially not by himself.

'Well, at least he's sitting more still than the kids at the primary school I've just come from,' the photographer said, his eyes on the body. 'So, I assume I won't be needing this then, will I?'

He lifted a hand to reveal a glove puppet in the shape of a squirrel.

No one laughed.

'And just what the holy hell is that?' Sowerby asked.

'This is Mr Squirrel.'

'Yes, I can see that it's a squirrel ...'

'No, not *a* squirrel, *Mr* Squirrel; he's my friend, and he helps entertain the children and make sure the little buggers don't fidget too much when I'm trying to take their photograph.'

'You have issues,' said Sowerby with a despairing shake of her head.

Harry watched as the photographer made the squirrel wave a little fluffy paw at the pathologist.

'We'll leave you to it,' he said, and made his way back outside, forcing the photographer to step back.

Margaret and her daughter followed him out of the room.

'Photos shouldn't take long,' Sowerby said. 'Then we'll get the body removed so we can document the scene and get everything bagged up and taken away.'

'It's an odd one,' said Margaret. 'And I'm fully aware of just how enormous an understatement that is.'

'You're right though, it is,' agreed Harry. 'There's killing someone in the heat of the moment, there's killing someone after a bit of planning, and then there's something like this. What's the motive behind any of it?'

'That's your job to find out, isn't it?' said Sowerby. 'So, why don't you crack on with that, and leave me to the bit I can do?'

There it was again, Harry noticed, that sharpness. He was tempted to ignore it, but if something was up, he needed to know. So, he gestured for Rebecca to move away from the others.

'I think we need to have a little talk,' he said.

'I don't think we do,' Sowerby replied.

The look Harry gave her was more than enough to let her know he wasn't about to take that as an answer.

EIGHT

'Right, then,' Harry said, 'what's going on?'

'Nothing,' said Sowerby. 'Why?'

'Don't give me that,' Harry replied. 'Something's niggling you, and I need to know what it is.'

'Again, why? You're not the boss of me.'

'A blessing for us both, I think,' said Harry, 'but this is my investigation, and if there's a problem, I need to deal with it and make sure it's no longer a problem.'

'I don't know what you mean.'

Harry folded his arms.

'I know we're work colleagues,' he said, 'but I'm pretty sure that now and again we've strayed into the territory of being friends. Terrifying though that is for us both, make the most of it, and be honest with me.'

'I am.'

'Rebecca ...'

Still nothing.

Harry frowned.

'If you don't talk to me, I'm going to go and speak with our favourite photographer over there, ask if I can borrow Mr Squirrel ...'

Harry saw the pathologist's shoulders drop a little.

'You wouldn't dare.'

'Try me,' Harry said and held up his hand, wiggling his fingers.

'I hate puppets,' Sowerby said. 'Creep the hell out of me.'

'Well, get talking, then.'

'You really want to know?'

'Yes,' Harry said. 'I'm not saying I can help with whatever it is, but voicing what's on your mind might do you some good.'

'Lance the boil, you mean?'

'Something like that.'

The pathologist took a breath, then exhaled long and slow.

'I'm not sleeping, Harry,' she said. 'Haven't been for weeks now.'

'That's not good. Do you know why?'

'I keep getting ... flashbacks.'

'Flashbacks? To what? I imagine you're spoiled for choice in that area.'

For the first time since she had arrived at the crime scene, Harry saw a smile on Rebecca's face.

'Yeah, you're right there,' she said. 'And that's the problem; there's no one identifiable event I keep seeing. It's as though every damned crime scene I've ever been to is vying for a few moments of fame in my mind. I go to bed, I close my eyes, and there they all are, pushing and shoving and screaming at me to take notice. I can't bear it ...'

'And it's been like this for how long? Just a few weeks, or longer?'

'Yes.'

'That's not an answer.'

'A few weeks, that's all.'

Harry wasn't convinced and had an inkling what might be the cause.

'It's a year now, isn't it?' he said. 'Give or take.'

Sowerby didn't reply, just stared at Harry.

'I'm right, aren't I? It's been a year since that explosion over in Reeth, the one you were frankly bloody lucky to survive.'

And she had been, Harry thought, because he knew from personal experience what it was like to be caught in a bomb blast; his reflection reminded him of it every day, though the physical scars were nothing compared with the psychological. He knew what it was like to go without sleep.

'I'd rather not talk about it.'

'And I'm thinking that's probably your problem right there,' Harry said. 'Two of your team lost their lives that day. Just because you had counselling back then, doesn't mean that's the end of it, that it's all dealt with.'

'Well, I've not got the time right now to—'

Harry cut Sowerby off.

'Horseshit!' he said, his voice quiet, but no less formidable. 'This is one of those rare occasions where the person you're speaking to actually says *I understand* and isn't talking out of their arse!'

'Seriously, Harry, this isn't the time ...'

'And my guess is you've been telling yourself that for too long,' Harry said, not about to back down. 'Hiding how you feel deep down, because it's easier that way, or that's how it seems. Well, here's some news for you; it isn't, not at all. Because it never goes away, and that's what you really have to understand if you're going to move on at all. What happened to you, you can't ignore it, you can't run from it, you can't hide from it, but what you can do is learn to face it and to deal with it.'

'Who made you my therapist?'

'I'm not your therapist, Rebecca. I'm your friend,' Harry said. 'And believe you me, I don't say that lightly, or to just anyone.'

Sowerby reached out and gave his arm a squeeze.

'Aw, that's sweet,' she said, but Harry was having none of it.

'Sarcasm suits you most of the time, but right now, not in the slightest,' he said. 'This is serious. I know where this can lead. I've lost mates to PTSD, friends who saw taking their own lives as the only way out. So, this is how things are going to go ...'

'You can't give me orders, you know that, don't you?'

'It's either me or the squirrel.'

'Give me a moment ...'

Harry didn't.

'We're going to work this case together, as we always do, but at some point today, you're going to call whoever you need to call—I'm assuming you still have the contact details for the counsellor you worked with last year—and book an appointment. You are then going to tell me when that appointment is, and you are going to go to it.'

Sowerby went to protest, but Harry just kept right on talking, bulldozing his way through her words.

'You are also going to speak to your mum about this, because she needs to know and I'm damned sure she would be mighty angry to find out you had been hiding it from her.'

'Is there anything else?'

'Oh, I think that's more than enough to be getting on with,' Harry said, then as he turned to head back to the cordon tape. 'I'll call you later, about what's happened here, but also about this.'

'I don't like to be checked up on.'

'Sue me,' Harry said. Then, without waiting for a reply, he headed back to the cordon tape as the rest of the scene of crime team moved into the studio with their equipment.

'How are you doing, Boss?' Jim asked.

'Better than our friend in there, that's for sure,' Harry replied. 'What details do we have on him?'

'Like I said earlier, we've an address, and the name and contact details of his wife,' said Jadyn. 'Her name's Leslie.'

'Has anyone contacted her yet?'

Harry watched both Jadyn and Jim shake their heads.

'Not yet, no,' said Jadyn.

'Is Liz still in the car with the woman who found the body?' Harry asked.

'Sally Dent? Yes, she is,' answered Jim. 'Want me to go and fetch her?'

'No,' said Harry. 'I'll go over and have a quick talk with her myself, then I'll head off and speak with the victim's wife. If you could confirm her whereabouts, that would be useful.'

With nothing else to add, Harry headed over to the old Police Land Rover. He gave a gentle knock on the rear passenger window to get Liz's attention, who then opened the door and stepped out.

'How is she?' Harry asked.

'She's how anyone would be if they turned up to work and found someone dead in their office,' Liz said. 'She's calmed down, though.'

'I understand she knows the victim.'

'She does ...'

Harry noticed a change in Liz's tone, and moved away from the Land Rover, forcing her to follow.

'Something the matter?' he asked.

Liz glanced back at the Land Rover, and the woman sitting inside it.

'She's told me that she had a bit of a fling with him,' Liz said. 'I've not got any of the details yet, but I don't think it was all that long ago. She sort of just blurted it out, then clammed up about it. He booked some private pottery lessons with her, one thing led to another ...'

'And he ends up in her studio with his hands cut off,' Harry said.

'I know people react badly after a break-up, but this seems to be pushing things a little far, don't you think?' said Liz. 'I know she's going to be a suspect, but I'm just not seeing it.'

'You'd be surprised how unlike a murderer most murderers look or seem.'

'Even so,' said Liz.

'Most times, they're just the person next door. Only makes it even more terrifying if you ask me. It would be a whole lot easier if more of them did look like murderers, I can tell you.'

'That's not what I mean,' Liz replied.

'Then what do you mean?'

'You can't fake shock like this,' Liz explained. 'You could try, but this is real, I'm sure of it.'

'Does she have an alibi?'

'She was home alone last night.'

'So, that's a no, then.'

'There was some meeting up in the Market Hall in town. She said Lance was there, too, at the meeting I mean, and that was the last time she saw him. She went home after that.'

'I need to speak with her,' Harry said. 'You think she'll be alright with that?'

'If you'd been here when we first arrived on-scene, no,' said Liz, 'but she's okay now, I think. Still in shock, obviously, but she should be alright.'

Harry walked over to the Land Rover and ducked his head inside the rear of the vehicle.

'Sally Dent?' he said.

The woman opposite was petite. She was wearing blue denim dungarees and scuffed brown leather boots. Her hair was dark and pulled back in a rough ponytail, held in place by a scrap of leather pinned in place by a thin piece of short, sharp wood. The blanket Liz and Jim had given her was resting on her shoulders and she was nursing a plastic cup of tea. She looked at Harry, sipped the drink.

Harry took out his ID.

'I'm Detective Chief Inspector Harry Grimm.'

'You're not going to arrest me, are you?'

'I just need to ask you some questions, that's all,' Harry explained. 'Mind if we have a little chat?'

'I didn't ... I didn't do *that* ... I couldn't. You have to believe me. I don't even know why he was in my studio!'

Harry slipped into the Land Rover, closing the door softly behind him. The woman shuffled away to jam herself up against the other door.

'How's the tea?' Harry asked, wondering if she was about to do a runner, though to where he had no idea because, with most of his team here, she wouldn't exactly get far. But blind panic was a powerful force and it could make even the most rational of humans do the most irrational of things. Even kill someone, he thought, though he kept that to himself.

'What?'

'The tea,' Harry asked. 'I could do with a mug of the stuff myself.'

'It's very sweet,' Sally said. 'I don't usually have it with sugar.'

'Did they bring you any biscuits? Can't have tea without biscuits, right?'

Sally shook her head.

'No, I suppose not.'

Harry leaned out of the door.

'Liz?'

The PCSO walked over.

'There's a bag over in Jadyn's car, I think; Jim bought a load of sandwiches and whatnot down when I arrived. Can you go check to see if there are any biscuits left? I didn't see Matt get his hands on them, so we might get lucky.'

Liz dashed off and returned barely a minute later.

'You're in luck,' she said, handing Harry the bag.

Harry turned back to face Sally.

'Here you go,' he said. 'Cockett's shortbread, so should be good. I mean, when is it ever anything else?'

Sally reached into the bag and took a biscuit.

Harry did the same.

'Good, aren't they?' he said. He was just about to start with a few questions, when a scream and a thump ripped the moment apart, and Harry found himself staring into the wild eyes of a woman on the other side of Sally's window.

NINE

'You killed him! You killed my husband! That's what you did; you murdered him, didn't you? I know you did!'

Harry watched as Sally scuttled away from the woman on the other side of the window, who was now banging so hard against the glass that he thought it could shatter at any moment.

Then the door opened.

Harry reached over to grab hold of Sally, opened his door, and pulled them both out, away from the other woman. Sally's tea went everywhere, scalding his lap.

'You bitch! You mad little bitch! You killed him! You slept with him and you killed him!'

'Liz! Jadyn! Anyone!' Harry roared. 'Help here! Now!'

As Harry dragged Sally further away from the Land Rover, he saw the woman lunge into the vehicle to chase after them, only to be stopped before her head had even made it past the door. Liz and Jim blocked her way, and Matt and Jadyn were at the other door, blocking her exit.

'Here, come on, I've got you,' Harry said, leading Sally further away, and trying to ignore the large wet patch on his trousers.

The other woman, who Harry assumed, based on what she was saying and doing, was the victim's wife, Leslie, was putting up quite the fight. He watched his team work hard to calm her down. She had some lungs on her, too, his ears ringing from the shouting.

'You know her, I assume?' Harry asked Sally.

Sally gave a sharp nod. Harry noticed her eyes weren't so much filled with fear at what had just happened, but rage.

'She's Lance's wife,' Sally said. 'We don't get on.'

'I gathered that,' said Harry.

Matt waved to indicate that they had everything under control. Harry called Jadyn over.

'What's she doing here?' he asked Jadyn. 'I asked you to confirm her whereabouts, not invite her over to the crime scene for a chinwag!'

'I didn't!'

'Then what exactly did you say to her? Why the hell is she here?'

Jadyn shook his head.

'I've no idea,' Jadyn said. 'I was about to go and try to contact her when she just turned up.'

Harry looked over to see that the rest of the team had somehow managed to calm Leslie down. Though she was still making a scene, her rage had turned to tears and wailing.

He asked Jadyn to look after Sally for a moment, then called Matt over and took him to one side.

'What's the story, then?' he asked once they were out of earshot.

'She drove down here of her own accord,' said Matt. 'At least that's what I've gathered from what she's said between all of the shouting. And there's been quite a bit of that, hasn't there?'

'Bit weird, though, isn't it?' Harry said, spotting a small red sports car parked up the road. 'To just come wandering along to a pottery studio looking for your husband. Who, it turns out, is dead.'

'She's saying that her husband—that's Lance—never came home last night, and she guessed he would be here, like. She came round to confront him, or maybe both of them, I think.'

Harry looked over at Sally.

'Liz said something about her and our victim having an affair, or that they'd had one and it had ended badly.'

'Not sure at what point an affair doesn't end badly, for all parties,' said Matt. 'Anyway, she arrives here, sees all of what's going on—the police, the white suits—and puts two and two together—'

'And attacks our witness,' said Harry.

'Something like that.'

A guttural yell split the air, the sound a twisted mix of rage and sorrow. Harry looked over to see Liz leading Leslie away from the Land Rover and along the road, towards Jadyn's car. She opened one of the rear doors and helped Leslie to sit down.

'She's good at that, isn't she?' Matt said.

'The screaming and the wailing?'

'Yes,' said Matt. 'Don't usually see people have that kind of reaction, though.'

'How do you mean?' Harry asked.

'Shock, it usually has people stunned into silence, doesn't it? And she's very much not that.'

'I'm going to have to speak with her,' Harry said. 'But that would probably be better done up at the office, I think, rather than here.'

'Want me to take her there?' Matt offered.

'Yes,' Harry said. 'Grab Jadyn's keys, leave the ones for the Land Rover with me. See if you can at least make her comfortable. Obviously, she's aware now of what's happened, but not the details, so make sure you keep those to yourself. She'll know that soon enough. I'll be along in a bit, once I've had a chat with Sally.'

With that decided, Harry and Matt went over to Jadyn and Sally and explained what was going to happen. Harry saw Sally relax a little at the news that Lance's wife was to be taken elsewhere.

Once Matt had taken Lance's wife away, Harry led Sally back to the Land Rover.

'Once we've had a little chat, I can drive you home,' he said.

'But I've work to do,' Sally replied. 'I'm behind as it is. I need to get into my studio.'

'I'm afraid that's not going to be possible for quite a while yet,' Harry said.

'How long?'

'Your studio is a crime scene,' Harry explained. 'The people you've seen in the white suits, they're documenting everything now. We need to be absolutely sure that any evidence we could possibly need has been collected before we hand the place back to you.'

'Yes, I know, but how long? Is it a day, a week, a month?'

'Honestly, usually no longer than a day, perhaps two.'

'Okay,' Sally said.

Harry twisted himself in the seat so that he was facing Sally a little better.

'Where were we?' he asked, taking out his notebook.

'You were going to ask me some questions,' Sally said. 'I don't know what about though because I've told you I didn't do ... that. I didn't. I couldn't. His hands ... I mean, I just can't imagine ...'

'Can we just run over a few details?' Harry asked. 'If you could confirm your name for me?'

'But you know it already.'

'I do, but just to confirm it ...'

'Sally Dent. This is my pottery studio. Do you want my home address and telephone number as well?'

'If that's okay.'

Sally removed a scuffed wallet from a pocket and handed Harry a small card.

'There you go,' she said. 'All my contact details are on there.'

Harry slipped the card into the back of his notebook.

'If you're alright to do so, it might be best if you tell me exactly what happened,' Harry said. 'No rush, just take your time.'

Sally was quiet for a moment, thoughtful, then said, 'You're not charging me, are you?'

'Pardon?'

'You're not arresting me, anything like that? Do I need a solicitor? I don't want to say anything if it will be used against me, or whatever it is the police say to people before arresting them.'

'Look, right now, all I'm trying to do is to work out what happened, and to do that, I need you to just tell me as much as you can. You're not under arrest, just helping with an investigation. Obviously, you don't have to tell me anything, though I would advise against it.'

'Why?'

Harry really wasn't in the mood for all the questions. Which gave him a choice, and that was to either suck it up and keep answering them, or to nudge Sally in the right direction.

'Let me ask you a question, nice and direct,' he said.

'Okay ...'

'Did you kill Mr Lance Hamilton?'

Sally's eyes went wide.

'What? God, no, of course not! I've already told you that! No! I wouldn't! I couldn't! Why the hell did you ask me that?'

'Well, right now, all I've got is your word to that effect,' Harry said.

'But you must know that I didn't do it!'

'The only way I can know anything at all right now, is if you tell me everything you know; why you're here, what time you got here, how you know Lance, everything.'

Sally pursed her lips, like she was trying to keep whatever words she needed to say trapped inside.

'How did he get into your studio?' Harry asked. 'I'm assuming it's kept locked.'

There was a slight pause, as though Sally was trying to stop herself from talking, but just couldn't.

'I was sleeping with him, okay?' she blurted out, her voice loud and sharp. 'I was sleeping with him and had been for a couple of months, and now I'm not. Well, of course I'm not, not anymore, because he's dead, isn't he? But you know what I mean; we were a thing, then we were no longer a thing, and you know what, him being dead? I couldn't care less! There, I've said it. Happy?'

'Let's roll this back a bit, then,' Harry said, reeling a little from the anger in Sally's voice. 'How did you first get to know Lance?'

'I've known of him for years,' Sally said. 'It's a small place, Hawes, isn't it? I've seen you around plenty often enough, too. You're dating that gamekeeper from over in Carperby, aren't you?'

Harry smiled a little, hearing someone he'd neither spoken to nor seen before telling him such precise details about his own life. But that was the Dales, wasn't it? Everyone knew everyone else.

'You said you were sleeping with him,' he said, moving on. 'Were you friends beforehand, then?'

Sally shook her head.

'He was a client,' she said. 'I do private lessons as well as group ones, and he booked a few. No idea why, really. Boredom, I think. His business seems to run itself and he was looking for something to fill his time. One thing led to another and, well, you can guess the rest.'

'Did you know he was married?'

'Of course I did!' Sally laughed. 'Not like it mattered.'

Harry parked that comment for the moment.

'How long did the affair last?'

Sally shook her head and laughed.

'Affair? It was never long enough to become an affair. And anyway, you can't have an affair with someone if their marriage is a sham, can you? Which is why all of that makes no sense.'

'All of what?'

'Her screaming and yelling,' said Sally.

'So, what happened between you?' Harry said.

'He promised more than he could, or wanted to give, that's what,' Sally said. 'And I was an idiot to even get involved, I know that. Plus, he was, well, just a bit, I don't know, obsessive, possessive. Scared me, to be honest. Liked it rough, too, if you know what I mean.'

'How so?'

Sally fell quiet.

'Was he abusive?' Harry asked.

'It was all consensual, until it wasn't. He didn't take kindly to being told no. I didn't know he had taken one of my spare studio keys. I've a few because I'm always losing them. And like I said, I hadn't got around to getting it back. I found him hiding in the kiln room one night, naked, and sweating in the heat of the place. He expected me to be excited by it all. Trust me, that man naked is not exciting. Even when he's tied up.'

'What did you do?'

'I kicked him out, that's what!' Sally said.

'But you kept seeing him?'

She nodded.

'Why?'

'Wish I knew. He had charisma, I'll give him that. I forgave the weird stuff because he could charm the knickers off a nun. Anyway, him and his wife, they've not been happy for years, and she's been knocking around with one or two blokes on the side, that's for damned sure. I think he just wanted to see what it was like, if I'm honest, see if the grass really was greener.'

'Did you break it off?'

Sally shook her head.

'Oh, he did that. A week ago, if that. Turned up for his lesson—he was still using those as a cover for turning up to have some fun—and just called it off. No warning, nothing, and then expected everything to carry on as normal. He even wanted us to have the lesson! Can you imagine? *Yeah, sorry darling, I know I'm really weird, but I don't think this is working for me. Anyway, how's about we have a go at making a vase?*' She tapped her temple. 'Insane!'

'The lesson didn't go ahead, then?'

'I threw him out, along with everything he'd made, most of which I tried to hit him with as he ran off.'

There's clearly no love lost between Sally and Lance, Harry thought, and he'd put people away with far weaker motives than being dumped, that was for sure.

'And today?'

'I came to work late this morning and there he was, sitting in my chair and—'

Sally's voice caught in her throat.

'Do you know how he got in there?'

'The door was open when I arrived,' Sally said. 'Like I said, he had a key cut. I took it off him, but he must've had another. Mind you, I'm awful at leaving the place unlocked, usually because when I've the kiln on, it can get pretty hot in there; everything on the shelves, that all has to go in for firing. I can't leave anything out, or the heat will dry it up. I've two kilns in the other room. On sunny days, it's even worse.'

'What time was that?' Harry asked.

'I left the house late-ish, because I had a lie-in for once, plus I was a little hungover after the bottle and a half of wine I drank last night when I got home. Probably got here about ten-thirty, eleven at the latest.'

'You didn't touch anything?'

Sally's shock at being asked such a question wrote itself on her face.

'God, no. Why the hell would I? Why would anyone? I didn't even go into the studio. I opened the door, saw him sitting there, and that was enough.'

'Did you notice anything about the body?'

'Like what?'

'You were the one who found Lance,' Harry said. 'So, what did you see?'

'I saw a body,' said Sally, 'like I've said. Lance, sitting in a chair in my studio. And ...' Her voice caught, but she forced it out anyway. 'And ... his hands ... they were missing.'

Harry looked back over his notes.

'I need to ask you something else,' he said. 'This is a little difficult, so I just want you to be aware of that, but I also need you to be as honest with me as you can be.'

'Of course.'

'After what you said about Lance's behaviour, that it was a little strange, was Lance ever violent at all? Did he abuse you in any way, emotionally, physically?'

Harry waited.

'No,' Sally said.

'You said his behaviour was strange, and what you described, it certainly sounds that way.'

'Yes, but that's not abuse, is it?'

'He hid in your studio naked. And you mentioned something about him being tied up.'

'He liked a bit of kink.'

'That sounds like a little more than kink,' said Harry.

'Don't think I don't see what you're doing,' Sally said. 'Lance is dead in my studio with his hands gone, and here I am having just been dumped. So, if he had been violent, maybe I took his hands as revenge, right? That's it, isn't it? That's why you asked? And right now, you've only my word that I didn't do it.'

'Asking questions is what I have to do,' Harry said, 'no matter how difficult they may be to hear or to answer. I'm a detective. It's my job.'

Sally looked away for a moment, and when she turned back to face Harry, he saw a hardness behind her eyes.

'If you want the truth of it, then here it is,' she said. 'The whole thing was a bloody mistake. I should've known better, but I was bored and I found the whole thing oddly exciting and thought, why the hell not? I'm not proud of it, but it's what I did, what we both did actually, because it wasn't just me, was it? It takes two to tango, Detective, and I can tell you now, though we certainly didn't tango, we did plenty. Yes, some of it shocked me a little, but it was always consensual. Lance may have been a bastard in the end, a weird man with some odd interests and ideas maybe, but he never hit me. Quite the opposite, actually; no one's ever praised me or complimented me so much in my whole life. As I said, if there was one thing he could be, it was charming.'

Harry gave Sally another moment or two to see if she wanted to say anything else, but it was clear that she was done. He called Jim over and asked him to drive her home.

'I'll probably be in touch again,' he said, as Sally clipped herself into the front passenger seat.

'Suit yourself,' Sally replied, 'but I've nothing else to say.'

'Maybe not, but you never know,' said Harry. 'And on that, I need to advise you to keep all details about the case strictly confidential.'

'I've zero interest in talking about this with anyone,' said Sally. 'Why would I?'

'You'll want to at some point, but that's a different thing entirely,' said Harry. 'Right now, though, this is about keeping things close, so that we have the best chance at getting ahead with the investigation. And we certainly don't want the press involved.'

'The press? Why not?'

'Because they're all bastards, that's why,' said Harry, and stepped back onto the pavement. He watched as Jim turned the Land Rover around and headed off. Then, with the afternoon already getting on, and after a quick chat with Jadyn, to make sure he kept him up to date with what was happening, he set off on foot towards town, to the office at the community centre.

TEN

Walking into the community centre, Harry narrowly missed thumping into a large man standing like a bouncer on the other side of the door. The man turned around, saw Harry, and beamed.

'Harry!'

Then to Harry's surprise, he found himself clamped in a bear hug.

'Hello, Dave,' Harry said, eventually prising himself from the iron grip of Dave Calvert. Dave had been the first person he ever actually spoke to in Hawes when he'd arrived a couple of years ago. Since then, he had provided Harry with a much-needed friendship outside of work, as well as many pints in various pubs across the dale.

'I just popped in to see if you were around,' Dave said. 'Don't suppose you've got a minute to spare, have you?'

'Not really, no,' Harry said, glancing behind Dave and deeper into the community centre. 'Is it urgent?'

'Two minutes, that's all, I promise.'

'You take that long to order a pint and a packet of crisps, what with all the stories you end up telling, even if no one's listening.'

'Scout's honour.'

'You were in the Scouts?'

'It's part of the reason I fell in love with being outside.'

Harry knew Matt was fine to deal with Lance's wife in the interview room at the back of the building. A few extra minutes wouldn't matter.

'Come on, then,' he said, and led Dave into the office.

Inside, Harry gestured to a chair at a table, and Dave sat down, the chair beneath him looking small and somewhat fragile.

Harry pulled out the chair opposite.

'Two minutes,' he said, repeating Dave's promise. 'And I'll be holding you to that, so get a move on.'

'It's about the PCSO thing,' said Dave.

A while back, Dave had come up with, in his mind, the great idea of becoming a PCSO. Harry hadn't been so sure, but had finally warmed to the idea, helped in the main by the team's enthusiasm for the idea. Though Dave had worked offshore most of his life, he'd decided a change was required, and apparently this was it, along with his goats, whose nutritious milk he was looking into turning into artisan cheese.

With the PCSO thing, Harry was able to genuinely show some interest. As to the goat cheese? He couldn't think of anything worse. He'd finally grown used to Wensleydale cheese, but only with cake. As for goat's cheese? No, there was no way he was going anywhere near it, even if it was Dave's pride and joy. He'd been close enough to goat's cheese to smell it, and that was enough. The stuff had the same stink to it that his hands did after stroking one of Dave's goats, and why the hell anyone would want to eat a cheese that smelled like that he just couldn't fathom.

'What about it?' Harry asked, shoving his deep-seated horror of goat's cheese deep down inside him, hopefully to be forgotten about forever, or longer, if he was lucky.

'I just wanted you to be the first to know ...'

Harry leaned forward.

'Know what, Dave?'

Dave grinned, his face lighting up.

'I've been accepted,' he said. 'My training programme starts in a couple of months. Can you believe it? Brilliant, isn't it? Me, a PCSO!'

Harry laughed.

'You're still sure you want to do it, then?'

'Of course I'm sure!' Dave replied. 'And it's a bit late now to change my mind, isn't it? Anyway, as I'm sure you know, I only do things if I'm absolutely committed to them, and I'm committed to this. It's my way of giving something back to the community, isn't it?'

'Yes, I suppose it is that,' said Harry. 'So, how long's the training?'

He should probably have known the answer to that himself, but he couldn't remember; it had been so long now since he'd had anything to do with PCSOs who weren't already deeply into their roles.

'Five weeks at the training centre, so lots of classroom stuff. It's going to be weird being back in school, isn't it? Do you think the chairs and desks are tiny and covered in graffiti and chewing gum? Not been anywhere like that in decades. I nearly got expelled, you know? No, wait ... I did ... Bloody hell, it really was a long time ago, wasn't it?'

'Expelled? For what?' Harry asked, but could tell that Dave wasn't listening.

'Anyway,' Dave continued, 'as well as roleplaying through various scenarios, learning the law, that kind of thing, I've then to complete five weeks of tutoring in the workplace.'

'You're looking forward to it, then?'

'Absolutely,' Dave said. 'Are you?'

The question caught Harry off guard.

'Am I what?'

'Looking forward to it?' Dave asked. 'Me being a PCSO.'

'Should I be?'

'I don't know, should you?'

Harry could see that Dave was being absolutely deadpan serious; the man wanted to know, so Harry had to give an answer.

'I think it'll be good for you, yes,' he answered. 'And everyone certainly seems to think you'll be an excellent PCSO. Including me, actually, and I don't say that lightly.'

'Well, as I'll be having you tutoring me, there's no doubt about that, is there?'

Harry sat back in his chair.

'What was that?'

'Tutoring me,' Dave said. 'You're the DCI, so you'll be in charge of what I learn when I'm out of the classroom and in the workplace.'

'Me tutoring you?'

Harry was saying the words as much for himself as for Dave. It wasn't that he didn't know he would be doing it, or that he didn't want to, more that all of this had come around so quickly that he was surprised by its arrival. And no one had really mentioned it, at least not for a good while.

'For five weeks,' said Dave. 'We talked about it, remember? Of course you do. It was all part of the application process, making sure the workplace training was easy to arrange, which it was. I've been talking it through with Gordy and Matt since then, like; didn't want to be bothering you with it. And Jim and Liz are happy to have me shadowing them, showing me the ropes.'

'You wouldn't have been bothering me with it at all,' said Harry.

Dave looked at his watch.

'There,' he said, 'two minutes. Well, closer to three, but not bad going, like.'

'That's it?' Harry asked.

'Nowt much else to say, not for now, anyway,' Dave said. 'It starts in a couple of months, but that's not actually that long, is it? And I've been working on my fitness, following a little plan your Jen gave me. She's a bit of a taskmaster, isn't she? First few days I could barely walk, but I'm doing okay now. I'm no racing snake—I mean, just look at me!—but I'll certainly be fast enough should anyone decide to test me by buggering off when I shout out, *You're nicked!*'

'You do know that we don't say that,' said Harry. 'This isn't The Sweeney. Plus, being a PCSO, you'll not be arresting anyone, ever.'

'Don't worry, I know.' Dave smiled, and slapped one of his huge meaty hands down onto the table, the sound like a cannon going off, Harry thought. 'Just pulling your leg.'

Dave stood up and moved over to the office door.

'You know, I really appreciate it,' he said. 'Your support, the team's; it means a lot.'

'Don't get all gushy, Dave,' said Harry. 'Doesn't suit you. Or me, for that matter. Next thing you know, we'll have hugging, and neither of us wants that, I'm sure.'

'I'm just letting you know, that's all,' said Dave. 'It won't be forgotten. And there's nothing wrong with a good hug now and again; does you good, Harry.'

'I'm yet to be persuaded.'

Dave opened the office door.

'If you're kicking your heels one night this week, you should come up and see how things are going with the goats.'

'Should I?'

'Yes.'

'How can I say no?'

'Easily,' said Dave. 'Mainly, because you're not a fan of goats. But I'd like to show you what we've been up to.'

'We?'

'Phil's decided to go in on the whole cheese thing with me,' Dave said.

Phil was a friend of Dave's from down the dale. He was also a childhood friend of Grace's dad, Arthur, owned a Shire horse called Harry, and was notorious for making the worst pork pies anyone had ever tasted. Not that this ever stopped him from making them. He had also looked after Dave's goats when he had been working away, so what Dave had said made a lot of sense.

'You've tasted his pies, right?' said Harry.

'I have,' said Dave, 'and I survived. But don't worry; any cheese making, that'll be down to me, with Phil more on the animal side of things. Better division of labour. Well, I'll be off.'

Dave opened the door, but Harry stopped him before he could step through into the community centre's lobby.

'Look, Dave, just so you know, and I don't say this lightly, it'll be good to have you on the team once your training's done,' he said, shaking the big man's hand. 'Weird, yes, and probably more than a little terrifying if I'm honest, but good.'

'Thanks, Harry,' Dave said.

Harry asked, 'What are you on with for the rest of the day, then?'

Dave gave a nonchalant shrug.

'Nowt much,' he said. 'Bit weary after this thing I went to last night in the Market Hall. There's only so much of people shouting at each other instead of listening that I can put up with; gave me a proper headache. So today, I'm going to be taking it easy, and making the most of a life by having a bit of leisure time.'

Harry laughed at that.

'How are those wildlife cameras doing?'

'The ones up at Snaizeholme? I've some cracking footage of badgers and squirrels and a good few deer, too. That is something I'm doing today, actually; heading out to check them this evening. But until then? You know, I'll probably just go have a little stroll, maybe over to Hardraw and back, grab a bite to eat, have a kip down by the river.'

'Don't fall in.'

'There's not enough water in it to drown me.'

'You can drown in a pint of water.'

'Really? How the hell do you fit in the glass?'

Harry shook his head and laughed.

'Well, you enjoy the rest of your day then,' he said. 'I'd best get on, though; some of us have jobs to do.'

'That you do,' said Dave, and then left the office and headed out of the building.

With Dave's news dealt with, Harry wasted no time and headed down the short hall to the interview room, knocked, and waited. From the other side of the door, he heard chair legs scrape on the floor.

The door opened and out slipped Matt, pulling the door closed behind him.

'How are you doing in there?' Harry asked. 'How is she?'

'Well, she's calmed down, so that's something,' said Matt. 'Not really said much since we arrived, and I've not pushed her, either. Figured I'd wait until you came along.'

'What have you said to her about her husband?'

'Not much,' Matt replied with a shrug. 'I've not specifically said, *Mrs Hamilton, I'm afraid to tell you your husband is dead*, but she obviously knows. That's clear enough. All that screaming and yelling was a bit of a giveaway, I think.'

'She's calmer though, yes?'

'From one extreme to the other really,' said Matt. 'Screamed herself out at the crime scene, I reckon. I've given her tea and biscuits. You want anything before we head in?'

Harry shook his head, then checked the time to see that the afternoon would soon be drawing to a close.

'Not just yet. Best we just crack on, I think, don't you?'

'Yeah, probably for the best,' Matt agreed.

Harry pointed at the door.

'After you, then, Detective Sergeant.'

Matt opened the door.

ELEVEN

Rebecca Sowerby wasn't having the best of days, and right there and then, as she walked back to the studio from one of the SOC team vans, all she really wanted to do was march after Harry and tell that craggy-faced, grumpy, and uniquely smug git exactly what she thought of him, which wasn't much right then. Still, telling him would make her feel better, that was for sure.

That he'd said what he said, and then just walked off, had annoyed her more than a little. And now, an hour or so later, she was still seething. Who the hell did he think he was, taking her to one side and speaking to her like that? It wasn't as though he held the monopoly on suffering after a bomb explosion, was it? No, it bloody well wasn't!

What she had been through, that was so far and away from what Harry had experienced that to even think he could draw a comparison, was laughable. And anyway, she didn't have a problem, did she? So what if a year had passed since the explosion in Reeth? She had survived it, and she had moved on, because that's what she had always done, how she had stayed sane. Life had to continue, so there was no point in dwelling on things because that was unhelpful and unhealthy.

A shout brought Rebecca up sharp. Looking up, she saw the

photographer walking towards her. He was waving at her with that bloody ridiculous squirrel-shaped puppet on his hand again.

'I'm done,' he said, coming to stand in front of her.

'The squirrel,' Rebecca said. 'I told you ...'

The photographer lifted the puppet to his face and stared at it.

'Don't think she likes you,' he said, then made the squirrel rub its face as though upset.

'You've made him cry,' he said.

'It's a puppet,' Rebecca said, her voice rising in pitch along with her temper, 'and this is a bloody crime scene! Quite literally, too, if you haven't noticed.'

The photographer then used his free hand to clamp it over the squirrel's head and cover its ears.

'Don't say that!' he said.

'What?'

'That he's a puppet,' the photographer whispered. 'You'll upset him.'

Rebecca leaned in close enough to smell the photographer's truly awful aftershave.

'If you're not gone from my sight in the next thirty seconds, I'll rip his bollocks off.'

'He doesn't have bollocks,' the photographer said. 'He's a glove puppet.'

'Exactly,' Rebecca replied, and after looking the photographer up and down just slowly enough for him to get the message, pushed past him and on towards the studio.

Arriving back inside the small room, Rebecca wanted to be anywhere other than where she was right then. She could also still hear Harry's voice rattling around in her head, demanding that she do this and that and all that other stuff she didn't have time for, and why the hell wasn't she just back home enjoying a day off like she had planned? She wanted to scream. No, she wanted to let rip with such violence that her entire being simply burned up in a single moment of pure, unadulterated anger.

Rebecca had been looking forward to a weekend of doing not

much at all, because she felt like she not only deserved it but needed it. The lack of sleep was driving her to distraction, and nothing she did seemed to help. She'd tried apps on her phone designed to help you sleep, but all they had done was give her access to her phone, which meant she had spent too many nights constantly staring at it and doom-scrolling or playing pointless games. She'd tried meditation, but found herself to be absolutely incapable of emptying her mind, or at least quietening it enough to help her relax and drift off. She'd even given herbal teas a go, stopped drinking caffeine, avoided cheese, bought a few novels to read, but nothing had worked. Nothing!

As for today, she'd planned to get up late, mooch around in her dressing gown, eat late and well, then maybe head out in the afternoon to mooch around a bit more. The whole idea had been to get away from the day job, to just enjoy being her, to try and relax, no distractions. But then she had been called out to something early on, and just as that had been drawing to a close, the call had come in from the team over in Hawes. So, instead of heading back home, she had simply continued driving further up the dale, leaving her plans for the day in ruins behind her.

Seeing her mum turn up in that ridiculous new vehicle had annoyed her more than it should have done, that was true. What her mum did was her own business, not hers, but she was tired. No, she was exhausted, and she was grumpy, and it had been something to let off steam about.

A young woman from the SOC team, whose name Rebecca couldn't remember, came over.

'We're ready to move the body now.'

'And?'

'And, well, I'm just letting you know.'

'You don't need my permission,' Rebecca said. 'Just get it done.'

The young woman stood staring for a moment, then turned on her heel.

Rebecca knew she had been too sharp, and as she considered going over to apologise, a yawn caught her unawares.

Dear God, I really am tired, she thought, as another yawn chased the first into the afternoon air.

A few minutes later, and with the body moved, Rebecca got on with directing the team to document everything they could from the crime scene, and to take anything that could be regarded as evidence. While she was watching them bag and box things up, she yawned again, only this time, when she opened her eyes, the sensation made her dizzy and she instinctively reached out to steady herself. Her hand fell against one of the shelving units in the studio and Rebecca found herself staring in horror as, almost in slow motion, it started to tip.

'Shit!'

Time slowed to the flow of treacle.

With no real hope of stopping the shelves from toppling over, she still jumped forward to try and stop the inevitable.

'Don't ... please, just don't ...'

Catching hold of the shelves, all Rebecca could do was stare as the pots and jugs and everything else stacked up on each shelf did their level best to give her a heart attack, rocking and tipping and threatening to leap into the unknown and smash on the floor.

Rebecca held her breath.

The pots rattled, tipped, then stilled.

At last, she exhaled, relief flooding through her. Then she saw one piece, a huge thing that was more sculpture than anything else, its sides twisting in and out like flames, with tiny gaps cut into the clay with astonishing care and skill, teeter on the edge of the top shelf, and fall.

Rebecca dropped to her knees and caught the creation in her hands just centimetres from the floor. She held it for a moment, staring at it, aware then how fragile it was, how easily broken. The clay was damp, she realised, the piece still to go into the kiln, and the top section, which seemed to work like a lid, wobbled just enough to make her heart stop.

'Everything okay?'

Rebecca looked up to see another member of her team staring

at her from the studio door. She didn't answer right away, her mind still on what was resting in her hands. If she let go now, just let it fall, it would still shatter. She felt much the same herself.

'Yes,' she said at last, pushing herself back up and resting the piece on a shelf. 'Bit of a close call though.'

'Tell me about it; I've knocked into these shelves three times now. I'm amazed none of us has broken anything! Do you want us to check the other room any more than we have?'

'The one with the kilns?'

'Yes. It's been photographed, but it looks undisturbed. We've found no evidence to suggest anything happened in there that could be linked to what took place in here.'

'Nothing at all?'

The figure in white shook their head.

'We found condoms, though, which made us all laugh a bit.'

Rebecca did a double take.

'Please don't tell me they were—'

'Used? No, just a couple of boxes of them on a shelf.'

'Why keep them in there, though?'

'You never know when the mood will strike, right?'

'I do, and I can't see it ever being in a small, dark room with a couple of kilns for company, can you? Anything else?'

'Nothing.'

'Then we can probably leave it,' Rebecca said. 'Let's stay with this main room.'

Left alone again, Rebecca carefully made her way to the studio door and stepped outside, where she removed her facemask, closed her eyes, and took a deep breath.

All she could think about right then was the pot or vase or whatever the hell it was supposed to be that she had caught, and how close it had come to ending up in a thousand pieces. Then a wave of tiredness crashed over her and once again she heard Harry's words. She knew then that she had no choice but to accept that the gruff detective had hit closer to the mark than she wanted to admit, so she headed back to her vehicle to find her phone.

TWELVE

Sitting down at the table in the interview room, and with Matt to his left, Harry looked over at the woman opposite, Lance Hamilton's wife, Leslie. She had dark brown hair, pulled up with a large hair clip, a single streak of grey stretching back from her forehead, and at that moment a face devoid of emotion. Harry had seen this before, those in shock so wrung out over what they had just experienced that their faces were little more than a shell. And that shell could crack easily, exposing whatever mess was behind it. She was wearing jeans, a plain white shirt with a small cardigan, and a blue silk scarf tied around her neck.

In an attempt to help her feel a little more relaxed, Harry did his best to make himself look at ease and approachable, which wasn't easy, not when he knew better than anyone what he looked like.

The last time he had seen her, Leslie had been screaming blue murder at Sally Dent, who in turn had seemed terrified at the sight of the woman on the other side of the Land Rover's passenger door window. Now, however, Leslie seemed calmer, her face red and blotchy from tears. He noticed her rub her cheek, as though in pain.

Harry introduced himself, only to be cut off by Leslie.

'He's dead. I know he's dead,' she said before Harry could say anything. 'I can't believe it, but I'm right, aren't I? He's dead, and that's why you were at her studio. All those people in white suits ... Lance is dead. I know it. The bastard.'

Harry stored that last comment for later in their chat, thinking that approaching it right then would potentially take the conversation from calm to hysterical in a beat. It was an odd thing to say, though, considering her emotional display earlier.

'We have good reason to believe that the body found in Sally Dent's studio is that of your husband, Lance,' he said. 'Though he's already been identified, we will still need you to confirm it.'

As hard as it always was, Harry believed times like this were made simpler and cleaner by stating the facts and just getting on with things. No one ever benefitted from someone failing to get to the point, especially not in cases like this. There was rarely any point in pussyfooting around the issue of death, he thought. However, her opening words had already dealt with any possible awkwardness, so Harry thought he might just as well push on.

On the table between them sat a jug of water and a couple of glasses.

'When?'

'That will be arranged with the mortuary,' Harry said. 'The sooner the better, though. And one of my team can accompany you, as well.'

'I can take you over,' Matt said. 'Not a problem at all.'

'Now?' Leslie asked.

'A bit too soon, perhaps,' Harry said. 'But tomorrow would be good, I think.'

'None of it is good, is it?' Leslie said.

'Do you fancy a tea?' Harry asked, then looked over at Matt, who rose to his feet.

'Grand idea,' the detective sergeant said. 'We've coffee as well. And biscuits.'

'Black coffee,' Leslie said.

'Tea for me,' said Harry.

Matt left the room.

'I need to ask you a few questions,' Harry said. 'But is it okay if we just confirm a few details first? Name, address, contact number, that kind of thing?'

Leslie agreed, and Harry wrote down what she told him.

'I've seen you about,' Leslie said, as Harry rested his pen on the table. 'Never up close, though.'

'Probably for the best,' said Harry, attempting a bit of humour. He knew many would think this was the worst of times for laughter, but more often than not, he had found that the darkest times were when humour was needed more than ever.

'How long have you been here?'

'In Hawes? Around two years now, I think,' Harry said. 'Doesn't seem like it, that's for sure.'

'Your accent ...'

'Somerset,' Harry said. 'Can't see me ever losing it now, either. I think it's part of my DNA.'

'Why would you want to? It's better than sounding like you're from round here, don't you think?'

Harry noticed that Leslie's accent wasn't local either. Though it had been eroded by her time in the Dales, London was clearly still the place which had shaped it. He could hear an echo of the city streets at the back of her words, and the more she spoke, the clearer it became.

'I'm going to assume, then, that like me, you're not local?'

'God, no,' Leslie said, as though to suggest otherwise was the worst. 'Can you imagine?'

Yes, I can, Harry thought, but kept that to himself.

Matt came back into the room and placed a tray on the table. He handed Leslie her coffee, leaving Harry to reach for his own mug.

Harry was about to ask a question when Leslie looked at him. 'And you're happy here, am I right?'

Harry nodded.

'Yes, very,' he said.

'You're lucky,' Leslie replied. 'I can't stand the place. Never have been able to. But what choice did I have? I'm here, so I had to make the best of it. Not that Lance helped. Well, he did, because he always thought money was the answer. He had a point, I suppose. It's nice, isn't it, to have enough, rather than be broke? But it doesn't make you happy. It can't.'

'The Dales, they're very different to living in a city,' Harry said.

Leslie laughed.

'It was Lance's idea, you know? Not mine. Why would I ever choose a place like this? Middle of nowhere, nothing to do. And trying to get a job around here? Forget it. Impossible.'

'What is it you do?' Harry asked.

'I'm an actor,' Leslie said. 'Well, I used to be, anyway. Not anymore, not properly anyway, not after moving here. Like I said, finding work was a non-starter.'

'How do you mean, not properly?'

'I'm a member of the amateur dramatics group,' Leslie said. 'It's hardly the same. How can it be? But it's the only place I feel at home, which isn't saying much, but it's all I've got.' She looked at Matt briefly, before turning her steely gaze back on Harry. 'Am I under arrest?'

'No,' Harry said, 'you're not. You're here because I thought it best to take you somewhere private for a chat, simple as that. At this stage, we're just getting as much information as we can, as quickly as we can, from anyone who knew your husband, and to make sure you're supported through this difficult time.'

'Is that why your friend here is taking notes?'

Harry looked across at Matt to see his notebook out on the table.

'Just procedure,' he said. 'We'll show you the notes at the end of the meeting, so you can make sure everything is accurate and sign off on them.'

Leslie scratched at the scarf around her neck and asked, 'Did she kill him?'

'Right now, we are working on establishing exactly what happened to your husband,' Harry said. 'At this moment, it's too early to know how he ended up at the studio.'

'I bet she did,' Leslie said. 'Though I can't say I blame her.'

Harry remembered Leslie's comment at the start of their conversation and caught Matt's eye. In the DS's expression, he saw his own concern reflected. But he decided to not delve any deeper into it, not yet anyway.

'When was the last time you saw your husband?'

'Last night,' Leslie replied. 'There was a meeting in town, about housing in the area. I don't think anyone really believes they can do anything about it, though, but at least they're trying to think of something.'

'And you were there because ...?'

'I work for a local accountant, Andrew Wilson,' Leslie said. 'No acting jobs, remember? I was there to support him, take the minutes, that kind of thing. He was the chair for the meeting, seeing as no one else volunteered. Not exactly exciting, but it was an excuse to get out for the night.'

'And your husband was there as well?'

'Of course he was,' Leslie said, shaking her head in mock disbelief.

'Why, of course?' Harry asked.

'Because he's nosy, that's why. He owns a lot of properties across the Dales, and elsewhere, too, I might add. Done rather well for himself. He knows people don't like him. He also thinks what he does is good for the local economy, brings money in, that kind of thing. Loves to tell people all about it.'

'You said it was his idea to move here, not yours,' said Matt, joining in.

'He had some kind of epiphany or something,' Leslie said. 'One minute, he's happy where we were, next, he's all about selling up, and before we know where we are we've moved somewhere he believed was better and healthier for us, especially for my son, who as you can imagine, didn't exactly appreciate moving schools at fifteen. Poor kid, can you imagine?'

'When was this?'

'Ten years ago, give or take,' said Leslie. 'Ten long, marriage-ruining years. Not that we were massively happy before then, but life was busy enough in the city to ignore any of the problems. Fine wine and dining out takes your mind off things, as it were. Here, though, it's like the hills have eyes, like they know what's going on, can see it, make it worse somehow.'

'You didn't get on, then?' Harry asked.

'I loved that man with all my heart at the beginning, I promise you that,' said Leslie, and Harry believed her. 'But things grew jaded. We drifted apart, but it was never horrendous. Then we moved here, and that killed it. If he was still alive, Lance would tell you the same, I'm sure.'

'You weren't happy together.'

'That's what I just said, isn't it?' said Leslie. 'Neither of us were.'

Harry remembered his chat with Sally, of Sally finding Lance in the kiln room.

'Can you tell me about when you came to the studio earlier today?' he asked.

'What do you want to know?'

'Why were you there?'

'It wasn't obvious, then?'

Harry sat back, waited.

'He didn't come home last night,' Leslie said, and Harry noticed that she was rubbing at the scarf around her neck again, the action like a nervous tick. 'He still wasn't around this morning, either. I checked the garage, discovered that ridiculous new car of his car was gone. I say new, it isn't, but it is to him.'

'What is it?'

'It's ridiculous is what it is,' said Leslie. 'Some old, red thing, a Jaguar, I think. It's nice, I'll give it that, but hardly practical or reliable. I've never driven it.'

'So, you find that he's not home and your next port of call is to go straight to a pottery studio,' said Matt. 'Why?'

Harry watched Leslie turn her eyes on Matt like headlights on full beam.

'Do I need to spell it out?'

'We can only work with what you tell us,' said Matt. 'A reason for you being there would make things considerably clearer.'

Leslie turned back to look at Harry.

'He was sleeping with her,' she said, voicing what Harry already knew. 'He's been trying all kinds of interests and hobbies over the years, and pottery was just another, so he added in a bit of adultery as well. I knew straight away it was going on. But then, we've both deviated from the path of true love, if you know what I mean, so I could hardly be angry at him, could I?'

'You seemed angry to me,' said Harry. 'Upset, even.'

'I was in shock!' Leslie replied. 'All those people in white suits. I knew something was wrong. And then, when I saw that bitch, I knew, I just knew!'

Harry said, 'But if you didn't care that he was having an affair, and by your own admission have been unfaithful yourself, why did you try and find him? And why react like that?'

'Because ...' Leslie began, but then her voice caught in her throat and she held a hand up, a silent request to be given a moment to gather herself.

Harry saw a single tear slip down her cheek.

When she spoke again, her voice was thick with emotion, and she rubbed at her neck once again.

'I've had enough! I woke up this morning to a life I never wanted, in a place I simply cannot stand, and I was angry! I went there because I tried that bitch Sally Dent's house and she wasn't in. I knew she would be at her studio, that I'd probably find him there as well, banging her over a potter's wheel or whatever it is they get up to, and I wanted it all to end, to just stop, so that I could get off this god-awful ride and start again, that's why!'

Leslie's voice echoed around the room as though it was trying and failing to find a way out. Then she scratched at the scarf again.

'Are you okay?' Harry asked.

'What?'

He pointed at his own neck.

'Your neck,' he said. 'You've scratched and rubbed at it a few times.'

'That? I do that when I get nervous,' Leslie said, dropping her hand from her neck.

Harry asked, 'Why did you accuse Ms Dent of killing your husband?'

'Well, did she?' Leslie asked. 'Did she kill him?'

Harry said, 'As I've already explained, Right now, we are trying to work out exactly what happened to your husband.'

'Do you know of anyone who wanted to harm your husband?' asked Matt. 'Someone who had a grudge, perhaps?'

'No, I don't,' Leslie said. 'Not specifically, anyway, but you should've been at that meeting last night; I'm surprised he got out of there alive!'

'Can you give us a list of everyone who attended?' Matt asked.

Leslie reached into her bag and pulled out a notebook. 'You'll find the minutes from the meeting in there,' she said. 'I'm not sure everyone who attended is mentioned, though. You'll have to ask Andrew for that.'

'Can I keep this?' Matt asked, holding up the notebook.

'Be my guest.'

Harry thought then that it was probably best to bring the conversation to a close. After allowing Leslie to read through the notes Matt had made, he told her that one of the team would be around to the house later on.

'We'll need to carry out a search of the place,' he explained, as gently and as carefully as he could. 'Just to see if we can find anything that might help us work out what happened, and why.'

'Feel free,' Leslie said. 'I've nothing to hide. Lance has an office, with his computer and filing cabinet and all that kind of stuff. Not somewhere I ever ventured into.'

Matt showed Leslie out and Harry waited in the office for him to return, plonking himself down in a chair that complained a little too loudly.

'So, what do you think?' he asked when the detective sergeant returned.

'I don't rightly know,' Matt said. 'I mean, how can anyone not love living round here? Makes no sense to me, that, no sense at all. Joan and I, we've never been happier, couldn't think of moving. And we get to bring up our little girl here, too. We're blessed, Harry.'

'I was thinking more about everything else she said, or didn't say,' said Harry, putting a stop to Matt's unstoppable urge to worship Wensleydale.

'You think she's a suspect, then?'

'She's unhappy, and she's lashing out and not making much sense, probably to herself as much as to us.' Harry then wanted to kick himself. 'We didn't check an alibi, did we?'

'She mentioned a meeting,' said Matt.

'So did Leslie, actually.'

Matt said, 'If you want, I can crack on with chasing up all the names from the minutes she gave us. We need to start somewhere, and that seems as good a place as any, doesn't it?'

'Yes, but I think we should have someone head over to have a look around his house first. I'm not saying there's anything there that will help, but you never know.' Harry glanced at his watch. 'Where the hell has the day gone?'

'Time flies whether or not you're having fun,' Matt said.

'Dave was looking for me when I arrived,' said Harry, then told Matt what Dave had told him.

'Three PCSOs,' Matt said. 'Is that a full set, then?'

'Dave probably counts as two.' Harry laughed and went to flick through the minutes that Leslie had handed him when the office phone rang. Matt answered.

'Anna?'

Harry was surprised to hear that name; Anna was the local vicar and also the partner of his detective inspector, Gordanian Haig. He wondered why she'd be calling when Gordy wasn't there.

When Gordy had requested a couple of days off, it hadn't actually been for her, but for Anna.

'She's not been herself for a while,' the DI had explained. 'Something's up, but I don't know what it is. I think she needs to get away, just to breathe a little.'

Gordy had then said how Anna's life could seem very suffocating. There was no letup. The job of being a vicar, if you did it properly and took the role seriously, was exhausting, because there was never really any escape. Everyone knew where you lived, would call when they knew you were in, which was generally mealtimes, and Gordy couldn't remember the last time she'd been around at Anna's and enjoyed a meal from start to finish without being interrupted.

'She carries everyone's problems and issues with her,' Gordy had explained. 'The job she does, she's a therapist, a friend, a confidant, as well as a leader, someone the community as a whole depends on. And I think sometimes the pressure just needs a release.'

They'd talked some more, with Gordy saying she had noticed Anna becoming more reserved over the past few months, but never coming out and saying something was wrong, always putting on a brave face, telling her to not worry.

'But I do, because that's what being in love with someone involves. You care, and you want to help and you worry; it's not all fun and running through the clover, is it?'

Harry had happily agreed to the time off, suggesting three rather than two days, and Gordy had taken them. She would be back tomorrow, and Harry had hoped the break would do Anna some good, but watching Matt on the phone, he saw the man's usually cheerful face fall dark. And that was a worry.

The call ended.

'Is Anna okay?'

'Anna's fine,' Matt said, and Harry allowed himself to feel a little relieved. But then he saw just how grave Matt's expression was.

'Why did she call?' Harry asked. 'What's happened?'

'It's Gordy,' said Matt. 'She's just been rushed to hospital.'

THIRTEEN

Matt watched Harry leap out of his chair, keys already in his hands, and rush over to the door.

'Where is she? Northallerton?'

'You can't go,' Matt said, but Harry cut in.

'I bloody well can! What happened? If it's Northallerton, I'll be there in the hour and—'

'Harry ...'

Harry yanked the door open so violently Matt half expected it to come off in his hands, shattered into splinters.

'Harry! Stop!'

Matt was a little surprised to see that raising his voice actually worked, as Harry paused mid-step through the door.

'Take a minute,' he said, as Harry hesitated in front of him. 'You can't be everywhere, you know that.'

Matt wasn't sure that Harry believed it.

'Watch me!'

'I'm serious.'

'And so am I!'

For a moment, neither of them moved, but Matt readied himself to chase after him. He had known the DCI for just over two years now, and although Harry's rough edges had been smoothed a little, and his gruff nature eased just enough to make him a little more approachable than a pit bull with a headache, the man was still a force of nature. If Harry decided to do something, there was little anyone was going to be able to stop him.

At last, and to Matt's relief, Harry eased the door shut.

'What happened, then?' he asked, now facing the detective sergeant. 'Is Gordy okay? I mean, I'm going to assume she isn't, seeing as she's being taken to hospital.'

'It was a hit and run,' said Matt, and saw his words light a fire in Harry's now-wide eyes.

'What? Where?'

'They'd spent the morning at a nature reserve over near Masham,' Matt explained. 'They were making their way back to Anna's vehicle, which they'd parked in town, when they were crossing a road, and a car flew round a corner and lost control. Anna said Gordy pushed her out of the way but was caught by the car as it went past. It nearly spun out, the rear end knocking Gordy off the road and into a field. The driver must've managed to get it back under control and raced off.'

'Did they get a registration number? What about the make of the car? Who's on this?'

'They have officers on it,' Matt said. 'They were at the scene within minutes thanks to another driver stopping to help; they called emergency services and did enough first aid to make sure both Anna and Gordy were okay.'

'Except Gordy isn't okay, is she?' said Harry.

'No, not exactly. She's been fortunate, by the sound of things, but then Gordy, she's tough.'

Harry raised a thick finger to point it directly at Matt as though he were giving him instructions.

'Right, we need to call the team that's on this and get over there, make sure Gordy and Anna are—'

'Harry,' Matt said, cutting in, but keeping his voice calm as he did so, well aware that Harry's fuse was shorter than ever right then. 'Masham isn't our area. I know it's not far outside it, but that doesn't matter. We can't just go racing over there and take over. There's ruffling feathers, and then there's you landing in the middle of it all like an Exocet missile and blowing everything to shit. And don't tell me that's not what you would do, because we both know it is. A part of me would be right behind you, too, but we both know it's a bad idea.'

'I can't just sit here, though,' Harry said.

'No, you're right, you can't,' said Matt. 'Not least because we've an investigation to be getting on with, like, haven't we? What's happened to Gordy and Anna, that's being dealt with.'

Harry moved away from Matt, who found himself instinctively putting himself in front of the office door, barring the way like an impromptu bouncer.

'I'd still like to send someone,' Harry said. 'Only seems right.'

'We need everyone on what we're dealing with over here,' Matt said. 'If Jen was around, I'd say we could send Liz or Jim over, but right now, we can't. Best thing we can do is to do our job here and wait to hear from Anna; she said she'll be in touch as soon as she knows anything more.'

'How's she doing herself?' Harry asked. 'Was she hurt?'

Matt shook his head.

'Not too much. Just a few cuts and bruises, and she thinks her right arm will be numb for days thanks to the stingy nettles Gordy threw her into.'

The faintest of smiles crept onto Harry's face, which helped relax Matt a little.

'And she's with Gordy now, right?'

'She is,' said Matt. 'She was given a check over and was fine to drive. She followed the ambulance. And where they were, it wasn't too far from the hospital, just a half hour or so. She's going to keep in touch.'

'That's something.'

Matt stepped away from the door.

'So, what do you want to do now?' he asked. 'You've had a chat with Sally, the pottery studio owner, and we've spoken with

Lance's wife. The SOC team will be busy at the crime scene for a good while yet, so that ties up at least Jadyn for now, doesn't it?'

'We need to work out Lance's last few hours,' said Harry. 'He was at this meeting, we know he never went home, and we know he somehow ended up at the studio. Which gives us a good number of missing hours, and it's in those that we'll find out what happened, and why. And hopefully who as well,' he then added, 'because I'm fairly sure Lance didn't cut off his own hands.'

'Sounds like as good a plan as any,' Matt agreed.

'Thinking back over what we've seen, it all looks rushed to me.'

Matt wasn't sure what Harry was getting at.

'How do you mean?' he asked.

Harry frowned, creasing the scars on his face deeper still.

'I don't rightly know,' said Harry. 'But there's something off about it. Like it's been set up to look like one thing, but it's either something else, or disguising something else.'

'You mean to put us off the scent?'

'Possibly. Just all seems a bit over the top. Why cut off his hands? Why put him where we found him?'

That last sentence caught Matt's attention.

'Put him there?'

'Well, I doubt very much that he marched in there of his own accord, sat down, held out his arms and requested that someone whack his hands off at the wrists. Which is what I mean about it all seeming a bit off.'

Matt thought Harry was going to keep speaking, but the DCI said nothing more.

'Best we get back down to the crime scene, then,' he suggested, and turned to open the office door.

Harry called him back.

'What about Dave?'

Well, that certainly came out of nowhere, Matt thought.

'What about him?'

'He's not doing anything today, is he?'

'I've no idea,' said Matt. 'Haven't spoken to him. But I'm not sure what that's got to do with anything. I know he's looking to be our next PCSO, but he's not one right now, is he? We can't have him going around knocking on doors or anything like that, not least because he'd probably break them.'

'That's not what I'm suggesting,' said Harry. 'I know he's not part of the team, not yet, but what he is, is dependable, and from what I gathered after talking to him, he's kicking his heels a bit today.'

Matt was confused, but doing his best to not be, which wasn't always easy with Harry's thought process.

'I'm still not following you.'

Harry didn't answer. He pulled out his phone.

'I'll see if he can head over to the hospital,' the DCI suggested. 'Those wildlife cameras of his can wait, I'm sure.'

'He doesn't need to go,' Matt said. 'Like I just said, everything's in hand. We can't go walking in there with our size 11s.'

'That's as may be, but I'd still feel a little happier if that hand was being held by one of our own,' Harry replied. 'And Dave's the closest thing we've got without actually sending one of the team, which we can't do anyway, as you rightly pointed out.'

Matt could see that he had no chance of talking Harry down on this. The man had made up his mind. But then, perhaps what he was suggesting wasn't such a bad idea after all. Anna would be focused on Gordy, plus she would be dealing with the accident herself, so to expect her to be keeping them up to date wasn't fair. If they sent Dave, he'd be there in a personal capacity, would undoubtedly love being called into action by Harry, and on top of all that, he was one of the most dependable people Matt had ever known.

'Call him,' Matt agreed. 'My guess is, he'll not only be pleased to hear from you, but will trip over himself trying to help.'

'Well, I hope he doesn't,' Harry said, putting the phone to his ear. 'You've seen the size of him; imagine the damage!'

He'll be dining out on this for months, Matt thought, laughing to himself, as Harry called Dave, who answered in seconds. The conversation was over in a couple of minutes.

'I'm going to assume he said yes,' said Matt.

'He's already on his way over,' said Harry. 'I've no idea what he was doing when I called, but by the time I'd finished, I'm fairly sure he was running.'

Matt laughed.

'God bless that man,' he said. 'Having him on the team is going to be quite something.'

'He's certainly not lacking in enthusiasm,' said Harry, then added, 'I need to call Walker though.'

Matt had to agree.

'Not the kind of thing you should keep from a detective superintendent,' he said.

'I'll meet you outside,' said Harry.

A few minutes later, and with Harry having spoken to Detective Superintendent Walker to inform her about Gordy's accident, Matt followed him down to the marketplace. The place was busy, with a couple of trucks dropping off goods to shops on the other side of the road, the pavements busy with locals and tourists alike, and a gathering of off-road motorbikes, their riders dusty from the trail, just pulling in to park up and no doubt head to the pub for a bite to eat and some liquid refreshment.

Like Harry, Matt was concerned about Gordy, but there really was nothing they could do beyond sending Dave, so he turned his mind back to the task at hand and marched at speed with Harry back to the pottery studio. Jadyn was at the cordon tape when they arrived, the SOC team still busy.

'Constable Okri, I've a job for you,' Harry said. 'I need you to go have a look around at the Hamilton's place.'

'I'll go there now,' Jadyn said.

'His wife mentioned he had an office, so maybe there's something there that'll give us an idea how he ended up down here.'

Matt asked, 'Where are Liz and Jim?'

He'd noticed they weren't there as soon as he and Harry had arrived.

'Liz nipped into town to grab us all some lunch,' answered Jadyn, 'but then she got called to something in the car park behind the primary school. Jim ran off to join her.'

'The car park?' said Matt. 'What was it, people arguing over parking spaces? I've had people threatening each other with everything from a car jack to boiled sweets and a flask of hot coffee over that kind of thing.'

'No,' said Jadyn. 'Someone's vandalized a car, quite badly too, I think.'

'Really?' said Harry. 'That seems rare for round here, doesn't it?'

'Why would anyone do that?' said Jadyn.

'All kinds of reasons,' said Matt. 'Booze is usually one, so is jealously, and you can never discount simple mean-spiritedness, along with a good dose of deliberate stupidity.'

'Nice car, too, by all accounts,' Jadyn added. 'An old Jag, I think.'

Matt and Harry shared a look.

'Did you just say it was a Jag?' Harry asked.

'Yes, a red one,' said Jadyn.

'Matt? We're off,' Harry said, then looked at Jadyn. 'We'll send Jim back down here to take over as scene guard. Then you get yourself off to the Hamiltons', understood? Here's the address.'

A heartbeat later, Matt was once again chasing after Harry and back up into town.

FOURTEEN

As he arrived in the car park, and having sprinted up the steps from the marketplace, Harry realised that he'd run the whole way without even thinking about it. But what surprised him more than anything was that he wasn't even out of breath.

He had been keeping up with his running for a good while now, thanks in no small part to Detective Constable Blades, who was no doubt racing up and down a mountain with the ease of a mountain goat at that very moment. He had lost weight, too, with Grace even commenting on it somewhat favourably. He wasn't about to break out with a six-pack, but it was quite the revelation to find himself wearing jeans he'd not worn in so long he was surprised they were still in his wardrobe.

Thinking of Grace, Harry quickly pulled out his phone as he walked over to where Jim and Liz were standing next to a red Jaguar and sent her a message. With the way things were going, he couldn't see any reason why he wouldn't be free that evening, so that was what he told her. Not waiting for a reply, he stuffed his phone back in his pocket.

Harry heard footsteps coming up behind him and turned to see Matt jogging over to join him.

'Bloody hell,' the DS said, 'you can't half shift when you want to. I did my best to keep up, mainly because you were blocking the wind, but no chance of that. Jen's been keeping at you, then?'

'She has,' said Harry, feeling a little smug.

'How did that race go?'

A couple of weeks ago, Harry had joined Jen on a considerably shorter race than the one she was on today, and it hadn't been the unmitigated disaster he had expected it to be. Though he would have never admitted it, and certainly not to Jen on the day of the race, he had been nervous about the whole thing. Not just at the thought that he might fail to finish, but also of doing it in the first place, because a race meant people. As far as Harry was concerned, people were better either avoided completely, or kept very far away from wherever he was, wherever that happened to be. It wasn't that he disliked people per se; he was just picky about those he spent time with.

'Race is perhaps a grand term for what I did, I think,' said Harry, leading Matt towards Jim and Liz. 'But it wasn't too bad, I suppose. I got to the end of it, so that's something. Even got a medal.'

'A medal? You should bring it to the office.'

'No, I don't think I should.'

Matt asked, 'Will you do another, then? Have you got the bug?'

'There's a big difference between an experience being not too bad, and one that you'd happily repeat,' Harry said, as they approached Jim and Liz. 'But you never know.'

'If Jen has her way, then ...'

'Don't remind me.'

Harry and Matt stood by Liz and Jim.

'Jadyn told you where we were, then,' said Liz.

'He did,' said Harry.

'You didn't need to come up, though,' said Jim, jabbing a thumb over his shoulder at the vehicle behind them. 'It's just a vandalized car, isn't it? We can deal with it. Not really detective stuff. Very much PCSO territory.'

'How's Mrs Hamilton?' Liz asked.

'As you'd expect, I suppose,' said Matt.

'We've sent her home,' added Harry, 'and we need Jadyn to follow on behind her and have a look around the place. Jim?'

'Yes, Boss?'

'You mind heading back to the crime scene and having a stint as scene guard? Jadyn's waiting for you to arrive before he can nip off.'

'Now?'

'Right now.'

'No problem.'

Jim jogged across the car park and off into town.

Harry called to him.

'Where's Fly?' he asked. He was used to seeing Jim with his faithful furry friend to the point where it was easy to believe they were inseparable.

'With Dad, up on the farm,' Jim replied. 'He's proving himself to be a little too useful. He's also developing a soft spot for Mum, mainly because she spoils him. Where's Smudge?'

'With Grace,' Harry replied, and left it at that as Jim turned and continued on his way.

Harry looked at Liz.

'As we're not going to have Gordy with us for a while, would you be able to step in and do a bit of the family liaising stuff?' he asked. 'Once Jadyn's done, head over there to see how she's doing. Jen will be around tomorrow, but I'd like Leslie to know there's support available.'

'Of course, makes sense,' said Liz, 'but what do you mean about Gordy? She's back in a couple of days, isn't she?'

Harry glanced at Matt, and decided to keep quiet until he'd heard more about how the detective inspector was.

'That she is,' he said, then quickly moved on and asked, 'So, what have we got?' his attention on the car. 'It's a bit of a mess, isn't it? You've run the plates?'

'We have,' said Liz. 'Still waiting on that. Shouldn't be long.'

'Who called it in?'

'A young lad who works at the chippy. I'm surprised no one reported it earlier.'

'People probably thought someone already had,' said Harry. 'You've his contact details?'

Liz gave them to Harry.

'He said he saw it here on his way home from work last night, but that it didn't look anything like this. Spotted it when he was heading into town earlier for work.'

'Last night? What time would that be, then?'

Matt said, 'The chippy closes at eight-thirty.'

'Nine-ish then,' said Liz. 'If you take into account cleaning up.'

Harry took a moment to have a closer look at the car. It was, or at least it had been until someone had taken a recent and savage dislike to it, a red Jaguar that had clearly been well-loved by its owner. Despite its age, the paint shone and sparkled in the sun, and the cream leather interior looked barely used.

To get it back into the showroom condition would take some work, he thought.

Deep scratches had been gouged into the doors, the wings, all over the bonnet. The roof was covered in thick, white paint, which had flowed over the edge and dripped down the windows like melting ice cream. All four wheels had been cut with something sharp and strong enough to render them not only flat, but out of action for good. The headlights had been kicked in, and on the bonnet, in more of the white paint, sat words Harry wasn't about to read out aloud this close to a primary school, never mind in public. But they made it pretty clear for anyone reading them that whoever had done this really disliked Mr Hamilton. Though whether the person responsible had then gone one step further and cut off the man's hands, Harry had no idea. It did seem odd, though. Another one of those coincidences he didn't believe in.

'Do we know how long it's been here?' Matt asked.

'No,' said Liz. 'We were waiting to hear back on the number plate first before we headed off to do door-to-door. Oh, wait, on that ...' Liz looked at her phone. 'It's just come in. Right, we've the owner and ...' She looked up at Harry. 'You're not going to believe this.'

'Actually, I am,' Harry said. 'Mr Lance Hamilton, right?'

That raised an eyebrow.

'How did you know?'

'His wife mentioned her husband's car,' said Matt. 'When Jadyn said where you were, he mentioned the description, which was why we raced up here. I say raced; Harry legged it and I did my best to just about hang on to his tailwind.'

'It wasn't a race,' Harry said.

'Then why did you run so fast? Anyway,' continued Matt, 'we can probably safely assume that it was Lance who drove it here yesterday evening before he headed into town to the meeting in the Market Hall.'

'Why didn't he drive home, then?' Liz asked.

'That's what we need to find out,' said Harry. 'As well as who did this and why, because you know what I'm like with coincidences.'

'No such thing,' said Matt.

'Exactly.'

'Maybe he came back to his car and found someone doing this to it,' Liz said. 'They got into an argument, and one thing led to another.'

'Possibly,' said Harry, 'but how do we get from vandalizing a car to a dead body in a pottery studio with his hands not just cut off, but missing? Which reminds me ...' He took out his phone.

'Who are you calling?' Matt asked.

'Sowerby,' Harry said, as the call connected. 'It's Harry,' he said.

'What?'

So, she's still in a bad mood, Harry thought.

'We've found Lance's car,' he said. 'Looks like he left it in the car park in town behind the primary school, and it's been fairly heavily vandalised.'

'Let me guess, you need us to come and have a look at it.'

'I'm afraid so, yes. Might be a connection. I'd be surprised if there wasn't,' he said. 'I was also calling about the victim's hands.'

'Send me the location and I'll be there as soon as I can,' Sowerby replied. 'As to the hands, I'm afraid that we've not found them. Wherever they are, they're not in the studio.'

'They can't have just disappeared,' said Harry. 'They have to be there.'

'No, they don't,' Sowerby replied. 'And they're not, because we've looked all over the place, and there aren't exactly many places here to look, really. Not like they'd be easy to miss, either.'

'But why take them in the first place?' Harry asked, not looking for an answer. 'Cutting them off is one thing, but keeping them, or whatever it is they've done with them?'

'People do the strangest things.'

'Don't they just?'

Harry finished the call.

'No hands, then?' Matt asked.

Harry shook his head.

'Sowerby will be on her way as soon as she can.' He looked at Liz. 'We'll need someone to stay with the vehicle until she gets here. And it's probably a good idea if you stay on-site, too, keep an eye out for anyone showing interest in what's going on. Then once you're done, head over to see Leslie Hamilton, like we said.'

'There's already been plenty of people showing an interest,' said Liz. 'Everyone who drives in to park up or comes down the path from the Creamery can't resist having a look. It's in plain sight, after all; you can't really miss it.'

Harry looked towards the road, which connected the top end of Hawes to the bottom end of Gayle.

'What about folk walking by?' he asked.

Liz turned to see where Harry was looking.

'I've not noticed anyone,' she said. 'But then, I've not really been looking.'

'Well, keep an eye out,' Harry said. 'Someone does this, and they live close by, they're not going to be able to resist walking up to have a good look at their handiwork.'

'So, what now?' Matt asked. 'If we've the SOC team coming up here to have a look at this, and Jadyn heading over to the Hamiltons' place, that frees us up a bit, doesn't it?'

'It does,' agreed Harry, and pulled out the contact details of the one who had called them about Lance's car. 'Matt, I don't suppose you're hungry, are you?'

'Always. Why?'

'I fancy a trip to the chippy ...'

FIFTEEN

When Jim arrived at the crime scene, Jadyn was more than happy to hand over the responsibility of being the scene guard. He knew the job was vital to ensure the integrity of the crime scene and make sure the only people accessing it were those involved in the investigation, but that didn't make it any more interesting.

The times he had done it, and there were plenty, he found it a bit tedious. Not that he'd ever shown that to Harry, not a chance of it. The DCI was someone he found the unshakable urge to always try and impress, sometimes to the point of wishing he could just shut up and stop. But Harry had a way about him that made Jadyn want to do his best. He was gruff and he could be a grouch with a short temper, but he was never anything other than fair, and they all knew that if anyone was going to have their back, it was Harry.

Some days, Jadyn couldn't believe how lucky he was to have had DI Haig bring him onto the team in the first place. Not only was he working for a great boss, he'd made some of the best friends he could imagine, and was now dating someone he'd fancied from the moment he'd first met her.

As far as Jadyn was concerned, Jen was one of the most interesting, exciting people he had ever met. She was an ultra-runner, a police detective, and best of all, she owned a lizard called Steve.

She was also a mean cook, enjoyed horror movies for some reason he couldn't yet fathom, and had shown enough enthusiasm for his small collection of records to make him think they certainly had plenty in common. And that had led to his decision to up sticks and move to Reeth; close enough to be more a part of Jen's life, but not so close as to get in the way or scare her off.

Having become briefly lost to his own thoughts, Jadyn realised that Jim was still speaking, so he tuned back in, hoping that he'd not missed too much.

'... is a bit rough,' Jim said, 'so just go careful. You know where you're going, right?'

'Sorry,' Jadyn said, 'can you just go over that again?'

'Which bit?'

'All of it.'

Jim laughed.

'You did seem to glaze over a bit. I was just talking about the track up to the Hamiltons' place, that's all. To get there, head up into Gayle, then take Gaits Lane, turn left at the end, and continue on the track at the sharp right. Make sense?'

'I think so. Don't reckon I'll get lost.'

Jim said, 'The lane is part of the Pennine Way, so that's probably signposted. I've not been up that way in a good while. I just remember that the road sort of gives up and becomes a track soon after. It's not four-wheel drive only or anything like that, though. You just need to drive carefully if you don't want to pinch a tyre and end up with a flat.'

With Jim's instructions now clear in his mind, Jadyn jumped into his car and headed off.

Driving through Hawes, he turned left at the primary school. He spotted Liz in the car park, standing next to a red Jaguar, and sent her a wave, smiling to himself when the wave was returned. It was a small act, but it made him feel at home.

In Gayle, Jadyn took a right before the bridge, and then an immediate left onto Gaits, which was so narrow that he found himself sucking in a breath to help squeeze through.

Threading his way along the thin lane, he passed between stone dales houses with small, well-kept gardens and window boxes filled with bright blooms, before crawling past the entrance to the ford across Gayle Beck on his left. Looking down to the water, he saw a couple of walkers approaching the crossing. He drove on, then wondered if he should go back, and slowed down. Not long after, he stopped his car, and with a shake of his head slipped the vehicle into reverse, then headed back towards the lane leading to the ford. Parking up, he climbed out and walked down towards the two walkers.

'Now then,' he said, as one of the walkers stepped into the shallow water, sending a crown of watery diamonds into the air, glinting in the sun as they splashed back down.

Both walkers turned to face him. Jadyn figured they were both very much in their sixties. They were each wearing lots of shiny new walking gear, including trekking poles and rucksacks, which he had a feeling had only been out of the shop for a few hours. Though it didn't take a detective to spot the price tag still hanging off the strap of one of them. They were each wearing large-brimmed hats, their faces greasy from generously applied sun lotion which, in a few too many places, hadn't been rubbed in all that well, and gave the impression that they'd both shaved that morning and forgotten to wash off the foam.

'Afternoon,' said the walker on the left, a man with a face so pale it looked as though he hadn't seen the sun in years, though perhaps that was the sun cream, Jadyn thought. 'Can we help?'

'No, but I can help you,' Jadyn said. 'If you're looking to cross the river, you'd be best to just head back to the bridge. It's safer that way.'

The other walker, a woman who was as pale as the man, said, 'I don't think we're about to get run over, or hit by a wayward tractor, do you?'

'That's not quite what I meant,' said Jadyn. 'The ford, it's not safe to cross on foot.'

'But there's hardly any water in it, is there?' said the man. 'And we've got our boots on, so we'll be fine, I'm sure. Thank you for your concern, but I'm sure you must have other more important things to do than bother two innocent walkers.'

'It's a little deceptive,' Jadyn said, ignoring the man's protests. 'The crossing is really slippery. I know it doesn't look it, but it is. I wouldn't want you falling and then having to call an ambulance.'

Jadyn saw the woman narrow her eyes at him.

'Are you saying this because we're old? That's ageist, that is. We're not helpless, you know, and we are more than capable of walking twenty yards across a river.'

'Please, I'm just trying to help,' Jadyn said. 'That's all.'

The man laughed.

'Well, that's very kind of you to care so much, but like I've just said, I'm quite sure that the police have better things to do than telling people like us what to do when all we're doing is out walking. '

'I'm not telling you what to do at all,' Jadyn said. 'And I can't stop you crossing.'

'Good,' said the woman, and turned away from Jadyn to face the ford. 'Come on, Love, let's get on, shall we?'

Jadyn looked across the ford and up the road opposite, which led on into Beggarman's Lane, to where a bench sat on the verge with a good view of the beck. He could see someone on it and offered them a wave, which was duly returned.

'You see that bench?' Jadyn said, pointing at it. 'Do you know why people sit on it?'

'Because they're tired?' the man said, his feet now in the water. 'That's generally what benches are used for.'

Jadyn shook his head.

'The view,' he said, 'of the beck, where we are right now, actually. Because if you sit there long enough, sooner or later someone who doesn't know the area well will come along and try to walk across. Everyone round here knows how dangerous it is to try walking across. It's only those who don't know the area who attempt it. And then ...' Jadyn clapped his hands together. 'That's you, falling over, because you won't make it. But if you try to, whoever that is, you're going to give them a bit of a giggle, that's for sure.'

'Rubbish,' the man said, striding off across the ford. 'It's perfectly safe.'

Jadyn went to warn the man again, but it was already too late. No sooner had the man finished speaking, his feet went from under him and he let out a cry.

Jadyn made a quick dive, grabbing the man under his arms as he fell. The act of trying to save him, though, sent his own feet from under him. He tried to stay upright, but the added weight of another person made it impossible.

For the briefest moment, Jadyn was vertical, wavering between standing and falling. Then gravity had its day, and the man fell backwards, driving the constable onto the scalloped, slime-covered surface of the beck.

The man landed on top of Jadyn, a considerably softer landing for him had the constable not been there to break his fall.

The woman rushed over and helped heave the man off Jadyn and onto his feet.

'Are you alright, Love? What happened? You fell so quickly.'

'I don't know,' the man replied. 'I felt sure I was fine.' He then looked at Jadyn. 'Did you do that on purpose?'

Jadyn blinked at the man, shocked by the question. He was also sitting in the beck, and acutely aware that his pristine uniform was now a soggy, algae-covered mess.

'I'm sorry, what?'

'Did you do that on purpose; make me fall into the water?' the man asked.

'I caught you,' Jadyn said, managing to get to his feet at last and walk carefully off the ford and back onto the road that led down to it. 'You didn't fall into the water at all, I did. You landed on top of me.'

'Did you catch me, though?' the man asked. 'Or did you do that on purpose? I was fine until you turned up, wasn't I?'

'On purpose? Why would I?'

Jadyn was looking for words that would somehow make sense of what the man was saying, when from over the other side of the road, a sound interrupted the moment. He looked over to see that the person on the bench had moved and was now standing on the opposite side of the ford. He was also clapping.

'Nice one, lad! That was bloody lucky, like, the way you caught him just before he fell on his arse! Can't wait to tell the lads down the pub about this!'

The clapping continued for a while longer, and when it died, Jadyn could hear laughter.

'Like I said,' said Jadyn, looking over at the surprisingly dry man, 'you're better to cross at the bridge.' Before the couple could say anything else, he turned around, headed back to his car, and continued on his way, his clothes sticking to him uncomfortably.

In his car, Jadyn wondered if he should go and get changed. But that meant a drive back home, and he didn't have the time. He had no choice but to crack on with the task Harry had set him, and hope that his appearance didn't get in the way of things.

Trying to ignore his soggy backside, Jadyn stared ahead as the lane continued along its narrow way, a thin grey thread stitching together clusters of huddled houses, then old meadows kept safe behind walls built by hands long lost to time.

At the end of Gaits Lane and turning left onto Mossy Lane as Jim had said, Jadyn headed up a slope, the great vista of Wether Fell now filling his windscreen. To his right, a field was home to a small flock of sheep, all of them seeking some attempt at sheltering in the shadows of walls. Then, on his left, he saw the inquisitive head of a horse staring out over the wall, watching him roll by.

Though Mossy Lane then took a sharp right, Jadyn continued forward, edging over the boundary between a well-maintained road, and a lane with a surface crumbling like thick icing on a cake.

Slowly he drove on, the surface beneath him growing ever rougher until the Tarmac was no more, and rough pebbles called him onwards. Potholes caught the wheels, sending unnerving thumps and bangs through the car, whipping the steering wheel from his hands. He slowed to a crawl, and half a kilometre of clangs and knocks later, a house came into view.

Jadyn pulled up outside, climbing out to see, on the opposite side of the valley and carved out of peat and rock by the babbling glee of Gayle Beck, the lonely line of Beggarman's Road heading out of Gayle, then up over the top to take the traveler on into Wharfedale.

He locked the car, then walked to the house. The building sat at the far end of a clean, cobbled yard, which was surrounded by several stone barns, all of which had been converted into what he assumed were holiday homes. Seeing that there was no doorbell, he knocked at the front door.

No answer.

He tried again, this time making sure the knock didn't just disappear into the house but came back at him as a dull echo.

Still no answer.

Jadyn lifted his fist again, ready to thump the door hard enough to make the heel of his hand numb, when he heard footsteps. Then the door swung open, and he came face to face with a woman wrapped in a large towel, a smaller towel in her hand to dry her hair.

'Oh,' Jadyn said.

SIXTEEN

'Well, what is it?' the woman asked, looking him up and down. 'And just what on earth happened to you?'

'I fell in the beck,' Jadyn said. 'No, that's not quite true, actually, I went to warn someone to not cross it and then I ...' His voice faded as he caught the look of disinterest on the woman's face.

'Is this about my husband?' she asked.

'Yes. I'm Police Constable Jadyn Okri.'

'And you expect me to let you in like that?'

'I can go and get changed.'

The woman sighed, then pulled the towel off her head and threw it to Jadyn.

'Give yourself a dry down with this,' she said, 'then come in.'

Under the woman's steely glare, Jadyn took the towel and gave himself a rub down.

'I think that's it,' he said, not entirely sure that it was.

The woman stepped back from the door and beckoned Jadyn in.

'I'll be back in a couple of minutes,' she said, then padded off down the hall and up a flight of stairs.

Jadyn wasn't about to presume he could just walk in and find somewhere to sit down, especially when he was so grubby and how the house was so pristine. So, he stood in the hallway, staring at the various pictures decorating the walls. Some were of a young woman in various theatre productions, others showed her with a young boy, full of smiles. He saw no pictures of a husband, but there were spaces on the wall where other pictures had once hung.

'What are you doing?'

Jadyn looked up to find the woman, now fully dressed in jeans and a blue and white striped top, with a thin, blue scarf around her neck, staring at him from the bottom of the stairs. He recognised her then from the pictures he had just been looking at.

'Waiting,' he said.

'Why didn't you go into the kitchen?' She tutted. 'Come on, this way.'

The woman turned, and Jadyn followed.

The kitchen was a large room with a flagstone floor and cabinets painted a soft grey-green. In the centre of the room was an island comprising more cupboards, a sink, and a ceramic hob. He saw a large oven and an even larger fridge freezer, which immediately filled him with envy. His own fridge was a touch on the small side, the freezer little more than a shoe-box-sized compartment at the top. This one, though, Jadyn reckoned he could fit enough food in to last him through the summer and halfway to winter. A large wooden dining table with six seats took up the rest of the room.

'Coffee?'

Jadyn realised he hadn't confirmed the woman's identity and asked, 'This is the house of Mr and Mrs Hamilton, isn't it?'

'It is,' the woman said. 'I'm Mrs Hamilton—Leslie—his widow.'

'I'm sorry; about what's happened,' Jadyn said.

'Was that a yes or a no for coffee?'

'What? Oh, right, yes, I mean no. I'm fine, thank you.'

Mrs Hamilton clicked the kettle on anyway. Then, after removing a cafetière from a cupboard and spooning in some fresh coffee, she turned around and walked across the kitchen to a washing machine.

'So, how can I help?'

Jadyn remembered what Harry had said and asked, 'Would it be okay if I had a look at your husband's office?'

'Of course,' Mrs Hamilton replied, pulling wet clothes out of the washing machine. 'It's through that other door over there, down the hall, and on your left.' She held out a hand expectantly. 'No idea what you think you'll find; he's not been in there for a good while now on account of him not actually living here.'

That statement took Jadyn by surprise.

'Where does he live, then?'

Mrs Hamilton pointed back out the way Jadyn had entered the house.

'You saw those converted barns? One of those. Went of his own accord, but not far enough, I can tell you.'

Jadyn stood up, and then, for a reason even he couldn't think of, walked over and shook Mrs Hamilton's still-extended hand.

She stared at him, eyes wide with shock and, Jadyn was sure, a fair amount of disgust.

'What on earth are you doing?'

'You held out your hand,' Jadyn said. 'I thought, I mean I ...'

'The towel,' the woman said, then pointed at the washing machine.

Jadyn felt like an idiot.

'Oh, right, yes, sorry,' he said, and handed over the towel, trying to ignore the green stains it was now covered in. 'I'll go to the office, then.'

'Take all the time in the world,' Mrs Hamilton said, throwing the towel into the washing machine. 'It's not like he's going to be back anytime soon, is it?'

Jadyn wasn't sure how to take that statement. A death so close would affect anyone badly, and there was no set rule as to how a person would deal with it. Some were angry, some were upset, some would be in silent shock for days. As for Mrs Hamilton, Jadyn couldn't quite work it out. Was she hiding behind snide remarks? Was it a case of building a wall to hide behind because without it she would fall apart? Or was it just irritation at the state in which he had turned up, wearing half of the riverbed of Gayle Beck on his uniform?

That's probably it, he thought.

Leaving the kitchen, Jadyn pulled on some disposable rubber gloves and shoe covers and followed the instructions she'd given and soon found himself in a small, neat study, with a desk, a filing cabinet, a bookshelf, and a record deck with a collection of records. A window in the far wall, across from Mr Hamilton's desk, showcased a view up the valley.

The walls were decorated with various photographs of a man Jadyn assumed to be Mr Lance Hamilton, either sitting behind the wheel of a red Jaguar or standing beside it. There were no pictures of Mrs Hamilton, or the boy he had seen with her in the photographs in the hall.

Pulling on a pair of thin, disposable rubber gloves, Jadyn couldn't resist a look at the deck and was impressed with the record collection. Mostly jazz, but with a good number of blues as well.

Back at the desk, he checked through the drawers, but found nothing. Though that wasn't helped by having no idea what it was he was really looking for. Then he did the same with the filing cabinet, the key for which was in the lock above the top drawer. He wasn't really surprised to find that it was full of files, most of which were either to do with finances or with houses.

Looking around the room, Jadyn could hear Harry's voice in the back of his mind: *Look for something that should be there but isn't, or something that is, but shouldn't be.*

Jadyn had come to realise that really, that's what being a detective was all about. Obviously, there was more to it, a lot more, but as clear rules went, he could think of nothing else that matched it. He rather fancied the idea of being a detective himself someday, not that he'd mentioned that to anyone, figuring he was still a little green to express such a thought.

He kept looking, looking behind things and in things, even under things. It was when he had decided that the room held no secrets at all that something caught Jadyn's eye. On the bottom shelf of the bookcase, one book didn't look quite right. He wasn't sure why, but following Harry's rule, he knew he needed to take a closer look.

Jadyn dropped to the floor in front of the bookcase to look at the books on the bottom shelf. There was nothing unusual about any of them, most of them paperbacks, except for the one that had caught his eye. He wasn't sure why until he looked a little closer and saw that the pages weren't pages at all and, on removing the book from the shelf, found it was a well-disguised box made to look like a book. He'd seen similar things before, clever little safes or secret spaces designed to look like something else.

Opening the box, Jadyn wasn't sure what he would find, if anything at all, and at first the contents didn't change his mind. Lifting them out, they were nothing more than a collection of hand-written notes, and he was about to put them back and leave the room, when he started to read the one on top. By the time he'd reached the end of it, then flicked through the rest of the pile, Jadyn already knew he needed to speak with Harry.

With the disguised book in his hand, Jadyn headed back through to the kitchen.

Mrs Hamilton was busy hanging out various bits of clothing, none of which looked to Jadyn like they were from this century, though he couldn't quite work out why. They just looked old and big. Not exactly high fashion. The towel was swirling around in the washing machine.

'Did you find anything?' she asked.

Jadyn hesitated, not sure whether he should share what he had found, though of course there was every chance that she knew about the box and its contents.

'Is something wrong?'

'No. Well, yes,' Jadyn said, and held out the book-disguised box.

'And what's that, then?'

'I was wondering if you could tell me.'

Jadyn walked over and showed Mrs Hamilton the contents.

'It's filled with letters,' he said, keeping the letters in his hand. 'They're all addressed to your husband, and, well, they're a bit threatening. And by a bit, I mean a lot.'

Mrs Hamilton looked at letters as Jadyn shuffled through them, then sat down at the dining table, the frown on her forehead deepening, pulling shadows down over her face.

'Are you okay?' Jadyn asked. 'Do you need a drink of water or something?'

Mrs Hamilton let out a short cry, stilling it immediately by covering her mouth with a shaking hand.

Jadyn wasn't sure what to do. She was shocked by the letters, that much was clear.

'They don't make nice reading,' he said. 'I'm sorry I had to show them to you, especially after what's happened, what you've been through.'

Mrs Hamilton looked up at Jadyn with a thin, broken smile.

'I'm ... I'm fine,' she said. 'Really.'

Jadyn asked, 'Have you ever seen them before?'

Mrs Hamilton shook her head.

'Never. I don't know what to say. Why didn't he tell me?'

'Your husband never mentioned them?'

'What were they doing in his office?' Mrs Hamilton asked. 'Where were they?'

'Bottom shelf of the bookcase.'

Mrs Hamilton was quiet for a moment, but eventually looked up at Jadyn.

'Sorry,' she said. 'I'm just in shock. I mean, after what happened to Lance, and now this? I don't know what to say.'

'I've not read them all,' said Jadyn, 'just had a flick through, but they all seem to contain threats. Do you know anyone who would do this? Someone who would want to threaten him like that? Or why?'

Mrs Hamilton said nothing, just stared, and Jadyn could see that she was in shock.

'I'm going to need to take them with me,' he said.

'Yes, of course,' Mrs Hamilton said. 'And I need to call Archie.'

'And he is?'

'My son,' Mrs Hamilton said.

Jadyn had heard no mention of a son until now, but then he remembered the pictures in the hallway.

'Does he know? About what's happened, I mean?'

'What?'

There was a distant look in Mrs Hamilton's eyes, and Jadyn felt as though she was staring right through him.

'Have you told him about his dad?'

'He's not his dad,' Mrs Hamilton said, the words spitting out of her like rounds from a gun. 'And no, not yet.' Then she seemed to relax, her face softening. 'Sorry,' she said, 'it's just all so much to take in, isn't it? I don't know where the day's gone.'

Jadyn slipped the letters into an evidence bag.

'I'll leave you to the rest of your day,' he said. 'One of our team will be around later to see if there's any support we can provide.'

Mrs Hamilton smiled, though her eyes weren't joining in, the lines at their corners like deep, painful cuts.

'I'm fine, honestly.'

She stood up and Jadyn allowed himself to be led back outside.

'Thanks for coming round,' Mrs Hamilton said, then closed the front door.

Outside, Jadyn walked back to his car, not entirely sure what to make of his visit. Mrs Hamilton was not herself, but that was understandable, though there was still something odd, as though she could switch her behaviour on and off at will. The letters were clearly a surprise to her and had upset her deeply, and Jadyn thought it was strange that she hadn't yet contacted her son about her husband's death. But then again, grief was something everyone reacted to differently, and perhaps this was just her way of dealing with the loss, he thought.

Jadyn dropped into his car, his trousers only slightly less soggy than they had been when he'd arrived, and headed back down the lane towards Gayle.

SEVENTEEN

The chip shop wasn't open.

'You look more disappointed than you should be,' Harry said, laughing to himself at the dejected look Matt was wearing. 'It is only four-thirty.'

'Yes, but any mention of food, particularly if it's fish and chips from this place, and I'm immediately hungry.'

'I didn't actually say that we were going to eat anything, certainly not fish and chips.'

'I love fish and chips.'

'Everyone loves fish and chips.'

'Not as much as I do.'

Harry cupped a hand against the glass of the chip shop window to shield himself from the sun and leaned in. He could see a few figures busying themselves behind the counter, obviously getting ready for when the shop opened at five.

'They're in,' he said. 'Give the door a knock.'

Matt did as Harry asked.

'Not sure they heard. Try again.'

On Matt's next knock, a man came to the door and yanked it open. He was about the same height as Matt, and wearing a white tunic, so clean it made Harry's eyes hurt to look at it too long.

'Now then, can I help?' the man asked. 'Though I'm not sure how, seeing as you're the police, and I batter fish. Not seeing the crossover, if I'm honest.'

'Best in the Dale, too,' Matt said.

'Much appreciated.'

Harry said, 'We're looking for a young lad who works here.'

'We've three of those,' the man said. 'One big, one medium-sized, and one nowt much more than an oversized sparrow. Which one is it? And what trouble is he in?'

'Do they work different shifts, then?' Harry asked.

'They do,' the man replied.

Harry waited for more, but no further details were offered.

'We're looking to speak to the one who was working last night.'

'Well, that should've been Jacob, but he called in sick, though if you ask me, all he's suffering from is being a lazy arse. So, it'll be Oliver you'll be wanting.'

'Is he around?'

'Oli's out back, as he's in today as well, which is his normal shift. Did a good job of stepping in at the last minute; he's good like that. A worker.'

'Can we speak with him?'

The man looked behind him, then left and right, before stepping out onto the pavement and pulling the door closed behind him.

'You can tell me,' he said.

'Tell you what?' Harry asked.

'What he's done,' the man replied. 'He's not squeaky clean, I know that, but who is? What I also know, though, is that all of that was a long time ago now and he's really pulled himself together, you see, and—'

'He's not in trouble,' Matt said.

Harry thought the man looked a little too surprised.

'He's not?'

'No,' Harry said. 'We just need to have a word with him about something he saw last night, that's all.'

'And you're sure he's not in trouble?'

'Should he be?' Harry asked, wondering just what on earth Oli had been up to, and when.

The man paused just long enough for things to get uncomfortable, before turning back into the shop and on the way back through the counter shouting, 'Oli? Oli! Get yourself over here, lad, the police want to have a word!'

A couple of minutes later, Oli appeared in the door. Harry understood now what the man had meant with his sparrow description. Oli looked around seventeen, was small, thin to the point of being almost transparent, and stared back at Harry with wide, fearful eyes.

'Hello, Oli,' Harry said, 'I'm DCI Harry Grimm, and this is DS Dinsdale.'

'I didn't do it.'

'What?'

'The car. I didn't do it. I saw it, but I didn't do it. I promise I didn't.'

'Well, it would be a turn-up for the books if you did,' said Matt. 'Most criminals don't commit a crime, then call the police about it.'

That seemed to help Oli relax a little, Harry noticed.

'Can you spare a few minutes?' Harry asked.

'Sure,' Oli said.

'Is there somewhere we can chat inside that's a little more private?'

Oli said, 'Yeah, there's a small office. Come on.'

Harry and Matt followed Oli into the chip shop and were soon shown into a room barely big enough for one of them, never mind three. A single chair was pushed under a desk, but having only one of them sitting down would've seemed a little odd, so they left it where it was and stood awkwardly close in the confined space.

'How can I help?' Oli asked.

'We just want to know about the vehicle,' Harry said, and took out his notebook. 'When did you first see it?'

Oli's expression became serious and thoughtful, but when he

spoke, the words fell out of him faster than dry rice from an upturned bowl.

'You know, I think I would probably have been maybe ten, eleven years old? Think I was just leaving the school, heading home, and this massive red sports car drove past, and I was all eyes, I can tell you. We got loads of sports cars in the area, even the occasional Lamborghini, though they're usually from up in Middleham when a rich horse owner is in town, that kind of thing, but I remember that Jag, because red was my favourite colour. Still is. I love red.'

'Oli,' Harry said, 'I didn't mean exactly when in your life. I meant more this week; might be a bit more useful.'

'Really?'

'Yes.'

'Yesterday, then,' Oli said. 'I was on my way home from work and there it was in the car park, like I knew it would be, all shiny and red, and I do like red, you know, and I had to take a few minutes just look at it. Would love a car like that myself someday.'

'No reason to say you won't have one,' said Matt.

Oli laughed.

'Working in a chippy? No chance.'

Harry said, 'You knew the car would be there? How?'

'He'd been in, hadn't he?' replied Oli. 'He's still got that new car grin folk have. Ordered chips, scraps, and a battered black pudding. He almost went for the battered Wensleydale Cheese, but then decided on the pud.'

'What?' said Harry.

'Black pudding,' said Oli. 'That's what he ordered.'

'No, I mean, you do battered Wensleydale Cheese?'

Oli gave an enthusiastic nod.

'It's all gooey on the inside, goes everywhere. Not good if you have a beard.'

Harry moved on.

'Who had been in?' he asked.

'The owner, Mr Hamilton,' said Oli. 'He comes in a couple of times a month, always goes for the black pudding, which was why I was surprised that he almost went for the cheese.'

'He's usually that predictable?'

'I've never seen him order anything else,' said Oli. 'But then, he didn't seem quite himself. Said he'd been at The Board Inn. Reckon he'd had a few too many.'

'How do you mean?'

'Slurring his words, seemed a bit unsteady.'

'And what time was this?' asked Matt.

'Just before we shut up shop,' said Oli. 'He said he was going to enjoy eating them on the walk home. I was surprised because I'd seen his car, hadn't I? But then, with how much he'd had to drink, I thought it made sense. Then he took his order and headed back into town.'

That statement confused Harry.

'But you just said he was going to eat them on the way home.'

'So?'

'So, turning back into town from here isn't on his way home, is it?' said Harry, then looked at Matt. 'The Hamiltons' place is out the back of Gayle, so why would he go back into town to get there?'

'Maybe he fancied a longer walk,' suggested Matt.

'To be fair, the black pudding is big,' said Oli. 'I'd want a long walk home to eat it, and a nap halfway, probably.'

Harry wasn't convinced.

'Which pub did you say he'd been to?'

'The Board Inn,' said Oli.

Harry stood up.

'Thanks for your time, Oli.'

'Do you know who did that to his car, then?' Oli asked, as he led Harry and Matt back to the front of the shop.

'Not at the moment, no,' said Harry.

'Well, it wasn't me, just so you know.'

Harry paused, then turned to stand in front of Oli, towering over him.

'That's quite the guilt complex you've got there,' he said.

'But I didn't do it,' said Oli. 'I wouldn't. I love that car. And it's red, remember? I love red! And now it's covered in all that white paint! I mean, who carries that much paint with them, anyway, just so they can pour it on a Jag? Makes no sense.'

'You're right, it doesn't,' said Harry, then stepped out of the chippy and onto the pavement.

Oli shut the door behind them.

'What do you make of that, then?' Harry asked.

'Hard to say,' said Matt. 'At least we've got Lance here at just before eight-thirty, so that's something.'

'Drunk, too,' said Harry. 'Though that seems a little early to me. And hadn't he been to that meeting Leslie mentioned? Must've finished early for him to head to the pub and get drunk enough to slur his words and stumble.'

'What now, then?' Matt asked.

Harry pointed over the road.

Matt groaned.

'You're having a laugh! First, you take me to a chippy where we can't buy chips, and now you want to take me to a pub where I can't buy beer? I'm going off you, you know.'

Harry crossed over the road.

EIGHTEEN

When Gordy came to, it took a few moments for her to realise where she was. At first, all she could make out were bright lights, but then shapes drew themselves from the brightness and soon she could see that she was on a bed. An annoying beeping sound came to her. She had no idea what it was, but what she knew she wanted to find it and stop it and never hear it again. Then more shapes emerged, grey blobs making odd whale-like noises at her from what she assumed were faces.

'Gordy?'

The voice. She recognised the voice, which was good, so she held onto that, kept staring at where the voice was coming from, tried to remember who it belonged to.

'It's okay, you're fine. It's not as bad as we thought. You're very lucky.'

Gordy was confused, disorientated, and a fist of panic reached into her chest and squeezed her heart. *What's not as bad as we thought? What's happened? Where the hell am I?*

'... leg, and concussion. You'll have to stay in for a while, just to monitor your condition, but somehow, and we don't know how, yet, maybe we never will, when the car hit you, you rolled over the bonnet, and that sort of launched you, like a ramp they think, and—'

'Anna?'

Yes, that was it, Gordy realised. *The voice was Anna's!* She felt hands grab her own, squeeze them.

'It's me, Gordy.'

'Where am I? What's happened? We were at that nature reserve, weren't we?'

'We were.'

'And now we're not.'

'No.'

'Your face is scratched. Have you been gardening again?'

Gordy watched as Anna lifted a hand to her face and touched the scratches.

'I'm fine,' she said. 'No, not gardening. It's nothing. I promise. I've been so worried ...'

Gordy was about to ask what about, when she saw that there was another figure in the room as well. They were standing behind Anna and against the wall, just far enough away to imply that whoever they were, they were giving them some privacy. But her vision was a little blurry, and she couldn't quite make out who it was.

'Who's that?' she asked.

Anna glanced over her shoulder.

The shadow behind her lifted a hand and waved.

'Now then, Gordy,' he said.

'That's Dave,' said Anna. 'Harry sent him.'

'Harry sent Dave? What on earth for? I don't understand!'

And she didn't, and now that panic was starting to spread, and Gordy had the sudden urge to get up, get out, and run like hell.

She pulled her hands from Anna's, looked around, the room now fully in focus, and realisation poured over her like molten metal.

'What the hell am I doing in hospital? Anna? Why am I here? What's happened? What's going on?'

Gordy was suddenly and acutely aware of everything around her, and not just the bed and that irritating beep, either. There were other sounds now, of people rushing around, of machines huffing and beeping and ticking and whirring. Smells came to her, none of them pleasant, a nose-curling cocktail of bleach and disinfectant, hot food, body odour, and stale coffee.

'Gordy ...'

Gordy saw genuine fear in Anna's eyes.

'I don't remember,' she said at last, once Anna had finished telling her how she had been hit by a car, but then only because she had pushed Anna out of the way first. 'I don't remember any of it. How can that be? How can someone be run into by a car and not remember it?'

'You saved me,' Anna said. 'You pushed me out of the way and you were the one who got hit. You could've been killed.'

'Evidence would suggest I wasn't,' said Gordy, attempting a smile.

Dave stepped forward.

'Good to see you awake,' he said.

'Did Harry really send you?'

'He did.'

'Why?'

Anna said, 'Because I called him to tell them what happened. I think he was about ready to commandeer any vehicle he could to be here himself.'

'He's in the middle of an investigation,' Dave explained. 'So, the entire team is tied up with it. So, here I am.' Dave put his hands out wide as though introducing himself to an audience considerably larger than two. 'Ta-da!'

Gordy chuckled, but pain shot through her body and her head exploded with black stars.

'You've spoken to the police?' she asked.

'Yes,' said Anna.

'They'll want to speak to me as well.'

'An officer is coming back later.'

Dave said, 'Harry's not happy that he can't get involved.'

'Regional boundaries do get in the way a little,' said Gordy. Then she added, 'Did you get the numberplate of the car? How did they lose control on that road in the first place? Makes no sense.'

'Thought you couldn't remember anything,' said Dave.

'Being hit, I don't remember that at all, but I remember where we were, because we'd parked in town, and we were making our way back, then ...'

Then nothing, she realised, nothing at all, not a damned thing.

Gordy realised that Anna was crying.

'I'm fine,' she said, squeezing Anna's hand. 'I probably don't look it, lying here attached to all kinds of machines, but I'm okay.'

Anna nodded, tried to dry her eyes.

Dave leaned in and said, 'I'm just going to pop out and give Harry a call; let him know how you're doing. Either of you want anything?'

Gordy, like Anna, declined, and Dave headed off.

'He's going to be our next PCSO, you know,' Gordy said. 'He's got his training to do, but I think he'll be fine.'

'He's not lacking in enthusiasm,' said Anna. 'When the police officer popped in to see us, he wouldn't stop asking them questions.'

'What did they say?'

'Very little. Hopefully they'll have something on a camera,' said Anna, but her words seemed to strangle her as she said them.

Instinctively, Gordy again reached out a hand.

'It's okay,' she said. 'I'm okay. That's all that matters, right?'

'I know,' said Anna, but Gordy could tell something else was going on.

'What is it?' she asked. 'What's the matter?'

Anna said nothing, faked a smile, shook her head.

'Don't do that,' said Gordy. 'Do not clam up on me. Also, don't run off, either, because that would be deeply unfair.'

Anna laughed, but the sound was chased by sadness. *And something else, too,* Gordy thought, *but what?*

'I'm waiting ...'

Anna took a deep breath, then breathed it back out so slowly Gordy wondered if it would ever end.

'When the car came at me,' she said, 'I saw it before you did. I was frozen, just stood there.'

'Natural reaction,' said Gordy. 'Sometimes, we just freeze. There's no blame here.'

Anna shook her head.

'No,' she said, 'it's not that. It's ...'

Again, her voice failed.

'Anna ... please ...'

Anna looked up and Gordy held her stare.

'I thought I was making it up, I really did,' she said. 'It made no sense, you see? I thought I was filling in the gaps, that kind of thing, making something of nothing, trying to come up with a reason for it, perhaps. I didn't mention it to the police because it just seemed crazy, but now, talking to you, remembering it, I'm not so sure. That I'm making it up, I mean. Because what if I'm not?'

Gordy's head was throbbing, her whole body ached, and there was the threat of a wave of pain from her busted leg just waiting for her over the horizon. Anna's inability to get to the point wasn't helping any.

'Making what up?' she asked.

'I recognised the car,' Anna said, as Dave knocked at the door, and with a nod from Gordy, came back into the room. 'And the driver.'

NINETEEN

Back at the office, and with what remained of the afternoon now being pulled thin by the evening ahead, Harry was nursing a mug of tea and having a half-conscious flick through the minutes from the meting Leslie Hamilton had given them. Doing so hadn't improved his mood.

The rest of the team had joined him for a chat before they all headed home for some much-needed rest, because the next day would be busy.

'You've not touched your cake and cheese,' Matt said, ignoring Harry's point about the notebook.

'Arguably, I didn't actually ask for it,' said Harry.

'Just because you didn't ask for it doesn't mean you don't need it,' Matt replied. 'And I tell you now, you absolutely need it.'

There's a certain logic to that argument, Harry thought, but he still didn't reach for a mouthful. Also, he still hadn't forgotten the item on the menu at the chip shop and found himself unable to look at the slab of cheese on his plate without imagining it as a thick, hot, gooey mess, bursting out of crunchy golden batter.

Harry turned to speak to Jadyn when something popped into his mind. 'When Leslie mentioned the meeting, I knew I'd heard mention of it before,' he said.

'Who from?' Matt asked.

'Our soon to be new PCSO,' said Harry.

'Dave? But he's over with Gordy.'

'I'll send him a message,' said Harry. 'Maybe he can shed a bit of light on Lance.'

Message sent, Harry then turned to look at Constable Okri.

'Sorry about the smell,' said Jadyn, noticing that he was under Harry's glare.

'And so you should be,' said Liz, wrinkling up her nose.

Harry had been lost for words when Jadyn had arrived at the office after being over at the Hamiltons' house, his uniform damp, green with slime, and stinking. The constable had gone over what had happened in lots of detail, including the letters and Mrs Hamilton's response.

Harry had given the letters a read through himself.

'Whoever wrote those letters, they didn't hold back, did they?'

'How do you mean?' asked Matt.

'You've read them,' Harry said. 'They're direct. There's stuff in there only someone who really knows him would know.'

'Like his wife, you mean?' said Liz.

'This is Hawes though,' said Matt. 'Hawes, in Wensleydale, remember? Most people know too much about everyone else. That's just the way of things up here, like, isn't it?'

Harry looked to Jadyn. 'Leslie said her husband had never told her about the letters, though, right?'

'She seemed really upset by them,' Jadyn replied. 'She didn't react like I was showing her something she'd done herself. I think she was shocked, but then on top of everything else, that's no surprise, is it? She was acting a bit strange really, meeting me at the door fresh out of the shower, then sorting out the washing, like it was just another normal day and not one where she'd found out her husband had been murdered.'

'People all react differently,' Harry said. 'Sometimes, just getting on with something normal helps. The familiar reminds you that life still goes on, and it's something you're in control of, at a time when everything else clearly isn't. Did she say anything about this meeting on Friday night?'

'No,' Jadyn said.

'What about the son she mentioned? Do we have any other details on him? A name, address maybe?'

'He's called Archie,' said Jadyn. 'That's the only information I've got, though; I was a bit distracted by the letters and the state of my uniform.'

Liz said, 'I headed up there after the car had been dealt with, like you said, but she wasn't in. I'll try again tomorrow.'

'Jen will be back then,' said Harry, 'so she can join you. And we'll need to keep an eye on Sally Dent at the pottery as well. She was keen to get the place up and running again as soon as possible.'

'Not easy after something like this,' said Matt.

Harry said, 'Tomorrow then, we'll have everyone in for a quick confab to chat through what we've got from today, see if we can get our hands on the list of attendees at the mysterious meeting, and then crack on with knocking on doors. If we have anything from the postmortem by then, we can go through that, plus the SOC team may well have something for us. You never know.'

'We definitely need to talk to everyone at that meeting,' said Matt. 'Particularly after what Oli told us didn't match up with what we found out at the pub.'

The chat with the barman had been brief, as the pub had been busy, and he had only been able to spare a few minutes. However, he'd managed to tell them that as far as he knew, Lance Hamilton had drunk only one pint, then a double vodka, which certainly wasn't enough to have him stumbling around and slurring his words, as per Oli's description of when the man had visited the chip shop for his supper.

'Plus, there was a bit of a set-to at the bar,' Harry said. 'Whatever happened at that meeting, it was enough to have some of them follow Lance and confront him.'

'Did the barman tell you who they were?' Jim asked. 'Did he recognise them?'

'No,' said Matt, shaking his head. 'He recognised them but didn't know any of them, not by name, anyway. He lives over in Kirkby Stephen, so not really a local.'

'We need to get to the bottom of whatever happened,' said Harry. 'Whether it's all linked to Lance's murder, I've no idea, but we need to find out.'

The smell in the room was growing a little ripe, and though he should send them all home now—especially Jadyn, the source of the pong—he still needed to speak to them about something else.

'Before you all head off,' he began, 'just a quick word about Gordy.'

The room hushed and everyone seemed to lean in just a little bit closer.

Harry explained about the accident, how Gordy had been hit by a car when she pushed Anna out of its way, but that she was doing fine according to Dave, and was awake and in good spirits.

'I've tried calling Dave for another update,' Harry added, 'but he's not answering. However, at least we know that she's doing okay. Obviously, she won't be back to work for a while, but I think we all know that won't stop her from trying to get involved.'

That raised a chuckle.

Harry stood up, ready to send everyone on their way, when there was a knock at the door, and before anyone was able to get over to open it, in walked Dave Calvert.

'Well, speak of the devil,' said Matt.

'This is a surprise,' Harry said. 'I've just told them about Gordy. Tried calling you to see if there was anything else but couldn't get through. And I've just sent you a message.'

'Driving,' Dave said. 'Always have my phone off when I'm driving.'

'You mean you've driven straight here from the hospital?' Harry asked.

'Yes,' said Dave. 'Don't think I broke the speed limit.'

'What? Why?'

'Figured it best to come over and speak to you in person,' Dave said, slumping down in a chair between Jim and Liz.

Harry didn't like the sound of that at all.

'What's wrong, Dave?'

Waiting for Dave to answer, Harry sank back into his own chair, aware that what he really wanted to be doing was jumping into his RAV and heading over to see Grace. Somehow, that seemed even more important than it usually did, and he wanted to get on with it and to find out why. But Dave was here now, and something was obviously up.

'The car,' Dave explained, clearly still frazzled from his journey over to Hawes from the hospital in Northallerton. 'Anna thinks she recognised it. Not only that, but—'

The room erupted, everyone expressing their shock at Dave's revelation.

Harry raised a hand, and that was enough to have them all calm down again.

'Finish what you were saying,' he said. 'She thinks she recognised the car and ... ?'

'The driver, too,' said Dave.

'How?'

'She says that he's one of her congregation and that he sits at the back of the church most of the time. Turned up about six months ago, keeps himself to himself, but that's about it.'

'And she's absolutely sure she recognised him?'

'I didn't say she was sure,' said Dave, 'but to me, she seems pretty certain, yes.'

'She's told the investigating team?'

'No,' said Dave. 'Not yet anyway, or not before I'd left. She thought she was imagining it, caught up in the stress and confusion of what had happened, trying to see something there that wasn't, that kind of thing. She was telling Gordy about it when I walked back into the room after talking to you.'

Harry was torn.

'This isn't our investigation,' he said. 'She needs to speak to the police who are dealing with it. We can't get involved, no matter how much we want to.'

'She knows that,' Dave said. 'Gordy's explained that to her in no uncertain terms, I can assure you, and Gordy's probably spoken to them by now anyway.'

'So, why did you race over here?' Harry asked. 'Why didn't you just call?'

'Because I didn't come alone,' Dave said, then he turned back to the office door and opened it, and in walked Anna.

TWENTY

Harry was sitting in the interview room. Opposite him was Anna. She looked pale, he thought, smaller, too, and the mug of tea he had provided was still untouched. He wished that Smudge was with him, the dog's ability to help someone relax almost a superpower.

After Dave's arrival, and then the appearance of Anna, Harry had dismissed everyone, advising them all to get home and grab plenty of rest for the days ahead. They had all protested, loudly too, about staying and helping, but Harry had been adamant; he would deal with it. He'd not had a chance to speak with Dave about the meeting at the Market Hall, so that would have to wait till morning.

Early evening was now threatening to disappear, and Harry was forcing himself to not hurry things along, simply because he wanted to get home to Grace. So, he waited, giving Anna the opportunity to take the lead and say what she needed to say. He had no idea what to expect, and was fairly sure that whatever Anna told him, he would have to immediately share with the team investigating what had happened to her and Gordy.

'It all started about a year ago,' Anna said, lifting the mug, then replacing it again without taking a sip.

'What did?' he asked, a little confused by the statement.

'At first, it was an email here and there, so I ignored it, because you get cranks, don't you?'

Whatever Anna was trying to tell him, it sounded to Harry like she'd jumped ahead a few chapters, missing out some key details.

'You need to start from the beginning,' he said. 'I'm not following you.'

'I prayed about it,' continued Anna, 'because that's what I do, isn't it? I'm a vicar, remember? If I can't pray, then what use am I to anyone?'

'Prayed about what?'

Harry remembered then the conversation he'd had with Gordy about her taking time off, not for herself, but for Anna. She'd mentioned how Anna had seemed up against it, bothered by something. Was that what Anna was talking about now?

'One night, after a particularly tough home visit,' Anna continued, 'I arrived home to an email that was especially vile. I was very tired, very upset, too, about what I'd just had to deal with; you know, I'm fairly sure there's no pain on earth like what a parent feels at the loss of a child. So, after that, I poured myself a glass of wine, and ... well, I'm not proud of it, but reading that email? It made me so angry, and I don't get angry, Harry. I just don't. But I was, and I responded; I typed a reply and hit send. Didn't think anything more of it till the following morning.'

Harry's mind was racing around trying to fill in the gaps, and there were a lot, because as yet Anna hadn't really told him anything.

'Dave said that you recognised the car and the driver,' he said, hoping to prompt Anna into explaining things a little so that he could understand where she was going with this.

Anna once again reached for the mug and this time took a sip, staring at Harry over the rim. To him, her eyes seemed haunted, as though she could sense an invisible threat, something in the shadows behind her, dangerous and prowling.

'Why can't people just be kind?' Anna asked, and Harry had nothing he could say to that. Well, nothing he was about to voice right there and then. 'Because really, that's the answer, isn't it? Kindness? If we were all simply more kind to each other, think how much better this world would be, and how quickly so many problems would be solved. That's all it takes, Harry; kindness. You understand that, don't you? I know you do. You may be this big, gruff, scarred man, with those eyes that have seen things most of us will never know about, but you're kind; I knew that as soon as I met you. It's a rare thing.'

'You replied to an email,' Harry said. 'Do you know who sent it? Are you able to tell me what it said? Have you kept them?'

'It was vile,' Anna said. Harry heard a hardening of her voice, something he had never witnessed before. 'The things it said, what I was accused of, not just doing either, but being, how it was people like me that would bring society down, that I had to be stopped ...'

Harry's worry turned up to ten.

'If you were receiving threats, Anna, from anyone, and in whatever form, it's a police matter,' he said. 'You need to tell me everything you know. Do you understand? Everything.'

'I couldn't tell Gordy,' Anna continued, almost as though she hadn't heard Harry speak. 'The emails, they'd mentioned her, not by name, but by association, because of who she was to me, and I didn't want her to know, to be involved. I was trying to protect her, you see? That's all I was trying to do. I prayed, and I thought it would all go away, but it didn't, Harry, it didn't, and now look ...'

Harry remembered the first time he had met Anna, how he had been struck by how she was just so wonderfully human. That she was a vicar seemed to only amplify that humanity. He was no religious man himself, but Harry had seen a brightness in her that he had witnessed in few others, a deep sense of care for the community she didn't simply live in but served. Now, though, that brightness seemed dimmed.

'I don't generally jump to conclusions, Anna,' he said, 'but my guess is that what you're telling me is you think the person who sent you these emails, it's the same person you saw in the car that hit Gordy.'

'It only hit her because she pushed me out of the way,' Anna said. 'It should be me in that hospital, not her. It was me he was trying to hit. Me!'

Harry held up a hand to stop Anna before she said anymore.

'You're wrong,' he said. 'No one should be in that hospital. Not Gordy, not you. Now tell me, who is it? Who is the driver?'

'The emails stopped,' Anna said. 'Just a few days before he turned up in the congregation. I didn't think anything of it. Why should I? There's no connection, is there? I didn't suspect him of anything, not at first, not for a good while, really. But now, looking back, I'm ...'

Anna's voice caught in her throat.

'In your own time,' Harry said, as his phone buzzed in his pocket.

He ignored it.

'I received one final email,' Anna said, then pulled a folded piece of paper from a pocket, opened it, and slid it across to Harry. 'I stopped off on the way back to print it off.'

'See you soon?' said Harry, reading the words on the paper.

'There's something else, too,' Anna said. 'At the bottom of the email. A bible verse.'

'Malachi 2: 1-3,' read Harry, none the wiser for having done so.

'Those verses have a title,' Anna said. '*Additional warning to the priests.*'

'And what do those verses say?'

'Turn the sheet over,' Anna said.

Harry did as she instructed, and as he read the passage, Anna recited it for him.

'And now, you priests, this warning is for you. If you do not listen, and if you do not resolve to honour my name,' says the Lord Almighty, 'I will send a curse on you, and I will curse your blessings. Yes, I have already cursed them, because you have not resolved to honour me. Because of you, I will rebuke your descendants; I will smear on your faces the dung from your festival sacrifices, and you will be carried off with it.'

'You know it by heart, then,' said Harry. 'God knows why, though; not exactly pleasant, is it?'

'I've read it a lot,' replied Anna. 'Vicar, remember? Knowing the bible is one of the things we're big on.'

Harry held the paper in his hand, tempted to screw it up and throw it at the wall.

'This,' he said, 'is a threat. You know that, don't you? This isn't just someone playing games. This kind of stuff, it's never a game. Ever. And it can't be ignored.'

'I know,' Anna said. 'I just didn't want to believe it, I suppose, that it was him. Does that make sense?'

'So, who is it, then?' Harry asked. 'And why do you think this is the same bloke who hit Gordy?'

'His name is Malcolm,' Anna said. 'And he's my brother.'

TWENTY-ONE

As revelations went, Anna's was such a surprise that Harry almost fell off his chair.

'He's your what now? Your brother? I didn't even know you had a brother!'

He already had one investigation to be getting on with, but then when did police work ever involve just doing one thing at a time? He wasn't Poirot. Good job really, he thought, because that moustache really wouldn't suit him. Not that he could grow one anyway, not since what had happened to him back in Afghanistan.

Anna gave the faintest of nods.

'Younger brother,' she said.

'They're always trouble,' said Harry. 'Trust me, I know that better than most.'

Somehow, that brought a flicker of a smile to Anna's face.

'It's why I couldn't tell the police, not right away,' she said. 'Gordy doesn't know either. I had to see you, tell you first.'

'Gordy doesn't know?'

Harry wasn't a fan of secrets.

'She's in hospital and needs to recover,' said Anna. 'Telling her will only add to the stress.'

'You'll forgive me, but I'm not sure what it is you're expecting me to do,' said Harry, 'What happened to you and Gordy, that's being dealt with by another team. I can't get involved, Anna; you need to go to whoever's the senior investigating officer. Who is it?'

'DCI Mason,' Anna said. 'But I can't, Harry.'

'What? Can't has nothing to do with it, and you know it. Call DCI Mason.' Harry held out his phone. 'Now.'

'You don't understand.'

'I understand that your brother tried to kill you. That's what I understand.'

'It's not like that. He didn't try to kill me.'

'He drove a car at you and put Gordy in hospital, Anna. If Gordy hadn't pushed you, who's to say you wouldn't have been killed? Have you thought about that?'

Anna went to speak, but fell quiet, and Harry had nothing to say right then to fill the silence. Her brother tried to hit her with his car? And he's not only been attending her church, but she thinks he's behind goodness knows how many threatening emails she's been receiving? How the hell had she kept all of this a secret?

'You can't protect him, Anna,' Harry said. 'That's not how this works.'

'How what works?'

'Life.'

Anna smiled, but any warmth was extinguished by the sorrow Harry saw in her eyes.

'We converted the same day,' she said. 'We were both part of a youth club, went to this big rally where some charismatic preacher was doing his thing. He asked people to go forward, and we both answered that call.'

'I'd love to be able to say I know what you're talking about,' said Harry, 'but I've not a religious bone in my body.'

'Souls don't need bones.'

Harry laughed, then sobered.

'I'm serious, Anna,' he said. 'If this was your brother, and you know how we can find him, then you need to help us do that.'

'I know,' Anna said, 'which is why I came to you, Harry. I know you, I trust you, and I need you to trust me. Malcolm, he's not himself. Hasn't been for a few years now, not since he lost his wife to cancer. He fell back onto the only constant in his life, his faith, looking for some way to channel the hurt. He needed to blame someone for her death, because to him, if God was all-powerful, then why did it happen?'

'It happened because that's life,' said Harry. 'He lost someone. He's not alone in that. Doesn't give him the excuse to do any of this.'

'It's not an excuse,' Anna said, 'it's a reason; he needed to blame someone, so he blamed me, said that because of who and what I was, that the family had been punished. It was nonsense, but he didn't want to see it. The change in him, it was dramatic.'

'Because of who and what you are?' Harry said. 'I'm not following.'

The smile Anna gave Harry was so warm, so genuine, he was momentarily lost for words.

'There's that kindness, you see?' Anna said. 'I wear a dog collar, remember? And I'm with Gordy. Some people have a problem with that.'

'Your brother being one of them.'

'Acutely so.'

Anna slid a small slip of paper across the table.

'This is his address,' she said. 'He never gave it to me because we never spoke. I was just happy to see him again. I followed him, though, one Sunday after church.'

Harry picked up the piece of paper.

'I can't go,' he said. 'You know I can't.'

'But you will,' Anna said. 'Not tonight, because I know he's not there. But tomorrow.'

'You know? How?'

'I called him,' Anna said, providing Harry with another jaw-dropping revelation. 'While I was following Gordy to hospital, I called him, and I said I'd seen him in the car. He was crying. I asked if he was home, and that shocked him, made him fall silent.'

'He didn't know that you knew where he lived, then?'

Anna shook her head.

'He said there was no point in my calling the police, because he would never go home now, knowing that I knew where it was. But he will.'

'You're sure?'

'When his wife died, we lost him to sorrow, but also to the past. He spent his time staring at photographs and videos. He would never leave those behind.'

Harry stared at the address. The correct thing to do was call the SIO, give them the information, let them deal with it. But correct didn't always mean right.

'I can have my team keep an eye on the place,' Harry said, not exactly sure how he was going to achieve that, having sent everyone home. Really, someone should've been on call, but with two staff away, and now the investigation into Lance Hamilton's death, the usual way of doing things had gone out the window. 'Do you have somewhere you can stay?' he asked. 'I don't want you going home, not with your brother out there having done what he did.'

'I've already sorted something,' Anna said, 'courtesy of your newest recruit.'

'Dave?'

Harry couldn't have picked anyone better.

'I'll call in for uniform from another team,' he said. 'I'll have someone sent over from Sedburgh, shouldn't be too much hassle; it's only for one night, and then one of my team can take over.'

Anna stood up.

'Thank you, Harry,' she said.

'I hadn't finished,' Harry replied. 'Everything you've told me and shown me, it still has to go to the SIO. DCI Mason needs to know. I'm going to give your brother twenty-four hours, that's all. You'll have some explaining to do, about why you kept this information to yourself for so long, but we'll cross that bridge as and when.'

'I understand.'

'Good,' Harry said. 'Now get yourself to bed; your eyes look like they're about to fall out of your face.'

Harry led Anna from the room and found Dave waiting in the office.

'Away then,' Dave said. 'Let's get you home to mine. The spare room is all made up. I'll throw some food together for us when we get back as well; nowt posh, like, but it'll be filling.' He looked at Harry. 'I'll keep you posted.'

'You do that,' said Harry, then Dave and Anna left, and Harry was alone.

The community centre seemed eerie in the half-light of the evening, the quiet so thick he had to force his legs to move to get himself out of the building.

Outside, the evening was warm, and the marketplace, though not busy, still showed life as people mooched past, slowly making their way from pub to pub, or home.

Harry had two calls to make, so he pulled out his phone, then saw that Grace had read his message but not replied.

On my way, he typed, then climbed into his RAV and pulled up the first number and called it.

'Well?'

'I've booked an appointment next week,' Sowerby said.

'Good,' said Harry, hung up, then a quick search gave him another number and that connected soon after.

'DCI Grimm,' he said. 'I need to speak with DCI Mason.'

The conversation was short and to the point, and as soon as it was done, Harry was on his way to Carperby.

TWENTY-TWO

Arriving at the community centre the following morning, Harry yawned as he pushed through the main doors, Smudge happily trotting alongside him, and considerably more awake. But then she always was, Harry thought. Since inviting her into his life, he'd never known Smudge to meet any new day with anything other than unbound enthusiasm, as though whatever it promised was bound to be the best thing ever. God, he wished he had her energy.

Harry hadn't slept well. His mind had been so full after such a busy day that closing his eyes seemed to do nothing more than amplify his thoughts to such a volume, he was surprised Grace hadn't been able to hear them as well. But she had slept on, much like Smudge, and Grace's dog, Jess, both of whom had once again managed to sneak upstairs in the night and settle down at their feet. Harry had drifted off eventually, but then woke at just gone three in the morning, to see every hour pass as he had laid there staring through the dark at the ceiling.

After a ludicrously busy day, which had then finished with Anna's visit and revelations and a quick chat with DCI Mason, Harry had headed back to Grace's. Despite his concern after leaving the clay shoot earlier in the day, Grace had seemed okay. They'd settled down for an evening of good food, which was left over from the picnic they had taken to the field, and a beer or two. With nothing much on the telly to watch, they'd instead gone for a walk with the dogs, which had included a stop at the Wheatsheaf Inn, before heading home again to fall asleep on the sofa, listening to music. Harry had had worse evenings, that was for sure.

The next morning, after he'd told Grace he would see her at his place that evening, he'd felt like Grace had wanted to say something, but she hadn't. He had left for work feeling as though something that should have been said hadn't been, and what it might be niggled at him all the way to work.

First at the office, Harry got the water boiling for tea, and no sooner had he done so, and Matt walked through the door.

'Now then, Boss,' he said. 'Hungry?'

Harry shook his head.

'Tired though,' he said, 'so it's coffee for me. Yourself?'

'Tea,' said Matt. 'I'll be back in five.'

'But you've only just arrived.'

'You may not be hungry, but I certainly am,' Matt said, patted his stomach, and was gone.

When the door opened again, Jen and Jadyn stepped into the room, both of them talking so fast and with so much enthusiasm that their voices came at Harry like a wave on a beach, tumbling over him in a crescendo of noise he just couldn't understand.

'How was the race, then?' he asked, cutting in.

'Amazing,' said Jen. 'Fifty miles, and I hit a personal best, too.'

Harry laughed.

'You don't seem like you've run five miles, never mind fifty.'

'You going to do an ultra, Boss?' Jadyn asked, as Jen settled down into one of the chairs, Smudge heading over to her for a tummy scratch, which she duly obliged.

'Of course,' said Harry, noticing Jadyn's inability to hide the smirk the question was riding. 'Doing one next month, after which I'm heading off to the Himalayas to solo Everest without oxygen, before paragliding back down. You should join me. Just make sure you don't slow me down.'

'I'm actually serious,' Jadyn said.

'That's what worries me,' said Harry, as the office door crashed open once again, and in walked Liz.

'Matt's on his way,' she said.

'Already seen him,' said Harry. 'He was hungry.'

'How does Joan put up with an appetite like that?' Liz asked. 'Their cupboards must be constantly empty.'

'Probably hides it behind the baby food to try and ward him off,' Harry suggested with a laugh.

After offering to make everyone a drink if they wanted one, Harry took himself over to the front of the room and pulled out the board, giving it a good wipe, so that they could crack on with working out what they knew so far about Lance Hamilton, and what they would be doing next. He also had the thing with Anna's brother, but that would be dealt with separately at the end.

Matt returned.

'Here you go,' he said, handing something over to Harry.

'I said I wasn't hungry,' said Harry, holding a warm white paper bag.

'And I know you better than you know yourself,' Matt said.

'Not sure that you do,' Harry muttered, and opened the bag as Jen came over to look at the contents.

'That's not going to help with your running,' she said.

Harry laughed.

'What, you mean this bacon sandwich is all that's standing between me and my career as an ultra-marathon runner?'

'Quite possibly.'

Harry reached in and lifted the bacon sandwich in front of his face. The smell was heavenly.

'Shame that,' he said, and went to take a bite.

'Think of all the work you've put in,' Jen said.

Harry paused, grease dripping down a finger.

'Look,' Jen said, 'I'm not telling you what to do—'

'Yes, you are,' said Harry.

'Well, yes, I am, but that's not the point.'

'Then what is?'

Harry noticed then that the room had fallen silent, not that it stopped Jen from having her say.

'All I'm saying is that you've worked hard, right? I know it's only one bacon sandwich, and I'm not saying you have to give them up or stop eating or anything like that, just that you shouldn't just fall back on old habits.'

Harry stared at the bacon sandwich. He knew Jen had a point. He'd progressed better these past few months with getting himself moving properly again than in the past few years. He looked at the rest of the team.

'Anyone want this?'

Jim entered the office at that exact moment, Fly at his heel.

'Me,' he said. 'I missed my breakfast.'

Harry handed the butty over, noticing a faint look of disappointment on Jadyn's face for missing out.

With the whole team gathered and doing his best to ignore Fly and Smudge play-fighting in the corner, Harry decided to move things on. He clapped his hands together to get everyone's attention, at the same time feeling a buzz from his phone in his pocket. When he eventually managed to fish it out, the call had gone through to voicemail. Rebecca Sowerby's name was on the screen. He quickly typed that he would call her back as soon as the meeting was over, and sent the message, receiving a thumbs-up emoji in reply. He looked at the team.

'Officer Okri?'

Jadyn stood up, marched over to the board, and got a pen ready.

'We've a couple of things to be on with today,' Harry said, 'so unless there's anything pressing from the Action Book, I suggest we just crack on. Would you mind just checking that, Jen?'

Jen grabbed the book, flicked through the pages, and shook her head.

'We're good,' she said.

Harry took centre stage.

'Let's deal with Mr Lance Hamilton first. Where are we and what do we know?'

Jim quickly ran through what had happened when he was called to the crime scene, and what he found. Jadyn and Liz then added their own details about when they attended, with Matt confirming it all, leaving it to Harry to continue with the story.

'Currently, we're waiting to hear from forensics, and the pathologist regarding the postmortem. Once they're happy that there's no reason to go back to the crime scene, then we can allow the owner back in, give her a chance to arrange for a clean-up.'

'Who?' Jen asked.

'Sally Dent,' Harry repeated. 'She owns the—'

'I know her,' Jen said. 'Not well, but enough to have a chat.' She turned to Jadyn. 'You didn't tell me it was Sally.'

'I didn't know you knew her,' Jadyn said. 'And I was a bit distracted.'

Harry noticed a sheepish look on Jadyn's face, and when he looked at Jen, he saw a faint blush to her cheeks.

'How do you know her?' he asked.

'She's a runner,' Jen explained, clearly pleased to be moving on with the subject and away from Jadyn's comment. 'I don't know her well, but I've bumped into her a good number of times. She's long distance as well.'

'But you live in Middleham,' said Harry. 'That's what, at least fifteen miles? You race together, then?'

'Eighteen by road,' said Matt. 'I dread to think what it is by foot.'

You're not the only one, thought Harry.

'And about halfway is Penhill,' said Jen. 'We've met there a few times, stopped to have a breather and a chat, usually late at night or early morning.'

Harry rubbed his eyes, his own tiredness amplified by the thought of being out running over Penhill in the middle of the night.

'Why usually?' he asked.

'Like me, she has to fit running round work, and she doesn't sleep well,' Jen said. 'She's fast, though, like a whippet. We've been in a few races together.'

Harry said, 'Well, once we have the all-clear, I'll leave it to you to go and see how she is. She may not have an alibi for the whole night, but I'm fairly sure setting up what we found, then calling the police about it is a little elaborate.'

'What we do know,' said Matt, 'is that she saw Lance in the early hours of the previous evening. There was a meeting in the Market Hall—'

'We still need to get our hands on the list of attendees at that meeting,' Harry said. 'We've Leslie Hamilton's notebook with the minutes in, but as we know, they don't contain the name of everyone who was there. That list is with Andrew Wilson, the accountant she mentioned..'

'I rang Leslie earlier,' said Matt. 'She gave me Wilson's contact details so I called him and he provided me with names, addresses, telephone numbers.'

'Where does he live?' Harry asked.

'On the way out of Hawes, just before you get to the auction mart,' said Matt.

'I'll be heading past there on my way to the mortuary this morning,' said Harry. 'I'll pop in and have a chat, see what he has to say about everything. And I need to speak to Dave, as he was there.'

'Already have,' said Matt.

'You've been busy.'

'I'm never anything else.'

Harry laughed at that but gestured for Matt to continue.

Matt said, 'Dave was a good source of information, and although we do need to head out and speak to everyone to double check what they were all doing after the meeting, I do have some names that are higher on the list than others. I've crosschecked it with what I got from the accountant as well.'

'Go on,' Harry said.

'Dave mentioned that a few people were unhappy to see Lance

at the meeting. Sounds like he left before it had been officially brought to a close, but that his leaving kind of hurried things along, after which a group then followed him over to The Board Inn, as we know already.'

'And Dave knows they did that because ...?'

'He headed over to catch up with a couple of people he knew outside the pub, watched them all go in, then saw them leave shortly after, followed a few minutes later by Lance himself.'

'Did he seem drunk to Dave?' Harry asked.

Matt shook his head.

'I asked him that exact question, and he said he wouldn't be able to say for certain either way. He did say, though, that it looked like Lance had spilled a drink on himself, his shirt was soaked.'

Matt handed a piece of paper to Harry.

'These are the names of everyone who Dave said followed Lance over to the pub,' he explained.

Harry read the names and recognised two of them immediately.

'Leslie Hamilton and Sally Dent? I don't recall either of them mentioning a pub visit.' He handed the list to Jadyn, who started putting them up on the board.

'Odd that, isn't it?' said Matt.

'A little.' Harry read the other names on the board as Jadyn jotted them down. 'We've also got the letters Jadyn found over in Mr Hamilton's office; someone was threatening him. There's nothing specific in any of them, no mention of severing hands, anyway, but they don't exactly make for pleasant reading. Lance's wife, Leslie, is claiming to have neither seen nor heard of them before. The one thing they do have going for them, though, is that they're hand-written, so I've had them sent to forensics; we might get something, we might not.'

'I ran off some copies,' said Jadyn, 'before I sent them off. We can all take them with us, then, can't we? See if they get a response.'

'Well done,' Harry said.

He gave everyone a minute or two to mull over what had been discussed, then realised Jadyn still hadn't finished writing the names on the board.

'Something up?' he asked.

Jadyn looked up.

'Sorry?'

'You're away with the faeries there,' said Harry. 'Daydreaming.'

'No, it's just I ...'

Jadyn screwed up his face as he tried to work out what it was that he was trying to say.

'It's just you what?' Harry asked.

Jadyn gave a shrug.

'No, it's gone,' he said, then without any further prompting from Harry, finished copying the names onto the board.

Harry decided it was time to bring things to a close and get on with the rest of the day.

'Right then,' he said. 'We know something happened in the pub, so I want to know what. I also want to speak with every person on this list, find out what they were doing there, why they followed Lance, and what they were doing last night. Matt, can I leave it with you to coordinate this with the team?'

'No bother at all.'

'Good,' said Harry. 'I'm going to speak with Sowerby, see where we are with things on that front, and I also need to check up on Gordy.'

The team fell quiet.

'I heard about what happened,' said Jen. 'How is she?'

Harry gave everyone an update on Gordy's condition, then said, 'There's something else, though; Anna came over with Dave last night, and I ended up having a lengthy chat with her.'

'She must be so worried,' said Jim.

'More than any of us could've known,' said Harry. 'Not only did she recognise the car and the driver, she knows him personally.'

An audible gasp lit the room like a firework.

'The car was aimed at Anna,' Harry said, 'but Gordy pushed

her out of the way and it ploughed into her instead. The driver, it turns out, is none other than Anna's brother.'

Another gasp, this time well-seasoned with swearing.

'I didn't know she even had a brother,' said Jadyn.

'You're not alone in that,' said Harry. 'Not entirely sure Gordy knows either, though I've not checked that little detail yet. Regardless, we know where he lives, or should I say where he moved to a while back, before turning up at Anna's church and attending Sunday morning services for a few months. We also know that Anna has been receiving abusive anonymous emails, something else she's kept secret. I requested help, and a uniformed officer was sent over to keep an eye on the place. Anna stayed over with Dave last night as well, just to be sure she was safe. Officer Okri?'

'Yes, Boss?'

'You'll be relieving the uniform currently standing watch,' Harry instructed. 'Anna thinks there's every chance her brother will go home at some point.'

Jen asked, 'But from what Jadyn's told me, I thought another team would be dealing with it? It's not our area, is it?'

Harry said, 'I've spoken with the DCI heading up the investigation. Jadyn will go over once we're done here and we'll see what the day brings. Any further questions?'

The only reply he received was Fly yapping at Smudge, who was lying on top of him, and squashing him into the carpet.

Harry said. 'Jadyn, hand the copies of those letters out if you could. Also, I'm sure word will have got around about what's happened. However, due to the nature of what happened to the victim, I'd prefer it if we kept it as quiet as we can. That means yes, you can inform people about Mr Hamilton's death, but that's it. No details about what happened are to be shared. Bar the person responsible, Ms Dent is the only one who knows any details, and she's been instructed to keep it that way. Is that understood? And remember, ABC principle: assume nothing, believe nobody, check everything.'

'Remember?' said Matt, and Harry saw him glance around at

the rest of the team in mild confusion. 'You've never mentioned that one before.'

'Really?'

'He's right, you haven't,' said Jadyn. 'It's good, though. Catchy.'

'We could have it put on a T-shirt,' suggested Jen.

'No, you couldn't, and no you won't,' said Harry. 'Let's crack on, shall we?'

A collective *Yes* from the team was all the confirmation Harry needed.

Exchanging a copy of the letters for the location of Anna's brother's house with Jadyn, Harry left the office. Outside the community centre, he jumped into his RAV to drive over to meet up with Sowerby, and to pop in on the way for a quick chat with Andrew Wilson.

Before setting off, he pinged Sowerby a text, just to make sure everything was good for him to pay a visit, and it was. As for Smudge, Harry left her in the capable hands of Jim and her best friend Fly. She didn't exactly seem bothered for him to be leaving and, though Harry would never admit it out loud, he would have preferred it if she was, even just a little.

TWENTY-THREE

Andrew Wilson's house was a grand Victorian villa, complete with bay windows, a neat front lawn protected by a low wall topped with iron railings, and stained glass adorning the front door. Harry wasn't surprised; he'd yet to meet an accountant not doing well for themselves.

He pushed through the gate, which opened smoothly on well-oiled hinges, strode up a flagstone path lined with flowers, and pressed the doorbell.

From deep inside the house, Harry heard an elaborate, electronic chime ring out.

'Just a minute ...'

The voice was distant and echoey.

Harry turned away from the door and watched a tractor trundle down the road, pulling a large trailer. The farmer, who was tucked into his cab between three excited border collies, raised a hand to wave at Harry, which Harry returned, though for the life of him, he had no idea who it was. But then that was Hawes, wasn't it? People waved at you, said hello. He couldn't help but think that the world could do with a bit more of that spread about.

'Hello?'

Harry turned around to find himself staring at a man wearing a military uniform, though Harry had no idea what country it was from, or what century. The material was either black, or a blue so dark it was impossible to tell the difference, and as Harry walked over, getting closer didn't help him any. A wide-brimmed hat was on the man's head, the jacket pulled in by a leather belt, from which hung a holster and a scabbard.

'Morning,' Harry said. 'I'm DCI Harry Grimm. Mr Wilson, yes?'

'I believe I've already spoken to one of your team, Mr Grimm.'

'That would be Detective Sergeant Dinsdale, and we're grateful for the information you provided.'

'The list of names? Oh, it was nothing. Not a problem at all. Happy to help. I've a written copy in the house as well that I can get for you if you'd like? Can I ask what this is about?'

Harry was now at the front door and was able to take in the full splendor of the outfit Wilson was wearing.

'I'm wondering if I should be asking the same,' said Harry. 'I'm a military man myself, but I've not seen a uniform like that before.'

'Do you like old movies?' Wilson asked, and Harry saw a glint in the man's eye. 'The theatre perhaps?'

Harry was trying to place the accent. There wasn't much of it, and it was definitely northern, but not from the Dales. A while back, he'd have said all northern accents were pretty much the same, but not now. There were subtle differences, even locally, and he'd noticed that folk over in Swaledale sounded the same but different to those in Wensleydale.

'Movies yes, theatre no,' answered Harry. 'Not that I don't like it. I just don't think I've ever had the time to give it a chance.'

'So many people say the same,' said Wilson. 'Shame really; it's the purest of ways to witness the acting craft.'

Harry could hear the man's enthusiasm for what he was talking about in his voice. This wasn't just an interest; it was a passion. Someone else with a hobby, he thought.

'Can I come in?'

'To my house?'

'That would make the most sense, yes,' said Harry.

'Of course, please ...'

Wilson stepped back into the house and allowed Harry to move past him, before closing the door. He then gestured to a door on the left.

'If you head through there, we can chat in my study.'

Harry did as asked and stepped into a house that not only looked clean and tidy, but smelled it, too. This was a home where everything had its place, the pictures on the wall neatly spaced out, the tiled floor of the hall polished to a shine. The air was filled with a heady scent of flowers, and he spotted plug-in air fresheners in a couple of sockets along the wall.

'Nice house,' Harry said. 'Spotless.'

'Just had it decorated,' Wilson said. 'Needed a bit of sprucing up.'

Harry headed through to the study and briefly wondered what it would be like to own a house large enough to contain one. He had never been a fan of studying, learning better through practical work and experience than from the pages of a book. Not that he didn't see the value in it, quite the opposite in fact. It was more that he would get restless if forced to sit down for too long. How anyone had the strength of will, and the focus and determination, to do anything like a masters or a doctorate he had no idea. And as for writing a novel? Not a chance of it. There was no doubt a lot of truth in the notion that everyone had a book inside them, but as far as Harry was concerned, that was exactly where his was going to stay.

The study was mostly how Harry expected it to be; a large desk in the bay window, atop which sat a computer screen, filing cabinets dotted around, and the walls lined with bookshelves. It was just that, right then, he couldn't actually see much of the bookshelves, hidden as they were behind numerous costumes.

'Take a seat,' said Wilson, gesturing to a couple of armchairs relaxing by a small coffee table.

Harry glanced over at the desk.

'Nice, isn't it?' Wilson said.

'I'm a little jealous,' said Harry, walking over for a closer look. 'Not just of the desk, either; that computer doesn't look cheap.'

'It isn't,' said Wilson. 'The days of hand-writing letters to your clients are long gone, thankfully. I work from home. No point wasting money on an office when my house is more than big enough to accommodate one.'

'You don't write any at all?' Harry asked.

'Haven't done in years,' he said. 'Even my signature is electronic.'

Harry took one last glance at the desk, then sat down and took out his notebook.

'You're probably wondering about all of this, I suspect,' said Wilson, waving a hand at the various garments hanging around the walls. 'We're doing Calamity Jane, you see? It's my first ever go at directing. I'm in the play, too, as you can see.'

'Ah, that explains the uniform,' said Harry.

'Lieutenant Danny Gilmartin; Calamity's love interest, except of course he isn't, not in the end. You'll have to come see it.'

Harry avoided responding to that, and said, 'I just need to ask you about the meeting you chaired a couple of nights ago.'

'Have you ever trod the boards?'

'What?'

'The boards,' said Wilson. 'Have you ever acted, been on stage? I think you'd be good. Brooding. Yes, you'd brood well, I'm sure. I'm thinking of doing Dracula next, and if you're interested—'

'I'm not,' Harry said.

'The offer's there.'

'Back to the meeting, if that's okay,' said Harry, keen to move on from the image now in his mind of him looking awkward and idiotic on stage as he tried to remember his lines.

'The one about housing? It's a real issue around here, you know. I was hoping it would be a little more constructive, but it's a start, isn't it?'

'You organized it?'

'I did. Community action and all that.'

Harry said, 'I understand things got a bit heated.'

'It is a shame, but yes, they did,' said Wilson. 'But then, I knew it would as soon as he turned up.'

'Who?'

'Lance Hamilton. I'd made a point of not mentioning it to him when he was round the other week, hoping it would pass him by. Wishful thinking though really, in a place like Hawes.'

'He was round here?'

'I'm his accountant,' said Wilson, then he laughed. 'You know, I could have just saved myself some time and turned that meeting into a social for my clients. I usually do a Christmas bash, you know? Wine, nibbles, that kind of thing.'

'How do you mean?'

'About the nibbles?'

Harry managed to stop himself from rolling his eyes.

'About your clients,' Harry said.

'Mr Hamilton is my largest client,' Wilson explained, 'not just in terms of turnover, but profit as well, but I'm also the accountant for a lot of people round here.' He leaned forward conspiratorially. 'There's not much happens around here that I don't know about. But confidentiality is what I pride myself on, so I hope you're not here to ask any, you know, compromising questions.'

Harry said, 'Should I be?'

Wilson sat back and smiled.

'You know what they say, small towns, big secrets; Hawes is no different. I probably know more than most. Now, can I ask what this is actually about?'

After what Mr Wilson had just said, Harry wasn't so sure.

'You know Mr Hamilton well, then?' he asked.

'Not socially, but yes, I know him well enough. We meet regularly. I sometimes think I know his business better than I do him. Why do you ask?'

'What actually happened at the meeting?' said Harry. 'I understand you went to the pub afterwards?'

Wilson looked thoughtful for a moment.

'Yes, Leslie and I had a brief chat after the meeting,' he said. 'Then we wandered over to the pub for a drink, but we didn't stay, not after what happened. It was all a bit tense, if you know what I mean.'

'Not exactly, no,' said Harry.

'Too much anger in the air,' Wilson said, his voice lowered to just a little louder than a whisper. 'Lance seems to attract it. If I'm honest, I think he likes to wind people up. I've tried to tell him so many times not to be like that, but he doesn't seem to care. A strange man, but then who of us isn't rather odd in some way?'

'Not sure I understand,' said Harry.

'What I mean is,' said Wilson, 'on the one hand, Lance will happily tell you how moving to the Dales changed him, how everyone should come here for the good of their health, and on the other, he seems to get a kick out of making money and not being liked. Odd, really. But it pays the bills, doesn't it? I can't be picky about my clients, more's the pity.'

'Was there an argument?' Harry asked.

'I think something had happened before we arrived at the pub,' Wilson said. 'There were arguments at the meeting, yes, but it got more physical at the pub. Aldwin Fothergill and Jeff Weatherill both looked as though they were going to strangle him at one point, and just before that, Sally had given him this enormous slap just before walking out. You should've heard it!'

This was all news to Harry.

'Do you know why she did it?'

Wilson glanced out of the window, as though checking to make sure they couldn't be seen talking, then leaned forward.

'I think they were having an affair,' he said. 'Not that it's for me to judge. Plus, of course, his own marriage was already over. Poor Leslie. He's treated her so badly. He hit her, you know? The day of that meeting. Though Leslie wouldn't talk about it. Awful, really, don't you think?'

'Are you married yourself?' Harry asked.

'No,' Wilson said. 'I'm not. Are you?'

Harry shook his head.

'You're with that gamekeeper, though, aren't you?' Wilson said.

Harry was once again taken aback by a stranger who knew intimate details about his life.

'Do you know why Mr Forthergill and Mr Weatherill were angry enough to do what they did?'

'No,' Wilson said. 'Not a clue. I think they were just riled up, really.'

'And after the pub, what did you do then?' Harry asked.

'Came back here with Leslie, Lance's wife,' Wilson said, then looked a little shocked by what he had said. 'I don't mean to imply there's something going on. There isn't. Not at all. She's married, isn't she? Well, not really, but Lance is a client, and that would be inappropriate. Anyway, we were rehearsing, you see, because she's Calamity Jane, and we went through the script a few times. She's also responsible for costumes and took some back with her to clean.'

Protesting a little too much there, Harry thought. Leslie hadn't mentioned anything about going to Wilson's house after the pub, though, had she? Something to check up on. Though the shock of what had happened was enough to knock details out of her mind, that was for sure.

Harry checked his notes.

'I think that's it for now,' he said, getting to his feet.

Wilson showed him out of the study and to the front door.

'Here,' he said, and handed Harry a folded sheet of paper. 'This is the list of everyone from the meeting. I wrote the names down beforehand, you see, because I wanted to make sure I had an idea of who was going to attend. And Leslie ticked them off.'

Harry took the list and stuffed it in his pocket. Then he made his way back up the path, only to stop halfway, having remembered the copy of the letters Jadyn had given him.

'Sorry,' he said, doubling back to show the letters to Wilson, 'I meant to ask. Do you know anything about these?'

Mr Wilson glanced at the letters.

'No. Should I?'

'Just checking, that's all,' Harry said, thanked the man for his time again, then headed back up the path.

At the gate, he turned around to see Mr Wilson with his hat raised in farewell.

I really do meet the oddest people in this job, he thought, climbing into his vehicle.

TWENTY-FOUR

Arriving at the address Harry had given him, a small house hidden down a narrow lane between Askrigg and Woodhall, Jadyn drove just far enough along to park up out of sight, but close enough to still see the house. He hadn't spotted any other police vehicles on the way, and he couldn't see any now, either. That wasn't good.

A quick walk up and down the lane, and Jadyn knew he was the only police officer anywhere nearby. Harry had told him he was there to take over from another officer. He now wondered if that other officer had ever turned up in the first place. If not, he wouldn't like to be on the end of whatever Harry would have to say about it.

Slumping back down into the seat, Jadyn was suddenly hungry. He knew that he shouldn't be, because he never skimped on breakfast, which he knew was by far the most important meal of the day. Well, sort of. Lunch and dinner came close. Even so, sitting there in his car midmorning, he was hungry. It was as though the simple act of being tasked to sit in his car and keep a lookout for a person of interest was a trigger.

This wasn't the first time it had happened either, and had he known he was to be sent out after the meeting, then Jadyn would have sorted himself out a much-needed snack. He was a little disappointed in himself. A quick search of the glove compartment, the door pockets, under the seats, yielded nothing bar a boiled sweet so hairy it looked like it could grow legs and growl. So, he was left with no choice but to ignore the grumbles in his stomach and focus on the job.

The house was, as far as Jadyn could tell, a typical Dales cottage. Sat between two other similar cottages, it gave the impression of being squeezed into shape, as though the pressure of the buildings on either side of it had forced it to be as small as it was.

Not that small *is* a bad thing; quite the opposite, thought Jadyn. Though this place did look a little rundown. The small garden at the front was overgrown, the windows mired with muck no doubt kicked up by passing traffic. It had an air about it of dejection, which contrasted dramatically with the scenery wrapped around it like a scarf of watercolour artwork.

The day was bright, the air clean, and thin clouds cast themselves across the blue sky like nets on the sea. Wherever Jadyn looked, pristine countryside stared back, with rich green pastures and their dry stone wall boundaries laid out to all sides. Beyond them rose the fells. Though not great, towering mountains casting the valley below in ominous shadow, they still wore a deep presence, and in muted majesty gave the Dales a panorama without equal.

Jadyn yawned. Not a good sign. He opened the window, turned the radio on, and stretched. Another yawn came, stronger than the first. He tried to put his mind to something other than falling asleep.

Tracking back over the last couple of days and everything that had happened, he mulled over what the team knew, which didn't seem to be much, thought back over the crime scene, then his trip out to see the victim's wife, how she'd greeted him at the door having just got out of the shower, the washing she was busy with, the letters he had found, her clear confusion when he'd shown them to her, the mention of her son, Archie.

Jadyn sat up as though jolted by electricity. Something was

there, just at the back of his mind, wasn't it? He closed his eyes to force himself to work out what it was. Something was linking being out at the Hamiltons', speaking to Leslie, and the meeting that morning. But what?

Then he had it.

He grabbed his phone.

Harry answered.

'Constable Okri? I'm halfway to the mortuary. This had better be important.'

'Boss, I've just realised something.'

'That sounds like an epiphany to me,' Harry said. 'Dangerous things. What was it?'

'Archie,' Jadyn said.

'You've lost me.'

'Leslie's son is called Archie,' Jadyn said. 'Remember?'

'Not exactly, no, but I'll take your word for it.'

'Those notes from that meeting,' Jadyn continued. 'The ones Matt got from Dave. There was an Archie on that, too.'

Harry was quiet for a moment.

'Wasn't a Hamilton though, was it?' he said. 'If it was, I'd have noticed.'

'No, it wasn't,' said Jadyn. 'But then he wasn't Lance Hamilton's son.'

'Yes, he was,' said Harry. 'Mrs Hamilton said so.'

'Yes, he was, but also he wasn't,' replied Jadyn. 'He's Leslie's son, but he's Lance's stepson.'

'So, he'd have a different surname,' said Harry.

'It's not much, I know, but I've just realised, and I know what you think about coincidences, right?'

'No such thing. Well done, Jadyn, that's a good spot. Send that through to Matt. He's coordinating the interviews, so it'd be good to give them a heads-up on that. How's things at the house?'

Jadyn considered lying, but the truth was out before he could stop it.

'There was no officer when I arrived,' he said. 'House looks quiet.'

'Could you repeat that?' Harry asked.

So, Jadyn did and, when finished, held his phone away from his ear while Harry tried to melt it with his rage.

'Didn't think you'd be too impressed,' he said, once Harry had stopped swearing.

'You just stay there and keep on with what you're doing,' Harry said. 'And again, well done on the Archie thing. Good detecting there, Constable.'

Conversation over, Jadyn put his phone down and focused again on the house. But no sooner had he done so than his phone buzzed.

'Yes, Boss?' he said, fully expecting it to be Harry, seeing as they'd only spoken a few seconds ago.

'She's passed out! I don't know what to do!'

The voice at the other end was very much not Harry's. It was younger for a start, and Jadyn had no clue what they were talking about, and assumed it was a wrong number.

'This is Police Constable Jadyn Okri, I think you must have the wro—', he said, but the other voice interrupted, racing ahead with scant regard for punctuation.

'She's like totally fallen down! She was just standing there, and we were talking, like, and laughing, and Gaz, he'd just told this joke, right, and I thought she was just taking the piss, you know? Like the joke was so funny she'd passed out laughing, and we were all laughing because it was properly funny, but then she didn't get up, and I tried to get her to, but she wouldn't, and I kept trying and now she's not moving, and—'

'Right, calm down,' Jadyn said, jumping in. 'Can you give me your name?'

'I'm Owen,' the voice said. 'You were at our school, remember? You said to call you if we needed to. And you gave us that card with a number on it.'

Jadyn remembered.

'You said someone's collapsed?'

'Beth,' said Owen. 'She's just lying there. She's breathing, but she's not moving. I didn't know what to do, so I called you.'

'You need to call an ambulance,' said Jadyn. 'Immediately.'

'They don't come though, do they?' said Owen. 'You're police. You're quicker.'

'You still need to call an ambulance.'

'But they'll take hours!' Owen replied, and Jadyn heard the desperation in his voice. 'I know because my gran fell, didn't she? And she was on the floor for two days before the ambulance came.'

'I'm not a paramedic!' Jadyn replied, fairly sure that Owen was exaggerating a little. 'Owen, listen to me. I need you to call an ambulance right now. Do you understand? Where are you?'

'What?'

Jadyn clipped his seatbelt.

'Your location, Owen; where is it?'

'Why?'

'Because I'm on my way.'

'You are?'

'Yes.'

'I'll text it to you.'

'Call that ambulance, Owen. Now!'

Jadyn hung up, and a few seconds later, his phone pinged. He read the address and put it in his satnav. Then he quickly called Jim, explained, hung up, and punched in a call to Harry.

'Me again,' Jadyn said, as Harry answered his call.

'What now?'

'There's a problem ...'

Jadyn then quickly explained the situation, not giving Harry a chance to interrupt.

'How long will Jim be before he gets to the house?'

'Ten minutes max,' Jadyn said.

'Then get shifting,' Harry said. 'And keep me posted on that kid.'

Call over, Jadyn put on his blues and twos and was soon howling up the dale, destination Leyburn.

TWENTY-FIVE

With the two phone calls from Jadyn rattling around in his mind, Harry continued with his journey to the mortuary, where he was met by the pathologist, Rebecca Sowerby. The lack of an officer on the scene when Jadyn had arrived would be something he'd deal with later. Right now, he had other things to be getting on with.

'So, what've we got?' he asked, deciding to keep things brief and to the point in case Sowerby was still not quite herself. It wasn't that he wasn't concerned, just that he figured the best approach was to leave her be for now; he'd said his piece, and that was that. And she'd said that she had booked an appointment, so that was all he could ask for in the end. He may have come on a bit strong with what he'd said, but he'd never been one for holding back if something needed to be said. Lance the boil, instead of leaving it to fester.

'A body,' Sowerby said. 'Surprised, right?'

Was he hearing things or was that a hint of the pathologist's sense of humour back? A good sign, then.

'That all depends on whose body it is,' he replied.

After changing his shoes for rubber boots, and donning a white lab coat and facemask, Harry followed Sowerby into a room of glistening stainless steel, strange sounds, and unpleasant smells. He stood opposite her, a steel table between them, and on it a white sheet, hiding the reason he was there.

Harry had noticed over the years that of all the smells that lingered, it was the ones associated with a place such as this that clung to his clothes the most. Yes, there were those crime scenes where a body had gone undiscovered for enough time to allow nature to get to work with a good dose of decomposition, and that took less time than most people expected.

However, it was the unique aromas of the mortuary which seemed to be the most tenacious when it came to following you around for the rest of the day. It reminded Harry of back when people could smoke in pubs, and the next day everything would need to be washed, just to get rid of the stink. Didn't matter if you'd smoked or not. The stale, acrid reek of the smoke had seeped into the fibres, and the washing machine called. A faint whiff, and Harry would be whisked back to goodness knew how many such rooms, staring down at bodies in various states of decay, the evidence of what had happened to them, the violence, raw and visceral. That stayed with him, too, he thought, the numerous images of the dead laid out in clinical cleanliness, a photo album of man's inhumanity to man he did his best to leave unopened.

Sowerby said, 'Just so you know, the victim's wife, she's coming over later today to ID the body.'

Harry realised then that he'd not checked in with Matt, who had offered to accompany Leslie when they had spoken to her the day before.

'I'll check to see who's coming over with her,' he said.

'No need,' said Sowerby. 'She's coming on her own. I mentioned that it might be best if someone was with her, but she was adamant she would be alright with it. Ready?' Sowerby didn't wait for Harry to give her an answer, and reached for the top of the sheet, pulling it down to reveal the head, shoulders, and torso of the victim, Lance Hamilton.

'Take me through it, then,' Harry said, his voice muffled by his facemask.

'There's not much to tell, really,' Sowerby said, 'but starting here ...' She pointed at Lance's left cheek. 'You can't really make it out on the surface, but this area is bruised. Something struck him, not hard enough to break bones or anything like that, but if he were alive now, the bruise would be visible.'

Harry remembered that the accountant, Andrew Wilson, had said something about Sally Dent slapping Hamilton in the pub.

'Anything else you can tell from it?' he asked.

'From the shape, I'm going to say that it was caused by a hand,' Sowerby said. 'We've been able to make out a shape which we believe resembles fingers.'

As well as what he had learned from Wilson, Harry thought back to what they knew so far about Hamilton's last movements, and his time in the pub after the meeting in the Market Hall. He remembered that Matt had spoken to Dave, who'd said he'd seen Hamilton leaving the pub, shirt wet, as though he'd spilled his drink. If Sally had slapped Hamilton, and knocked the man's pint from his hand in the process, then what had been the cause of her attack? And why hadn't she mentioned it?

'What else?' Harry asked.

'Beyond the obvious?' Sowerby asked, pointing at Lance's wrists.

'You mean there's something else?'

Somerby said, 'It would've taken anywhere between two and ten minutes for him to bleed out,' she said. 'He would have gone into shock fairly quickly. But there's something else that I think helped to incapacite and ultimately kill him..' She reached to a steel trolley to her right and retrieved a clipboard, handing it over to Harry.'Toxicology report. Your victim – or maybe even the murderer – may well have been suffering from insomnia.'

Harry read what was in front of him, then stared questioningly at Sowerby, none the wiser.

'Zopiclone?' he read out loud, not really sure if he'd pronounced it correctly.

'It's a class C controlled medicine,' explained Sowerby. 'A nonbenzodiazepine sleeping pill, and don't try saying that with your mouthful.'

Yes, thought Harry, Sowerby was very much more herself than the last time they'd spoken. Had she listened to him?

'Not over the counter, then?'

'No. And there's a hefty whack of the stuff in his system,' Sowerby explained. 'Not enough to knock out a horse, but certainly enough to send our friend here to the Land of Nod and for a good long time, too. Whoever had been prescribed it wasn't exactly following the directions on their prescription.'

'So would a high dose of it render Lance unconscious?' asked Harry.

'Depends,' she said. 'A drug like this can also cause a type of sleep-walking.' 'A type? You mean there's more than one?'

'There's the kind where you just get out of bed, stumble around a bit, stub your toe, wake up wondering where you are, then go back to bed a little confused, perhaps even scared. Then there's the other kind.'

'And what's that, then?' Harry asked, not liking the darker tone in Sowerby's voice.

'You get up and do things, and when you wake up, you can't remember any of it; that kind.'

'Do things?' said Harry, repeating what Sowerby had said. 'How do you mean? What things? Sounds bloody terrifying.'

'It is,' said Sowerby. 'Driving's one. People have woken up in their car in a hedge, no idea how they got there or why they're in their pajamas.'

'Well, Mr Hamilton here wasn't in a car, was he? He was found in a chair with his hands cut off.'

'There's eating as well,' Sowerby continued. 'Having sex, being violent. It's pretty sketchy if you end up taking too much, and it looks like our victim did exactly that.'

'Still though,' said Harry, 'I can't see that an overdose of a sleeping tablet would have him cut off his own hands.'

'On that,' said Sowerby, and moved her attention to Hamilton's wrists. 'We believe that the hands were severed by different cutting implements.'

'You mean knives.'

'No, I mean cutting implements,' Sowerby corrected. 'Very different. The one on the right, that was severed in one go, see?' She pointed at the wrist, which was now bloodless and had more in common with something in a butcher's shop window than something that had once been a living, breathing human being.

'Not really, no,' said Harry.

Sowerby swiped her hand in the air.

'Whatever it was, it went through the wrist in one quick sweep and that hand was off, though to where, we still don't know, do we? Went through flesh and bone cleanly, so it was definitely sharp and I'm going to suggest was either quite weighty or was used with considerable force, perhaps even both.'

'And that's different from the other wrist?'

To Harry, the wrists looked the same, just ragged things of flesh, dead and pale and crusted with blood dried black.

Sowerby moved her pointy finger to the other arm.

'With this one, we found more of a sawing or cutting action. Can you see? It's noticeably visible on the bone.'

No, I can't, thought Harry, so kept quiet.

'The right hand was taken first, the left sometime after. Less bleeding from this side compared with the other. Do you want me to explain that in detail, or are we good to go on?'

'We're good,' said Harry.

'Pity,' said Sowerby, 'because that's it, really. Bruise to the face, Zipiclone, and the wrists. Stomach contents comprised his last meal, which was black pudding and chips, and believe you me, it looks much the same half-digested as it probably did when he was eating it. We also found alcohol in his system.'

'How much?'

'Not enough for him do that to himself or let someone else do it,' Sowerby answered, and lifted the sheet to once again cover the body. 'The only other thing I have to report is back out in the office. Come on ...'

Harry followed Sowerby out of the mortuary and into the small office beyond the doors. The air here, though still haunted by the miasma of the room it was attached to, also carried the smell of coffee and pastries, not that Harry had seen or been offered one.

'Is this about those letters we sent through?' he asked, not expecting results on those so soon.

'No,' Sowerby said. 'But I believe a file of copies was sent back to your team.' She handed Harry an envelope.

Opening it, Harry found a copy of another hand-written note, the style different to the letters Jadyn had found.

'What's this?' he asked.

'Haven't the faintest idea,' Sowerby said. 'It was found in his jacket pocket in an envelope.'

The note read: *I know it's you. I've always known.*

'Well, that's not exactly helpful, is it?' Harry said. 'What the hell does it mean?' A thought struck him. 'Maybe he knew ...'

'About what?'

'Those letters,' Harry said. 'Maybe Hamilton knew who sent them.'

'That would make sense,' said Sowerby. 'Why the note, though?'

Harry frowned.

'That might be something only he knew and took with him to the grave.'

'Never got to deliver it, either,' said Sowerby.

'Not necessarily ...'

Harry fell quiet, deep in thought, staring at the note.

'Penny for your thoughts?' said Sowerby, but Harry said nothing, then slipped the copy of the note back into the envelope.

'We're done then, I suppose,' he said.

'I think so,' replied Sowerby.

Harry readied himself to leave, but hesitated.

'Look,' he said, 'about what I said last time, and how I said it, I hope that—'

'You were right,' said Sowerby, holding up a hand to stop Harry saying any more.

'I was?'

'You sound surprised.'

Harry laughed.

'You're okay, though?'

'I am,' Sowerby said. 'And thank you. For talking some sense into me.'

'It's what friends are for, right?' Harry replied.

'You're certainly one of the strangest,' said Sowerby.

Outside in his vehicle, Harry had another look at the note, his mind going over what Sowerby had just shared with him. Though he'd not said anything to her, he had found himself wondering if the note was linked to the letters Jadyn had found in Lance's office. It was certainly possible. And if that was the case, were they linked to what had eventually happened to Lance? It struck him as an odd turn of events, and it also didn't explain why Lance's note was still in his pocket. Had he meant to deliver it that night, but not got around to it? Or had he delivered it, an argument had ensued, and the killer had stuffed the letter back in his pocket?

With plenty to think about, and with a faint sense of hope that the team would uncover something useful in their chats with those who had been at the meeting, Harry headed back towards Hawes.

TWENTY-SIX

After a spectacular drive over the Buttertubs Pass, Matt arrived at the house of Jeff Weatherill a little after midmorning. The road had been quiet, and he had enjoyed making his way up out of Hawes and into the fells. When the walled boundary to the road eventually gave way to open moorland, it was as though the vast expanse open to him demanded that he sup deeply from it. It's impossible not to, he thought, because wherever he went in the Dales, he counted himself blessed.

Jeff and his wife lived on the edge of Thwaite, a small village at the top end of Swaledale, which was entered from the direction of Hawes by popping over the small bridge spanning Thwaite Beck. Thwaite itself was a cosy huddle of stone cottages nestled into the protective crook of the beck, which bubbled and bounced itself through the dale to then join up with various other slips of water, before eventually being swept away by the more powerful currents of the River Swale.

Matt had memories of being a lot younger and considerably fitter, having biked over the tops from Wensleydale to go exploring, wading upstream, looking for crayfish and minnows. Good days, though really no better than the ones he lived now. Life had changed and so had he, but the Dales were a constant throughout, an unchanging home that always welcomed him.

Thwaite itself was an old place and little had changed in over a hundred years or more. As one of the many stopping points on the famous Pennine Way, Matt saw a good number of brightly coloured walkers tramping through, most of them looking fit and well, though a few were clearly not in quite so fine fettle, as his old dad used to say.

Matt parked his car and turned off the engine. The Weatherills' house was, like all the houses in Thwaite, a stone building with a slate roof and clay chimney pots. It was obviously a home proudly kept, with bright window boxes and a flagstone doorstep that looked like it was cleaned and polished daily. And perhaps it was, Matt thought, because he knew a few folk, from older generations for sure, who still gave the threshold to their homes a weekly scrub. To the side stood a garage, the doors open, the interior empty. Matt peered in to see a space ordered and clean, the air rich with the smell of oil and grease. A workbench was tucked up under a window in the far wall, the other walls decorated with numerous hooks from which hung tools, all in fine order.

Matt walked up to the front door, which was of old wood, oak perhaps, beautifully polished and oiled, the grain shining through. There was no doorbell, but there was a large brass bell hanging below a slate name sign for the house, on which the word *Daleside* was etched.

Matt rang the bell, stepped back, and waited.

When the door opened, he found himself being nearly run into by a small woman in a boiler suit. She was carrying a toolbox.

Matt stepped back, and the woman skidded to a stop.

'The police? Bloody hell's bells! What now?'

'Mrs Weatherill?' Matt said, a little confused by the response.

'Yes, that's me,' the woman replied. 'Rachel Weatherill.' She pointed to an embroidered name tag on her boilersuit. 'Clue's right there.'

The tag read *Weatherill Services*.

Matt said, 'I'm looking to speak with Jeff, who I'm assuming is your husband?'

Rachel ignored the question, turned, and looked at the bell.

'Did you ring it?'

'Loudly,' said Matt.

'Bloody useless it is,' Rachel said. 'Looks nice, I'll give it that, and it's loud enough, but only if you're outside the house. Can't hear it inside at all. Need to get shot of it, but Jeff's not convinced. I keep saying it's just a bell, and there's no point having it if it doesn't serve a purpose, but there it still is, hanging around being useless. Much like him, if you ask me.'

'Don't suppose Jeff's in, is he?' Matt asked, hoping to hurry Rachel along.

'No, he's not, he's out working, and too bloody right he is, too, let me tell you.'

Matt heard anger in Rachel's voice but ignored it.

'Do you know where he is?'

'I don't. We're both run off our feet, now more than ever, and no thanks to him, either, I might add, the bloody idiot.'

There was that anger again, Matt noticed. Something was definitely going on, but he doubted it was relevant to the investigation, so he ignored it.

'Any chance you can be more specific?' he asked.

Rachel clenched her jaw for a moment, then pulled out a phone and tapped in a number.

'Where are you?' she shouted.

Jeff's reply barked from the phone in a broken electric tone, none of it intelligible.

'The police are at the door, and they want a chat,' Rachel said, her words slow, loud, and deliberate. 'What the hell have you done now?'

'What?'

'The police, they're here, and they want to talk to you.'

'I can't hear you.'

Rachel rolled her eyes.

'Where are you?'

There was a long pause, then Jeff said, 'Reception's terrible. I'm done anyway, so I'll be there in ten. Put the kettle on if you could.'

Rachel hung up.

'Fancy a brew?' she asked and, without waiting for an answer, led Matt into the house.

When Jeff eventually arrived, he strode into the kitchen like something out of a Tim Burton movie. The man seemed built entirely from long, thin twigs, which were all disconcertingly visible through his paint-spattered boiler suit.

'You in trouble, then, Love?' Jeff said, sitting himself down at the dining table, opposite Matt. 'What've you done to have us being visited by the police?'

Rachel poured Matt a mug of tea and placed it on the table in front of him. To Jeff, she gave no mug, but instead a scowl sour enough to curdle milk.

'Me?' she said, sitting down at the table. 'In trouble with the police? Are you really asking that question? I've never so much as driven the wrong way down a one-way street, as you well know.'

Matt took out his notebook and pencil.

'I'm just here to ask you a few questions, that's all,' he said.

'Questions?' asked Jeff. 'What about?'

'There was a meeting at the Market Hall a couple of nights ago,' said Matt.

'The one about housing?' said Rachel. 'We were both there. What about it?'

'Just wondering if you can tell me anything about it,' said Matt. 'I understand a Mr Lance Hamilton was there.'

Rachel was on her feet.

'Him? What the hell do you want to know about him for?'

There was a wildness in her eyes and Matt could see that Rachel was not someone to be trifled with. And judging by her response, he assumed that news of what had happened had not, as yet, got over the tops and down into Swaledale. Not that it would take long, but he wasn't about to help it on its way either.

'I'm just trying to get a clearer picture of events, that's all,' he explained. 'Gathering facts, that kind of thing.'

'Facts? I'll give you facts,' Rachel said. 'He's a bloody thief, that's what he is. Not that it excuses my husband's rampant stupidity, or his responsibility for what happened, but even so—'

'Rachel! Please!'

Jeff's voice was loud and desperate.

Rachel thumped back down into her chair.

'Is there something you need to tell me?' Matt asked, baffled by what was going on.

Both Rachel and Jeff shook their heads.

'Safe to say we're not his biggest fans, though,' said Rachel.

'How do you mean?' Matt asked. 'You said he was a thief.'

'He owns all these holiday cottages, right?' said Jeff. 'And yet he brings in contractors from outside to do maintenance, doesn't he? Not us. Not anyone local. The git.'

'Doesn't sound like you have much time for him,' said Matt. 'Was this raised at the meeting?'

'Lots of things were raised at that meeting,' said Rachel.

'It's his attitude I don't like,' said Jeff. 'And his face. Needs rearranging.'

Matt stared at Jeff.

'What?' said Jeff.

Matt took out the copies of the letters Jadyn had given him and handed them over.

'Can you have a quick look at these for me, please?'

Rachel and Jeff scanned the letters.

'Bloody hell, these are something, aren't they?' said Jeff. 'Who wrote them?'

'Do you recognise them?'

'Should we?' Rachel replied.

'Never seen them before in my life.'

Matt took back the letters, then said, 'If something happened at that meeting, or afterwards, then you need to tell me. And I have to say that with how you've both behaved since I turned up, something clearly did. Plus, and I'll say it again, you called him a thief. Why?'

'Because you only get as rich as he is by being one, that's why,' Jeff said.

Rachel said, 'It was just a meeting, and like all meetings that have happened forever, people argue, like, don't they? It's unavoidable. Differences of opinion, that kind of thing.'

'Who argued specifically?' Matt asked.

'Who? Everyone, that's who,' said Jeff. 'Though I'll admit, I might've had a few choice words to say about our Mr Hamilton, but that's not a surprise, is it?'

'Why isn't it?' Matt asked.

'You said you wanted to tar and feather him,' said Rachel.

'I wasn't being serious.'

Matt wasn't quite sure what to make of that, though it seemed to him that Rachel was seemingly intent on dropping her husband right in it. Though into what, Matt had no idea. He turned his attention to Jeff.

'Where did you park?'

'In the car park directly behind the chippy,' said Rachel, jumping in. 'Why? How's that relevant to anything?'

'Just questions I have to ask,' said Matt. Looking at Jeff said he said, 'Maybe you should tell me what happened.'

Jeff huffed.

'He was being a right stuck-up, know-it-all git, so I told him what I thought of him,' he said. 'After, me and a few others headed over to the pub, because we knew that's where he'd be. Had a word with him there, too.'

'Did your discussion turn violent at all?' Matt asked.

'I grabbed his collar, told him to watch his back,' said Jeff. 'Thought I'd put the frighteners in him a bit, if you know what I mean.'

'You threatened him, then?'

'I was angry,' said Jeff. 'That's all.'

'And what happened then?' Matt asked.

Jeff went to speak, but Rachel jumped in first.

'We left the pub, grabbed some fish and chips, then came home,' she said.

Matt noticed Jeff's eyes flicker between him and Rachel, but he said nothing.

'Can you confirm who was in the pub with you?'

'I can write the names down if you want?' Rachel said.

Matt handed her his notebook and pencil, and she did exactly that. The names corresponded with what he already knew.

'Is there anything else you can tell me?' he asked.

Silence, then Rachel said, 'She slapped him.'

'Who?'

'Sal,' said Jeff. 'Caught him a right corker, too. Knocked his pint out of his hand. He was covered. Bloody funny it was.'

'You mean Sally Dent?'

Both Jeff and Rachel nodded enthusiastically.

'Hell of a right hand on her, I'll give her that,' said Jeff.

'Do you know why?'

'Not a clue,' said Rachel. 'But the swing she had on it, whatever it was, she was raging, like. The sound of it!'

'Like someone had given him a right hook with a massive trout,' said Jeff, then he clapped his hands together loud enough to make Matt jump. 'Like that it was, only louder.'

'What happened then?' Matt asked.

'She left,' said Rachel. 'Handed Lance her drink, then off she went. It was pretty impressive.'

'She gave him her drink?'

'Add insult to injury, I guess,' said Jeff. 'And what was it she said? Something about the vodka numbing the pain of being such a bastard, or something like that, anyway.'

Matt was quiet for a moment, looking at his notes, thinking about what had just been said. Sally Dent had said nothing about the pub, but more worrying was that she'd not mentioned her set-to with Lance. Why, though? That bothered Matt.

Matt closed his notebook.

'Well, if there's nothing else—'

'There's not,' said Jeff, jumping in, then standing up. 'And I've work to crack on with.'

'Yes, you bloody well have, haven't you?' said Rachel.

There it is again, Matt thought, that heat of something between them, all nails and teeth.

Outside the house, Matt thanked the Weatherills for their time, then jumped back into his vehicle. The way they had both reacted throughout their chat was strange for sure, but it didn't put him in mind of people responsible for someone's gruesome death. Their response to the letters had seemed immediate and honest, but then they struck him as the kind of people for whom lying wouldn't come easily. Whatever it was they were thinking at the time, they both had very little problem expressing it, and he felt sure that if either of them had recognised the writing, they would have said.

Something was going on, though, he was sure of that. And it seemed as though Lance Hamilton was the cause of it, but for now, Matt had no idea what it could be. Anyway, after what he'd learned, he knew he needed to speak with Sally Dent, and he had a suspicion that Harry would probably want to be there, too.

He gave the DCI a quick call, and they arranged to meet at the office and go together. With that arranged, Matt headed back out of Thwaite towards the Buttertubs and then on to Hawes, while around him the Dales gleamed in emerald hues, and a buzzard soared above, its mewing call dancing up the valley before him.

TWENTY-SEVEN

Getting to the Fothergills' farm was easy; a simple drive out of Hawes and along past the right turn to Burtersett, continuing to eventually take a left down a gravel track, a mile or so before the hill leading up to Bainbridge, then over a cattle grid, and into the farm itself.

When they arrived, Jen and Liz parked up in the yard and opened their doors to be greeted by a mob of sheepdog puppies.

Liz managed to unclip her seatbelt, only to have her hands chewed gently by two black and white pups, their tails wagging so quickly, she wondered if they might take off, like small, furry helicopters. Beside her, Jen was having the same problem, only with three puppies, instead of two.

'I've had worse welcomes,' she said. 'How cute is this lot, then?'

Liz laughed as they both climbed out of their vehicle, spilling excited puppies to the ground, to then chase them, biting at their heels, as they made their way to the house.

'Over there, look,' said Jen, and Liz glanced over into a barn to see a sheepdog staring at them, tail thumping gently.

'Looks like their mum's enjoying the break,' Liz said, as the puppies moved from chasing them to trying to round them up, all the time bumping into each other and rolling around like tumbleweeds.

The door to the farmhouse opened and a man with wild grey hair, dressed in a simple checked shirt, jeans, and work boots came out to greet them.

'Sorry about this,' he said, before attempting to command the puppies back to their mum.

The puppies seemed to regard his orders as an excuse to attack him instead, and though he swore, Liz saw the warm smile on his face at the jumble of furry fun jostling for attention at his feet.

The man whistled.

The dog in the barn stood up and lolloped over to them. Seeing it, the puppies raced off to meet it halfway, and the dog turned around and led them all back to the barn. On the way, one of the pups grabbed hold of its mum's tail and used it as a swing.

'Little buggers, the lot of them,' the man chuckled. 'She's a good mum, though, that one, aren't you, Mist?'

The dog slumped down in the barn and her puppies piled on top of her.

'Mr Fothergill?' said Liz.

'That'll be me,' the man answered. 'But call me Aldwin. I can't be doing with all that formal nonsense.'

'We spoke on the phone.'

'That we did. And you'll be coming in for some tea, then. Karen's inside. We've had a busy morning of it, and we've a busy afternoon ahead as well. But that's farm life for you, isn't it? Not a career you'd choose if you wanted lots of holidays and weekends off.'

'We won't keep you long,' Liz said.

Jen added, 'Well, we might, if those pups come for a play again!'

Inside, the house was cool, the thick walls keeping out the heat of the day. The hallway was lined with photographs, a mishmash of various images of sheep, along with numerous shots of the various stages and ages of a girl's life, from toddler to adulthood.

'Is that your daughter?' Liz asked.

'That's our lass, Ivy,' Aldwin said. 'Named after my own Grandmother, like. Right through here ...'

He led them from the hall into a large kitchen lined with simple cabinets around a farmhouse table in the centre. The room, unlike the rest of the house, was warm, and Liz guessed that had a lot to do with the huge orange Aga against the far wall.

'They're here,' Aldwin called out.

Through another door, a woman entered, at her feet another sheepdog.

'Gus, on your bed,' she said, and the dog slinked across to a rug in front of the Aga.

She smiled.

'Now then, how do you like it?'

'Milk, no sugar,' said Liz, guessing the subject of the question.

'Same,' said Jen.

'I'll get those, Love,' Aldwin said, and his wife sat down at the table, directing Liz and Jen to do the same.

'So, how can we help?' she asked. 'And before you go on, we're going to assume this is about what happened to Lance Hamilton, yes?'

As a PCSO, Liz was aware that she could only investigate minor offences. Right now, she and Jen were not there to interview Aldwin and his wife as suspects, but simply to gather information.

She pulled out her notebook and went to speak, but as she did so, Aldwin brought over an enormous brown teapot, chipped enough to show that it was well-used, but not so damaged as to say it wasn't also well-loved. Then he fetched four mugs, followed by an old biscuit tin. He removed the lid and held it out in front of Liz and Jen.

'Biscuits,' he said. 'Made them myself.'

'He's a better cook than me,' smiled Karen.

'That's not true at all,' said Aldwin, lifting a biscuit. 'Though I have always been good with these, even if I do say so myself.'

He took a bite as Liz and Jen reached into the tin.

'You're not wrong,' said Jen, taking a bite. 'These are great.'

'Simple, too,' said Aldwin, still on his feet. 'Porridge oats, flour, butter, sugar, and a bit of syrup. Nowt to them at all. I'll give you the recipe if you want. One of my Grandmother's. She was a good cook, but her baking, well, that won awards up and down the dale.'

Liz had already finished her biscuit and took another.

'Thanks for your time,' she said, keen to get back to the subject in hand. Like Harry had said earlier, news was bound to get around. 'And as I said, we won't be long. Just looking for a few details about events a couple of nights ago.'

Jen said, 'There was a meeting at the Market Hall. We understand you were there.'

At that, Aldwin dropped onto a chair.

'Whatever's happened, it's got nowt to do with us,' he said. 'I had words with him, right enough, may have got a bit carried away, but that's all. Did he report me, is that it? I bet he did. Well, if he did, whatever he said, I'll tell you right now, it's rubbish, all of it.'

'There's been no report made against you,' said Liz. 'Perhaps you should tell us what happened?'

'Nothing happened,' said Karen. 'It was just a meeting for those of us concerned about housing in the area, that's all. You're both young, you'll know it's not easy, is it? To find somewhere to live, I mean.'

'No, it's not,' said Jen.

'Which is why we couldn't believe it when he turned up,' said Aldwin.

'Who turned up?' asked Liz.

'Lance bloody Hamilton, that's who. After what he's done, you'd think he'd stay away, but no, there he was, proud as anything, too. Not wishing to speak ill of the dead, but I can't see folk missing him now he's gone.'

'Can I ask what you know?' asked Jen.

'Not much,' said Karen. 'Just that Sally Dent found him dead round hers yesterday morning, if I'm right.'

'My thinking is God struck him down,' said Aldwin. 'Finally

had enough of his shite. The world doesn't need it, and good riddance to it, I say.'

Liz stayed quiet, hoping that the silence would encourage enough detail from Aldwin that things would become clear.

Aldwin went to speak, but Karen stepped in.

'Look, it's not that we disapproved of his business as such; God knows it's hard enough to make a living round here, and he's just been sensible, hasn't he, turning places into holiday homes? And it does bring folk to the area, no matter what others might say or think.'

'But he didn't need to go stealing our lass's place, did he?' said Aldwin. 'But he still did; just waded in and gazumped them. I mean, who does that, really? How mean and greedy do you need to be? Not that it matters now, though, does it? Need to check up on that, what it means with regards to the house sale. He's probably got it all sewn up though, screwing us over, even when he's dead.'

'So, your daughter, Ivy,' said Jen, 'was trying to buy a house, yes?'

'Her and her fiancé,' said Karen. 'She's pregnant, and they're looking to get married in a year or so, once all that's settled down. They were there, too, at the meeting.'

'And where do they live right now?' Jen asked.

'Here,' said Aldwin, with a wave of his hand at the room around them and the house beyond. 'The place is certainly big enough. But they want a bit of space for themselves, don't they? And who can blame them? They need their privacy.'

'Are they in?' asked Liz.

Karen and Aldwin shook their heads.

'They both work up at the creamery,' Aldwin said. 'Plus, they help out on the farm as much as they can. They'll take it over eventually, I hope. Which is amazing really, all things considered.'

'Farming's a hard life,' said Jen.

'It's not just that,' said Karen. 'Her fiancé, you see, he's not from round here himself, but he's fallen in love with the place. Seems more of a dalesman than even Aldwin here, and his family goes back generations.'

'Which makes it even more unbelievable, doesn't it?' Aldwin said, staring at Liz. 'I mean, how could Hamilton do that? What was his reasoning? He'd no heart, that's what it was. Has to be. And I think that's what stopped me from giving him a good leathering that night, because there'd have been no point, would there? It wouldn't have changed anything. It certainly wouldn't have changed him.'

'Did something happen, then?' Jen asked.

'There was a lot of arguing, that's for sure,' said Karen. 'And I had to pull this daft bugger away before he got himself into trouble.'

'He had it coming,' said Aldwin. 'And I'd have only roughed him up, that's all. A bloody nose and a bit of a slap, nowt else.'

'When you grabbed him by the collar in the pub, I thought you were going to strangle him!'

'I didn't though, did I? And that's what's important.'

Liz said, 'Can I ask what you did that evening? You were at the Market Hall, and then?'

'The pub,' said Aldwin. 'We followed Hamilton out. He left early, but we knew where he'd gone.'

'When we arrived, that potter woman, she slapped him,' said Karen. 'Knocked his pint out of his hand, too, and turned his cheek bright red! Then this idiot husband of mine, he decided to have a go himself, along with Jeff. But thankfully, Ivy managed to talk some sense into him.'

'And after the pub?' asked Jen.

'We came straight home,' said Aldwin. 'We can't be out for too long, what with everything that needs to be done on the farm. Plus, we've lost a few sheep to foxes, so I needed to be out that night to see if I could do anything about it. I'm not one for killing, but I need to protect my animals. And to be honest, I'm such a bloody awful shot, all I do is scare them, but that's good enough most of the time.'

Liz saw Jen check back over her notes, so she did the same. Then she remembered something. Reaching into a pocket, she pulled out the copies of the letters Jadyn had handed out to the team.

'Could you have a look at these, please?' she asked.

Karen took the letters, had a look, then handed them to her husband.

'They're horrible,' she said.

'Why are you showing us these?' Aldwin asked.

'Just wondered if you recognised them at all?' Jen asked.

'Why the hell would we?' said Aldwin.

'What about the writing?'

'What about it?' asked Karen.

'Do you recognise it?'

Karen shook her head, and Aldwin handed the letters back to Liz.

'I think that'll do for now,' said Jen, standing up, Liz following suit. 'We'll be in touch if we need to speak to you again.'

'Pop round whenever you want,' said Karen, leading them out of the kitchen and back to the front door, Aldwin following on behind.

'Don't tempt me,' said Liz. 'Those puppies of yours are a bit of a draw!'

'Well, they're already taken, I'm afraid,' said Karen. 'Ivy had first choice, obviously. Though I reckon he was keener than her!'

'Her fiancé?' said Liz.

'He's a big softy,' said Karen.

'Nowt like his father, that's for sure,' said Aldwin. 'And that's a blessing, I'm sure you'll agree.' He then handed Jen a sheet of lined paper torn from a notebook. 'And here's the recipe for those biscuits; jotted it down for you.'

'His father?' Liz said.

'I thought you knew,' said Aldwin.

Liz was confused.

'Know what?'

Aldwin and Karen looked at each other, then Karen said, 'Archie, he's Lance's son. Well, Leslie's son, and Lance's stepson.'

Liz was stunned, and judging by the look on Jen's face, so was she.

'Let me just get this right,' she said. 'You're saying that Lance Hamilton gazumped his own stepson?'

'Hard to believe, isn't it?' said Aldwin. 'They didn't exactly get on. That man, he was a total bastard to the end.'

A phone chimed from inside the house.

'That's mine,' Karen said, and popped back inside.

Liz followed Jen across the yard back to their vehicle, only to hear a cry from the house. They both turned to see Karen rushing out and speaking to Aldwin, who himself then gave a cry.

Liz dashed over, Jen overtaking her on the way.

'What's happened?' she asked. 'Are you okay?'

Karen was crying, and Aldwin looked in shock.

'It's Ivy,' Karen said.

'What is?' asked Jen.

'The baby,' said Karen. 'It's coming! Her water broke at work a few minutes ago. Archie is bringing her home now.'

'She's not going to the hospital?'

Karen shook her head.

'She wanted a home birth. It's all in hand. The doctor's been called, and the midwife is on her way now.'

Aldwin said, 'I'm going to be a grandad! Bloody hell, Karen, we're going to be grandparents!'

Then he threw his arms around his wife.

The sound of them both crying caused enough of a stir to have the puppies abandon their mother and run over to join in, dancing around everyone's feet.

Liz felt a tug on her sleeve.

'Come on,' said Jen.

'But shouldn't we do something?'

At that moment, Karen and Aldwin broke apart and Karen

said, 'We're fine. There's nowt you can do here anyway, so you just get on now.'

'Only if you're sure.'

'We're sure,' said Aldwin.

Again, Liz followed Jen back to the car.

'We need to speak with Harry,' she said once the doors were shut, but Jen was already on the phone.

TWENTY-EIGHT

When Jadyn arrived at the location Owen had sent him, which was a small housing estate in Redmire, he was relieved to find that an NHS rapid response vehicle was already on the scene.

Parking up behind it, Jadyn was quickly out of his vehicle and over to the house. The door was open, and he let himself in.

'Officer Okri,' Jadyn called out, to not cause any additional alarm.

With no response, Jadyn made his way through the house to the kitchen to find the back door open. Outside, he saw two paramedics and three teenagers, one of whom was lying on the lawn, and walked out to join them, introducing himself once again.

'You came, then,' said one of the teenagers, a boy whose hair seemed to have been caught in the act of trying to escape from his head, and frozen in place by industrial quantities of gel.

'Owen?' asked Jadyn.

The boy nodded.

'They arrived just before you,' he said.

'How is she?'

'Conscious, which is good news,' said one of the paramedics, as she held a facemask over the mouth of the girl on the ground. 'This is just to help her breathe a little easier, get some oxygen into her system, perk her up a bit.'

'She's okay, then?'

The other paramedic, a man with a shiny bald patch and a weathered face, said, 'As far as we can tell, yes, but we're still going to take her in to get her checked over, once we're happy she's okay to travel.'

Jadyn looked over at Owen and the boy standing with him and saw fear in both their eyes. And rightly so, too, he thought.

'And this is Gaz, yes?' he asked, pointing at the other boy.

Both boys nodded.

Jadyn looked over at the two paramedics.

'Mind if I take these two inside for a chat, find out what happened?'

'Be our guest,' said the woman.

'Teenagers don't generally pass out in their garden for no reason,' said the man.

'They've not told you, then?' Jadyn said.

'Told us what?' the man replied.

'Vaping,' he said, and saw both paramedics look at him in confusion.

'You're having a laugh,' the woman said.

Jadyn didn't answer, pointed at the open door back to the house, and said, 'Inside. Now.'

Once inside, Jadyn sat Owen and Gaz down in the lounge. Gaz seemed to have taken a completely different approach to his hair and had buzzed it off, giving him an unnerving Full Metal Jacket look.

'Right, then,' Jadyn said, 'where do you want to begin?'

Owen and Gaz stared at the floor.

'Let's start with something easy, then,' Jadyn continued. 'Whose house is this?'

'Beth's,' said Owen.

'And where are her parents?'

'Out.'

'Do you know when they'll be back?'

'Later.'

'Conversation not a strong point, is it?' Jadyn said. 'You were chatty enough on the phone.'

Owen lifted his eyes, but Gaz stayed staring at the floor.

'She's going to be alright, isn't she?'

'The paramedics seem to think so,' said Jadyn. 'But I'll need to speak with Beth's parents about what's happened, and to let them know where she is.'

Owen's eyes grew wide, and for the first time since sitting down in the lounge, Gaz looked at Jadyn.

'You can't,' Gaz said. 'They'll kill us.'

'They're not going to be very happy, no,' said Jadyn. 'And they'll be rightly worried about their daughter.'

Owen spoke again, this time his voice louder and more desperate.

'But you can't tell them what happened!' he said. 'You just can't! It was an accident, that's all. I—I mean *we* didn't mean for it to happen. Please, you can't tell them!'

Jadyn stared for a moment at Gaz, his mind caught on something he had just said.

'What do you mean, you didn't mean for it to happen?' he asked.

'It's not his fault, it really isn't,' said Owen.

'I'm not here to blame anyone, I'm here to find out what happened and make sure it doesn't happen again,' said Jadyn. 'And I think Gaz can speak for himself. Can't you, Gaz?'

Gaz was staring at him, mouth like a goldfish.

Jadyn gave the two boys a few moments of silence, enough to have them both fidgeting.

'It was me that got them,' Gaz said at last, blurting out the confession. 'They were cheap, and I didn't think this would happen, did I? We were just having a laugh, trying them out, that's all. We've never done it before, just thought we'd give it a go.'

Jadyn took out his notebook.

'What's that for?' Owen asked.

'You're not going to arrest us, are you?' said Gaz. 'You can't. My mum, she'll kill me.'

Gaz is certainly paranoid, Jadyn thought.

'Look,' he said, 'whatever happened to Beth, you don't want to happen again, do you?'

Both boys shook their heads.

'Then the best thing you can do is tell me where you got the vapes you used. And on that, where are they?'

'Where are what?' said Owen.

'The vapes,' Jadyn said. 'The ones you were using.'

Gaz stood up, left the room, then came back with a small haversack. He opened it and handed over a carrier bag.

Jadyn opened the bag and looked inside to find at least a dozen vapes staring back at him, perhaps more.

'That's a lot of vapes for three teenagers who've never vaped,' he said.

Once again, Gaz was showing too much interest in the carpet at his feet.

'Gaz,' Jadyn said, 'where did you get them?'

Gaz shook his head.

'Were you going to sell these?'

Gaz gave the faintest of nods.

'Would I be right in thinking then, after what's happened to Beth, that you won't be?' Jadyn held up the bag of vapes. 'Not that you'll be able to, I might add, seeing as I'll be confiscating this lot.'

More nods.

'Back to my original question, then,' continued Jadyn. 'Where did you get them? And I need to know, because if there's someone out there selling these, then I need to know about it and put a stop to it. You can understand that, can't you?'

'He'll kill us, too,' Gaz said. 'I can't!'

Jadyn put the carrier bag on the floor, then leaned forward, hands clasped, elbows on his knees. It was time to give Gaz a bit of a scare, he decided.

'You can either tell me here and now,' he said, 'or I'll have to take you in. And you know what that means, don't you?'

Gaz lifted his face to look at Jadyn.

'What?'

'It means that you'll end up in an interview room in a police station. You'll have to talk to someone considerably less understanding than me. Your parents will have to be called in because you can't be interviewed as a minor without their permission.'

'You mean I'll be arrested?'

Jadyn said nothing, instead just allowed Gaz's imagination to go to work. Of course he wouldn't be arrested, and neither would he end up in an interview room, but he needed him to understand the seriousness of the situation and that he had to help.

'I got them off Bug,' he said.

Jadyn was fairly sure he'd not heard right.

'Bug?'

'That's what I said.'

'And who's Bug, then?'

'Some bloke.'

Jadyn was trying to stay calm, but Gaz wasn't making it easy.

'Some bloke called Bug,' he said. 'I'm going to need a bit more than that, Gaz.'

'We go round the back of his dad's shop,' Gaz said. 'He's got us booze like that as well, fags, magazines.'

'Doesn't want his dad knowing,' said Owen. 'Makes him a bit on the side, like, doesn't it?'

'Bug gets the vapes from car boot sales, I think,' said Gaz.

'And you're sure that he's called Bug ...' Jadyn said, still unconvinced.

'He's well into eighties movies,' said Gaz. 'The Lost Boys, Breakfast Club, that kind of thing. Uncle Buck is his favourite.'

'Not sure what that's got to do with his name,' said Jadyn.

'It's just taking this piss, really,' said Owen, taking over from Gaz. 'Bug reckons he gave himself the nickname, but I don't believe him.'

'You've lost me,' said Jadyn.

Gaz said, 'There's a scene in Uncle Buck where there's this kid, and he's called Bug and that's where it comes from. His real name's Nat. See? Nat, as in bug?'

'Nat?'

'Nathan,' said Owen. 'Bug is Nathan—'

'Lofthouse,' said Jadyn, finishing off Owen's sentence.

'You know him?'

Jadyn saw confusion in the eyes of both boys.

'Not well,' he said. 'But I've a feeling we're about to become very well acquainted indeed.'

TWENTY-NINE

After taking calls from both Matt and Jen, and receiving updates from Jadyn and Jim, Harry had decided it was best that they meet up before doing anything else. He didn't want anyone rushing into any situation without all the facts, even if the ones they had didn't seem to either add up or make much sense.

Since it was now well past midday and so far into the afternoon that evening would be here all too soon, Harry had popped out to grab them all something to eat. Now, sitting with Matt, Liz, and Jen in the office as they munched on their various pies and sandwiches, he gave them a quick update on what had happened with Jadyn and told them that Jim was now monitoring Anna's brother's house.

As Sowerby had said, the copies of the letters that Jadyn had found at Laurence and Leslie's house had been sent through, but they hadn't been needed thanks to Jadyn making copies.

Forensics had sent through a report on the car, not that there was much to be read in it that was of any help. The car had been badly damaged by a person or persons as yet unknown, and that was that. They'd managed to provide an in-depth analysis of the paint that had been thrown all over it, but that was of no use because it was a common shade of something off-white-ish available in every DIY shop across the country and absolutely anyone could have ordered it from any number of websites.

'I've also checked in with Gordy,' he said, 'and she's doing fine. Should be out in a couple of days or so. How she didn't end up with broken bones is beyond me, but that's just the way things go sometimes, isn't it?'

'It's a miracle is what it is,' said Matt.

With Jadyn otherwise engaged, Jen was sitting beside the board just in case anything needed jotting down.

'Let's start with you, Matt,' Harry said, pointing at the DS.

'Well, Jeff and Rachel, they're not exactly a happy couple,' he said. 'Something is definitely going on there, though I've no idea what. What I did learn, though, was what I told you, Harry, about Sally giving Lance Hamilton a proper slap in the pub.'

'There's evidence of bruising on his face,' Harry said, remembering what he had seen in the mortuary with Sowerby. 'She must have hit him hard.'

'Knocked his glass out of his hand,' said Matt, 'then handed him her own.' He checked his notebook. 'According to the Weatherills, she told him it would numb the pain of being such a bastard.'

'Didn't know Sal had it in her,' said Jen.

'She's not like that, then?'

'What, the kind of person who slaps people and insults them? I don't think so, no. But then, I only know her through running, don't I?'

'Anything else?' Harry asked. 'Do we know what they did for the rest of the evening?'

'Grabbed a fish supper each and spent the evening at home,' answered Matt.

Harry looked at Jen and Liz next.

'What's this about Mr Hamilton and his son, then?' he asked.

'All we know is that his stepson, Archie, is engaged to Aldwin and Karen's daughter, Ivy, that they were buying a house together, and that he, Mr Hamilton, I mean, made the seller a better offer.

We've not been able to speak with Archie and Ivy yet, what with them currently in the process of becoming parents.'

Harry let out a sigh.

'Makes you wonder about people sometimes, doesn't it?' he said. 'Do we know why he did that?'

'He didn't get on with his stepson,' said Liz. 'Though why that would be a reason to basically nick his house, I just don't know. What they told us about the pub confirms what Matt just said about Sally Dent slapping Lance Hamilton. They saw it.'

Harry told them about his visit to see Andrew Wilson, but didn't get beyond the way the man had greeted him at the door before Matt was laughing.

'Next time you see him, we need to send you dressed as Wyatt Earp,' the DS said.

'Why?' Harry asked.

Matt didn't answer, as he was too busy laughing.

'You have to join the amateur dramatics group,' he said. 'Please. For us.'

Jen said, 'Matt's right. You'd be brilliant.'

Liz added, 'They'd sell out, I'm sure of it.'

Harry gave them all a moment, though judging by Matt's laughter, he needed a lot more than that.

'Well, when you've all had your fill of the idea of me being a thespian, perhaps we can crack on?'

Harry didn't give them a chance to say anything more, and quickly went through what Wilson had told him.

'So, his story confirms the slap from Sal,' said Jen. 'I'm amazed, really.'

'There's also what he said about Mrs Hamilton going back to his after the pub,' said Harry. 'She didn't mention that, and I'd be keen to know more.' He took out the list of names Wilson had handed him as he'd left, still folded. 'Not looked at this yet, but it's the list of attendees at the meeting.'

Then he went through everything he had learned from Sowerby. That done, he said, 'Right now, it feels like what happened to our victim is completely at odds with everything we've found out so far. I just can't place the violence and downright bloody weirdness of it with anything that we know so far.'

'I can't see Aldwin and Karen being responsible,' said Jen. 'They're obviously upset for the daughter's sake, not least because she's pregnant, but she's not homeless because of what he did, just inconvenienced for a while, that's all.'

Matt spoke next.

'Like I said, there's something going on between the Weatherills, but as far as I could tell, that's probably a relationship issue and nothing to do with Hamilton. Their business is busy, so they're probably just not seeing enough of each other.' He looked up at Harry at that point, and added, 'It can get a bit tense with Joan if I'm out a lot; you know what it's like, don't you? You need proper time together. And with this job, before you realise where you are, you've lost six months rushing around like a blue-arsed fly and left those you love way behind you.'

Harry had been about to say something, but Matt's words caught him off guard, and it took a moment or two before he could dial himself back into what they were talking about.

'And we've nothing on those letters, have we?'

'Not a dicky-bird,' said Matt.

'Where are we, then?' Harry said, as much to himself as to the rest of the team. 'Lance Hamilton was not exactly popular and didn't seem to mind much, either. Someone has been sending him threatening notes, but we've no idea who. He's gazumped his stepson, his marriage had fallen apart, and as Jadyn told us yesterday, he had moved out of the house, though not exactly to the next street or even the next village. I'll be honest, with all that going on, I can see why he had trouble sleeping.'

'Wait a minute,' said Matt. 'When we spoke to Leslie yesterday, she said she was there, at the crime scene, right? Said she was there because she'd not heard Lance come home.'

Harry pulled out his notebook.

'What she actually said was that he didn't come home, and that he wasn't there in the morning either.'

'That's what I mean,' said Matt.

'What are you getting at?' Harry asked.

'Lance had moved out, right? And like you just said, not exactly far away; he was just opposite the main house in a converted barn. If that's the case, then how would she know whether he'd got home or not? Was she spying on him? My impression of her was that she couldn't bear to be near him, so why would she care in the slightest where he was?'

Matt had a point.

'Maybe she was still jealous,' Harry suggested. 'That's pretty much why she came down to Sally's studio to find him, isn't it?'

Liz interrupted. She was holding a few sheets of paper in her hand.

'Matt, did you say it was the Weatherills you went to see?'

'It was, why?'

Liz held up the papers.

'These are the details we got sent over from forensics about that car, the one that was vandalised.'

'There's nothing in there,' said Harry. 'I've looked.'

'There's photos here of the logbook, though,' said Liz. 'A list of previous owners. Look ...'

Harry watched her hand the sheet over to Matt, who stared at it, then passed it over to him.

'What is it?' Harry asked, as his eyes fell on exactly what it was Liz was talking about, and he looked up at Matt.

'You have got to be kidding me.'

'I did wonder why they had such a nice garage,' said Matt. 'And why it was so empty.'

Harry stood up.

'Liz, I need you to go and have a chat with Leslie Hamilton, see what she's got to say about going over to Wilson's place. Whether it's important or not, I just don't like it when people keep secrets.'

'What about Archie and Ivy?' Jen asked. 'And Sal?'

Harry said, 'There's nothing we can do about Archie and Ivy at the moment, being as they're a little busy right now with the arrival of a baby, so we're best to just let them get on with the whole giving birth thing. We can chat with them tomorrow, assuming everything's gone well with the birth.'

'Won't they be a bit tired to have us turning up?' Matt asked. 'Speaking from experience, like, I've never been so tired myself. Joan was in labour for hours. Insisted on having all the windows open as well because she was so hot. The rest of us half froze to death.'

'Tired or not, we've got an investigation to push on with,' Harry said. 'They'll be fine, I'm sure. And I can be as sensitive as the next person.'

'If that next person happens to be Genghis Khan,' said Jen.

Even Harry laughed at that.

'Thanks for the vote of confidence, Detective Constable,' he said. 'As for Sally Dent, I'd like to speak with her myself, so leave that with me. Jen, I'd like you there with me, seeing as you know her, so I'll call you about that later on; she might be a bit more forthcoming if there's a friendly face in front of her, and mine's never been described as that, has it?'

Everyone laughed.

Harry then added, 'If you could check on Jim and Jadyn later, though, that would be helpful.'

'Will do,' said Jen.

Harry grabbed his keys. 'Matt, you're with me.'

THIRTY

By the time Harry and Matt had arrived in Thwaite, midafternoon had completely disappeared, and he found himself not just baffled by where time went, but why it had to get there so bloody quickly. He thought back to what Matt had said earlier, and wondered if perhaps the job was getting in the way with him and Grace. He'd never been all that successful at romantic relationships and knew that Matt had a point. Grace had never said anything, though, and she was plenty busy with her own life, that was for sure.

Standing outside the Weatherills' house, Harry reached up to ring the huge, brass bell hanging outside the door.

'Don't bother,' said Matt, lifting a fist and slamming the heel of it hard against the door three times.

Harry heard footsteps approach and stepped away from the door to avoid being hit by it when it swung out.

The door opened.

'Hello, Rachel,' said Matt, and Harry was sure he noticed just the hint of annoyance in the DS's voice, just enough to let them know that the reason he was there wasn't going to be a good one.

'Have you nowt better to do than harass people trying to make a living?' Rachel asked. 'I'm right in the middle of doing our monthly accounts. Can you not come back later?'

'No, we can't,' Matt said, and Harry was happy to let him take the lead. He had been here before, so it made more sense for him to do so.

'But I'm busy,' Rachel said, and lifted a hand to her forehead. 'I'm up to here with it, I am.'

Harry said, 'I'm DCI Harry Grimm. We will do our best to be as quick as we can. Just need to ask a few questions, that's all.'

'More questions?' Rachel asked, and looked at Matt. 'About what? You asked plenty of those earlier. What else is there to know? That Lance Hamilton is a bastard, we don't like him, and that's all there is to it.'

'Can we come in?' Matt asked.

'Do I have any choice?'

'You don't have to speak to us if you don't want to.'

'Then you'll think I'm hiding something, won't you?' Rachel said. 'And you'll be back with more questions and I'll never get anything done!'

She stepped back and Harry followed Matt into the house.

'Is Jeff around?' Matt asked, as they all sat down in the kitchen.

'He'll be back any moment. Is it him you need to speak to?'

Harry asked, 'How long will he be?'

Rachel went to answer, but the sound of the front door opening and then being slammed cut her off.

'Jeff?'

'Why's there another police vehicle outside again?' Jeff called back, and Harry listened to the man's footsteps as he walked through the house to find his wife. 'I hope they're not here asking us stupid questions about Hamilton again.'

Harry looked up as Jeff entered the kitchen wearing a boiler-suit, filling it out about as well as a few sticks of bamboo. He reminded Harry of a stick man drawn by a child around which ill-fitting clothes had been drawn and then scribbled in.

'Bollocks,' said Jeff.

Harry said, 'Mr Weatherill? Sorry to butt into your day like this, but there's a few things we need to clear up, if that's alright with you?'

'What's it about this time?' Jeff asked, then pointed at Matt. 'We told him everything earlier. If you've spoken to Hamilton and he's said something, then you can just turn around and tell him I said to piss off.'

Harry said nothing in response, waiting instead for Jeff to calm down. Eventually, the man's shoulders sagged, and he slumped down onto a chair.

'Go on, then,' he said. 'What is it?'

Harry looked at Matt and gave him a nod to crack on with why they were there.

'Can you tell me why you didn't mention that Mr Hamilton's car belonged to you until recently?'

Harry saw a look flash between Rachel and her husband so cold that he wouldn't have been surprised if the temperature in the room had dropped a couple of degrees.

'I told you,' she said. 'I told you something like this would happen, didn't I? Well, now look; the police are here, aren't they? Why, I've not the faintest idea, but I can guess.'

'Guess what, exactly?' Harry asked.

'Him and those stupid bloody card games he plays, that's what. I know he uses his own money, and he's never lost that much, but this time? This time, I could've killed him!'

Harry was confused.

'I think we might be talking at cross purposes here,' he said. 'Detective Sergeant Dinsdale was asking you about a car, not poker.'

'It's illegal, isn't it?' said Rachel. 'I knew it. I've seen it in the movies, the police busting up private poker games. It's about time, too, if you ask me; maybe this'll make him see some sense, though I doubt it.'

'It isn't illegal,' Harry said. 'Domestic gaming is permitted, so long as there's no levy made for playing, and it takes place in a private dwelling.'

'So, you're not here to arrest him, then? You can, you know; it would do him good. Lock him up for a few days, make him realise what an absolute dick he's been.'

Harry glanced at Jeff, then back to Rachel.

'We're here to find out more about a car we know you owned, which is now in the name of Lance Hamilton,' he said.

'Yeah, well, the only reason it's in his possession is because the man's a liar, a cheat, and a thief!' Jeff said. 'If there's anyone that needs arresting, it's him. He's a card counter, that's what he is. I can't prove it, but I will. That's why he won. The cheat. Honestly, when I get my hands on him—'

Harry held up a hand to stop Jeff from talking before he said something he would regret.

'Perhaps you should start at the beginning,' he suggested.

'You'll be going back years if you do that,' tutted Rachel. 'But he's never done anything as daft as this, believe you me. But he's really gone for it, hasn't he? I could kill him ...'

'I arrange poker games,' Jeff said, giving Rachel a hard stare, which was returned with enough heat to burn off his eyebrows. 'Started out as a bit of fun between friends, then others found out and wanted to join in. They don't happen that often because people work, don't they, have families? But when we can, we put them on. And I know the law enough to make sure no one has to pay anything to join in; you don't buy a place at the table. It's first come, first served, simple as that. If you miss out, then you just wait till the next time.'

Harry almost laughed; the idea that Wensleydale had some kind of underground poker thing going on was almost too much.

'No one pays, then?' he said.

'I get a few quid from everyone to cover food and drink, but that's it. I don't make a profit, not unless I win. And I do, because I'm good.'

'Doesn't make it right, though, does it?' said Rachel. 'You're an idiot.' She looked at Harry. 'I'm not saying he's ever done anything daft enough to risk the business or the house or anything like that, I just wish he had a healthier hobby, that's all.'

There's that word again, Harry thought, hobby. He wasn't liking it anymore, either, for hearing it more often. In many ways, the opposite was true.

Matt said, 'I'm trying to work out how any of that has anything to do with the car. And just to make sure we're talking about the same one, can I ask you to describe it?'

'Red Jaguar XJS,' said Jeff.

'Our wedding car, if you'd like to know,' added Rachel.

'My dad gave it to me a few years back,' said Jeff. 'It was his for years, lent it to us for the honeymoon.'

'And somehow it ended up in the hands of Mr Hamilton,' said Harry.

He watched as Jeff tried to make himself comfortable, but no amount of shuffling had the desired effect.

'It was a few weeks back now, and I don't know how he heard about the game, but he did,' Jeff said. 'I let him in, thinking it would be fun to see him lose.'

'Bit of an assumption, wasn't it?' said Harry.

'Like I said, I'm no slouch at the game myself,' said Jeff, 'and I made sure the other players were experienced as well. I've never liked him, and I'm happy to stand here and say that, so I thought we'd give him a good thrashing, that's all.'

'What happened?' Matt asked.

'It all got a bit carried away,' said Jeff. 'The pot got bigger, he really seemed to enjoy not just winning, but winding people up. He'd wiped everyone off the table except me. A couple of mates lent me a grand each to keep at him with the final hand, but it wasn't enough to match what he put in to see my cards. Then he suggests my car, and before I know what I'm doing, I've put that in the pot, too. I don't know what I was thinking, I really don't. I was just so bloody angry with him, with his whole attitude, and I had a killer hand ...'

Harry watched Jeff sink deeper into his chair.

'He'd had two straight flushes that night, so my thinking was there was no way that was ever happening again, like, was there? Only so much luck anyone can have. And there I was, staring at a straight flush myself. I couldn't throw my cards in and give up. I'd have been mad to!'

'He had a royal flush, didn't he?' Harry said. 'And you lost the car.'

'No one has luck like that,' said Jeff, anger setting fire to his tone. 'No one! It's impossible. That's why he's a thief, and that's why I followed him!'

THIRTY-ONE

'You what?'

Rachel's voice was loud and shrill enough to shatter glass. She was on her feet, staring at her husband. Then, before Harry or Matt could respond, she threw herself at him.

Jeff's chair fell backwards, and he and Rachel went with it, Rachel landing on top of him.

'Bloody hell!' said Matt, leaping out of his chair at the same time as Harry.

Harry grabbed Rachel, though doing so was like trying to wrestle snakes, her arms wriggling out of his grip as she did her best to lash out at her husband.

Jeff, Harry noticed, was doing everything he could to protect himself from the onslaught of flying hands, as Rachel whipped them at him, looking to strike him.

'Give over, Rachel, please!' he cried out, as Harry and Matt worked together to peel his wife away from him. 'Just stop, will you? Bloody hell! Stop!'

When Harry and Matt finally managed to drag her away, Jeff wasn't in the best of states, his hair ruffled, face flushed, eyes wide.

Harry pointed at a chair and looked at Rachel.

'Sit.'

Rachel didn't move.

'Please, Rachel,' he said. 'Fighting isn't going to solve anything.'

'It'll make me feel a whole lot better though, won't it?'

Matt helped Jeff to his feet, sitting him down in a chair a little further away from his wife than before.

Rachel sat down.

Harry looked at Jeff.

'Right then,' he said. 'Where were we?'

Harry waited, but Jeff remained quiet.

'Jeff?' he prompted.

Jeff looked up, glanced at his wife, mouthed the word, *Sorry,* then said, 'After the meeting on Friday night, I followed him. I know I shouldn't have, but him being there at all had really got to me. I don't really know what I was going to do, I mean, it wasn't planned or anything. All I could think about was him driving around in our car. I was just angry, that's all. I think my blood was boiling a bit.'

'You told me you took so long fetching our supper because the queue was long,' said Rachel.

'The queue *was* long,' said Jeff. 'I wasn't lying.'

Rachel, though, clearly wasn't listening.

'And even then, you didn't get the order right and had to go back after we'd got home, didn't you?' she said. 'How can it be that difficult? There's only two of us!'

'Probably best you explain what you mean by that,' said Harry.

Jeff fell silent again. When he finally spoke, Harry thought how the man's thinness seemed to have become even more fragile; he seemed more twig-like than ever, with more in common with a dead tree blasted by the wind than an actual human being.

'I followed him because I was going to give him a bit of a slap. There, I've said it. I'm not proud of it, but it's the truth.'

'Are you saying you were going to hit him?' Matt asked.

'No, I said I was going to give him a bit of a slap; that's not the same thing.'

'It is, actually,' Harry said. 'So, did you?'

'Slap him? No, I didn't,' said Jeff. 'I followed him after he'd been to the chippy, but I knew something wasn't quite right from the off.'

That statement caught Harry's attention.

'How do you mean, wasn't quite right?'

'For a start, he didn't go back to his car, and he wasn't heading home, was he? He just turned and walked off into town.'

'Maybe he fancied a wander around,' suggested Matt. 'Hawes is a nice place for a stroll on a warm evening.'

Jeff shook his head.

'Something wasn't right, I'm sure of it. He was stumbling, you see, like he was a few sheets to the wind, if you know what I mean.'

'What time was this?'

'No idea,' said Jeff. 'The meeting was at six, I think, but that was cut short by Hamilton. Then we went to the pub, but we didn't stay there long, so I'm guessing around seven.'

'You said Mr Hamilton was stumbling,' said Matt.

'He wasn't drunk though,' said Jeff. 'Can't have been; he'd not drunk enough in the pub to be like how I saw him, so don't ask me what was wrong with him. But it was odd.'

'What did you do?' Harry asked.

'What did I do?' said Jeff. 'Nothing, that's what. I could hear him muttering to himself, something about some letters, then something else about buying a house.'

That would be his son and future daughter-in-law, Harry thought.

'And that was it?' Matt asked.

'I did think about taking him to the doctor's,' said Jeff. 'But then I changed my mind. If he was that pissed so early in the evening, then it was his own stupid fault. I wasn't about to go wasting NHS' time, or my own for that matter, with the likes of him. No chance.'

Harry looked back over his notes, then back up again at Jeff.

'So, what colour's all that, then?' he asked, pointing a gnarly finger at the paint splatters on Jeff's boiler suit.

Jeff looked himself up and down.

'White oat and barley, or some such nonsense,' he said. 'You'll have to ask my client. Why?'

Harry sidestepped the question.

'You mentioned that Mr Hamilton didn't go back to his car.'

'So?'

'You knew where it was, then?'

'In the car park behind the school,' said Jeff.

'But that wasn't where you parked, was it?' Matt asked, and Harry was impressed that the DS had caught on to where he was going. 'And to get back here from Hawes, you wouldn't even drive past that other car park to see who was parked there, would you?'

'What are you getting at?'

'I think we're both just wondering how you knew Lance's car was in that other car park, that's all,' said Harry.

'I saw him drive up that way, how else?' said Jeff. 'Turned up the hill to Gayle. So, he must've parked up there, right?'

'What part of the order did you get wrong?' Harry asked, changing the subject again without warning.

'What order?'

'The one at the chippy,' said Matt.

'I ... I can't remember now.'

'It was your own supper,' said Rachel. 'You left it on the counter.'

'It's true, I did,' said Jeff.

Matt said, 'Do you know where I can buy that paint?'

'What?'

'I've seen it somewhere before and I'd really like some.'

'I've nowt left myself,' said Jeff, 'and you won't find it anywhere else. It was end-of-line stuff, so I got it cheap. Used it all up on the last job, except for about half a tin I left for touching up, that kind of thing.'

'What time did you go back to the chippy?' Harry asked, and he could see that Jeff was panicking a little, caught between the crossfire of questions.

'What? Oh, I don't know, it was closed when I got there. Had to bang on the door.'

'I told you it was, and you still went,' said Rachel. 'Why don't you ever listen to me?'

'I do,' said Jeff, but Harry cut in.

'So, if you knew that the chippy was going to be closed, why did you drive back to Hawes?' he asked.

'I ...'

'There must've been a reason,' Harry continued.

'I wanted my chips, that's all,' said Jeff. Then he blurted, 'And haggis! I wanted my haggis! That's what I ordered, that's why I went back.'

'What about Mr Hamilton's car?'

Jeff's panic was written in his eyes.

'What?'

'Did you go and look at it? It was yours after all, and you sound fairly aggrieved about losing it.'

'I don't know what you mean ...'

Rachel said, 'What have you done, Jeff? What did you do?'

'I've done nowt, I promise! Nowt at all!'

Jeff looked at Harry and Matt.

'Is this him? It is, isn't it? He's claiming I've done something, isn't he? What is it? Did someone scratch his car, is that it? Because I didn't and I wouldn't. And what makes you even think that I would?'

Harry said, 'We've not suggested that at all. You're the first one to raise it.'

Jeff shook his head.

'That's unfair, that is. Well, I can tell you for nowt, I've not touched his car, and I never would, because I had it for years and looked after it, and I want it back. So, you can tell him from me to sling his hook. And if he wants to accuse me of anything, then he'd best do so to my face, the bloody coward!'

Harry caught a look in Rachel's eye.

'Wait,' she said, 'this isn't about the car at all, is it? I mean it is, but there's more to it. Something's happened, hasn't it? That's why you're here again, why you were here yesterday. What's happened?'

Harry said, 'I'm sorry to inform you that the body of Mr Lance Hamilton was found on Saturday morning.'

The shock of his words slammed into Rachel and Jeff.

'He's dead?' said Jeff. 'What? How? He was fine when I saw him.' Shock turned to fear. 'Wait, you don't think I did it? You can't! I didn't! I would never!' He looked at his wife. 'Rachel, I didn't, you know I didn't! I was here, wasn't I? Tell them I was here! Tell him!'

'He was,' Rachel said. 'Other than that idiotic trip over to fetch his haggis supper, he was here.'

'Can you prove it?' Matt asked.

'Yes,' she said. 'We Zoom-called my sister and her husband for most of the evening. They emigrated a few years ago, live over in New Zealand now. They've a sheep ranch over there, the lucky buggers. We chat every couple of weeks, have a few drinks, catch up. I miss her.'

Harry said, 'We'll need to check that, and about your visit to the chippy, Jeff.'

'That's easily done,' Jeff replied. 'I didn't do it, whatever was done, really I didn't. I know I've said stuff, and I'll admit that when I went back over to grab my chips, I was hoping I'd see him again, but I didn't. I got my haggis and chips and came home.'

His voice faded.

Harry stood up, and Matt did the same.

'Thanks for your time,' he said. 'If we have any further questions, we'll be in touch.'

Rachel and Jeff led Matt and Harry out of the house.

In their vehicle, Harry spent a few moments just staring out through the windscreen.

'I'm beginning to feel like this is one of those investigations where the closer we get to what actually happened, the further we are away from understanding any of it.'

'You and me, both,' said Matt. 'And on that, shall we go have a chat with Sal and find out why she slapped Hamilton?'

Harry checked the time.

'You need to get back to that wife and daughter of yours,' he said. 'I'll give Jen a call and meet her over at Sally's.'

Matt went to protest, but Harry's stare was enough to stop him even opening his mouth.

'I'm going to message Jen and tell her we can leave the chat with Sally until tomorrow. I need to meet up with Leslie's son Archie as well. We all need a good rest before tomorrow.'

'I need more than that,' said Matt.

'You do? Like what?'

'Haggis,' said Matt.

'I dread to think of the state of your insides,' said Harry.

'Right now, they're hungry,' said Matt.

'You're always hungry.'

'We'd best get a move on, then, hadn't we?'

THIRTY-TWO

Harry dropped Matt back at the office to head home to his family, and to grab some haggis and chips on the way. He then called Jen to have her meet him over at Sally Dent's house in the morning, before putting in a quick call to Jadyn. He'd already checked in with Liz, who had said she'd been unable to get in touch with Leslie Hamilton, so that would have to wait until tomorrow. She'd busied herself instead with a call out to a local campsite, where two families holidaying in their caravans had taken such a dislike to each other that they'd ended up coming to blows. A couple of tennis rackets, a game of boules, and a portable toilet had all been involved in the fracas, but Harry had decided against asking for any further details.

'What've we got, then, Constable?' he asked.

Jadyn's retelling was fast and furious, but Harry rolled with it and waited for him to run out of breath.

'And the girl, Beth, she's okay?'

'She is,' Jadyn said. 'The parents are with her now, and I'm about to head back.'

'From where?'

'The hospital,' Jadyn said. 'I escorted them.'

'Of course you did,' sighed Harry, deciding it was probably best that he didn't point out that hadn't really been necessary. But still, Jadyn's actions would certainly shed a kind light on the police, and that could only be commended. 'What now, then?'

'I arrest him,' said Jadyn.

'What? Who?'

'Bug, I mean Nat; Nathan Lofthouse, the shopkeeper's son.'

'And you think you've enough evidence, do you, to go wading in there and dragging him away in front of his dad?'

'The lads, Owen and Gaz, and Beth as well, say he's who they get the vapes from.'

'Do you have that written down?'

'I've my notes,' Jadyn said, 'but no official signed statements or anything like that, not yet anyway, what with Beth and the paramedics and the hospital.'

'Exactly,' said Harry. 'Admirable though this urge of yours to go cracking skulls is, I think what you need is evidence, don't you? Teenagers are renowned for changing their minds about things.'

'You mean I can't go round there now?'

'No,' Harry said. 'Tomorrow, your task will be to get statements, to speak to the parents, to see if you can gather any further evidence, and then we'll see.'

Jadyn was quiet for a moment, then said, 'Okay, Boss. I'll see you tomorrow, then.'

'That you will, Constable,' Harry said, and made his way home, only to have his phone buzz as Jim called him.

'Anything to report?' Harry asked.

'Nowt,' said Jim. 'My time's nearly up, as well. I've about fifteen minutes left and then that's it.'

'No sign, then?'

'Very quiet,' said Jim. 'I'm going to give the dogs a run, as there's a footpath in the fields in front of the house, so I can still keep an eye out, just in case, then I'll head back.'

'Smudge okay, then?'

'She's with Fly,' Jim said. 'So yes, of course she is. I'll drop her back once I'm done.'

'Thanks,' Harry said, and hung up, then sent a text to DCI Mason to let him know that there was still no sign of Anna's brother. The reply he received made his blood boil.

Thanks. He turned himself in.

Harry typed a response, then deleted it immediately. DCI Mason would be hearing from him again, though, that much was certain. He then called Jim and told him about the message.

'When was that, then?' Jim asked.

'Not a clue,' said Harry. 'But I'll be finding out, that's for sure. I'm not a fan of anyone who thinks they can waste not only my time but that of my team.'

'I'll be seeing you a little sooner than expected, then,' said Jim.

Heading home, Harry had expected to find Grace waiting for him, so was disappointed to walk into an empty house. Thankfully, Jim turned up at the door not too long after.

'She's never any bother,' Jim said, as Smudge slipped into the house, brushing against Harry's leg as she mooched past. 'She could've stayed over. Mum loves her and you know what Fly thinks.'

'Nice to have her back, though,' said Harry.

'No Grace?'

'Not yet, no.'

'How are your mum and dad?'

'Same as always,' Jim said. 'Working too many hours, no time off, no holidays. Living the dream, Harry.'

Harry smiled.

'It's a tough life,' he said.

'It is, but they'd not swap it. Can't blame them, either.'

Harry heard something then in Jim's voice, and it was something he'd heard there before, no matter what the young PCSO did to try and hide it.

'Farming runs in the blood,' he said, seeing if Jim would take the bait.

'It does,' Jim replied.

Harry waited to see if Jim wanted to say anything else.

'They won't say it, because that's just the way they are, but I think they need more help than they'll admit to.'

'They've not had it easy,' Harry said.

'My brother, you mean?'

'I do,' said Harry, remembering that Jim's older brother had been killed in a tragic farming accident years ago. He didn't know the ins and outs of what happened, and it wasn't something that Jim ever talked about, but he knew that something like that, it would haunt a family.

'He was great,' Jim said. 'I looked up to him, you know? But when he was... I mean, when we lost him, I had to step in, do more.'

'And now you're a PCSO.'

'I needed to do something else as well. I couldn't just go into farming, not straight away, anyway.'

And there it was, Harry thought.

'You miss it.'

Jim gave a nod.

'I do, but I love what I do, being a PCSO. It's important, isn't it?'

'It is,' Harry said. 'But so is family.'

For a moment, Harry was sure Jim was about to say something, but instead he stepped away from the house.

'I'll see you tomorrow, Harry,' he said, then climbed into his vehicle and headed off.

Once Jim had left, Harry gave Grace a call to see when she was coming over. She replied to say she was running a bit late but would be there within the hour. And, true to her word, she was, turning up bleary-eyed, with Jess in tow.

Harry poured them a glass of wine each.

'Dad's been off today,' Grace said, walking through to the lounge to drop wearily onto the sofa. 'Mainly because I forced him to go home; he's not easy to persuade, even when he's half asleep on his feet and complaining about all his aches and pains.' She yawned, then added, 'You've lit the fire? But it's summer!'

'And it's cold,' Harry said. 'This house is always cold. Also, sometimes, it's just nice to do, isn't it? Makes you feel at home.'

Grace sipped her wine.

Harry went to say something, but hesitated. Talking about his feelings wasn't exactly a strength. Feelings were things to be pushed down deep, nice and safe.

'Hungry?' he asked.

'Starving,' Grace said..

'Then how about I do us some pasta, then we head to The Fountain for a pint or two? The dogs can come with us for the walk. It's a nice evening..'

'We can do better than pasta,' said Grace. 'Dad had some stew and dumplings in the slow cooker. He made enough for a family of twelve, so I bought some over.'

Harry led Grace through to the kitchen and once the food was heated up, they both scoffed it down like they'd not eaten in days, then headed off to the pub, Jess and Smudge trotting along beside them.

With a couple of pints of Gamekeeper poured, Harry turned from the bar to head towards the window, sitting against the wall between it and the fire.

Grace sat down beside him.

'You always sit here, you know that, don't you?'

'Do I?' Harry said, lifting his pint and taking a sip.

'Keep it up and we'll have to name it,' said Grace. 'Harry's Corner.'

'I'm that much a creature of habit?'

'We could even have a plaque put in.'

Harry smiled at that, then took another gulp of his pint, working out what it was he was trying to say, and how to say it.

'Yesterday,' he said, 'when we were shooting ...'

'You don't mean that pillock who turned up to complain about the noise?' Grace asked. 'Can you believe some people?'

'Yes, I can,' Harry said. 'But it's not that.'

'What is it, then?'

'Harry took a deep breath, then said, When Jadyn turned up, and I had to go, you didn't seem exactly pleased.'

'Well, I wasn't. But that's hardly a surprise, is it?'

'No. I suppose not,' said Harry, staring glumly into his pint glass.

'I mean it was our day out and then it wasn't any more. And let's face it, Harry, it happens quite a lot. Too much, probably,' she added ruefully.

'Our lives are busy, aren't they?' Harry said.

'You can say that again. But it also doesn't mean that we should just accept the status quo and continue as we are, does it? And if we're comparing lives,' Grace added. 'Yes, I'm busy, but I can switch off. Either you can't, or you choose not to, and I don't know which it is.'

'It's not that easy,' Harry began, but Grace cut him off.

'I didn't say I expected it to be easy,' she said, 'but it isn't easy playing second fiddle to the bastards you've clearly dedicated your whole life to catching!'

Everything Grace was saying, Harry knew to be true. His job had been his world for so long now, so all encompassing, that he'd neither adjusted to being with someone who wanted to be with him, nor given any thought as to how he would change his life to make space for that. In the end, he hadn't made much space for Grace at all.

'I'm sorry,' Harry said. 'I should've realised.'

'I knew about the job when we started seeing each other, said Grace. 'It's part of who you are, of course it is, but that doesn't mean I'm going to sing and dance every time it pushes its way into our life uninvited, does it? And neither does it mean that I'm going to just accept it and never want something more at some point down the line.'

'No, I can see that,' said Harry.

'And that leads me onto something else.' said Grace. 'Sometimes, zipping to and fro between three houses, really pisses me off.'

Harry noticed an edge to Grace's voice and realised this was all a little more serious than he perhaps had realised.

'All I seem to do is drive between where you, me and Dad live,' Grace continued, 'and a part of me would like to think that at some point that isn't going to be the case, that at some point you and me might look at being in one place together, rather than two places miles apart.'

Harry was again struggling to find words. Deep down, he knew this. That it was all there brewing on the horizon. I mean, moving in together was par for the course for most relationships if they were to have a future, and there had been no shortage of pointed comments to that effect from Matt and Jim and others on the team. It wasn't that Harry was against the idea outright. It was just something that also brought with it an undeniable sense of dread and terror too.

'Yeah, I know,' he replied. 'It's obvious really but I think I just got used to the status quo. Lazy really, relying on you doing most of the legwork while I bury myself in work'.

'And that's the crux of the issue right there,' said Grace. 'The job and you, sometimes it's impossible to know where one ends and the other begins.'

Grace stopped talking.

Harry sipped his beer.

For a moment, neither of them spoke.

'Anyway, you asked and there it is,' said Grace, breaking the silence.

'I see your point,' said Harry, watching Grace finish her pint.

'I'm not saying we move in together immediately,' said Grace. 'But what I am saying is that I'd like it to be out there as something that we might talk about now and again. No rush, just, you know, a possibility. Does that make sense? And I need you to know that it's normal and OK for me to be angry when you get called away for work, not have it trigger an existential crisis in you every time I let my unquestionably cheery and affable demeanour slip.'

Harry smiled and nodded at this. Then thought for a moment,

walking around his cottage in his mind. He hadn't been it long and it was the first place that he'd ever felt he could call home. Did he really want to give that up, to lose the place he could retreat to and lock out a world that had up until recently seemed to comprise mainly of criminal scumbags?

'Well, if we do ever decide to shack up together, I can't see my place being suitable.' he said uncertainly.

'Why not?' Grace asked.

'What I mean is, it seemed plenty big enough when I moved in, but that was just me and Smudge. With four of us, it would soon move from cosy to cramped. My mornings are punctuated by stubbed toes, walking into walls, banging into doors. And it really does need decorating, doesn't it? Trouble is, I'm hopeless at DIY.'

'Hopeless, or you just hate doing it?'

'Yes.'

Grace laughed.

'You want another?'

'Busy day tomorrow,' Harry said.

At this comment, Grace frowned, half jokingly, and Harry, spurred on by a rare moment of clarity quickly changed tack. 'I mean, it's my round, I'll get them in.'

And with that he made off to the bar, their empties in his hand and a mix of relief and foreboding in his heart.

THIRTY-THREE

Monday morning welcomed Harry with bright sunshine and the smell of dog breath in his face.

'If that's not Smudge, we need to have a serious chat about your oral hygiene,' he said, his eyes still closed.

'I'm not even in bed,' Grace replied.

Harry opened his eyes to see the curtains open and Smudge lying next to him, her face far too close to his own. At the bedroom door stood Grace.

'What time is it?'

'Six.'

'You off already?'

'I'm afraid so,' Grace said. 'I can't be doing with Dad getting to whatever job we're on first, because he never shuts up about it if he does.'

'I can believe it. You around later?'

'I am,' Grace said. 'I'll see if I can work it so what I'm doing has me finish up the day this end of the dale, but I'll let you know.'

Harry sat up, and Grace leaned over for a kiss.

'Say hi to Arthur for me,' he said, as she left the bedroom.

'I will,' Grace shouted back up the stairs, and then she was gone, the sound of the front door swooshing shut behind her.

Harry was sorely tempted to try and fall back to sleep, but already the job was filling his mind with what tasks he had on for the day, so he got up, showered, and after a feast of marmalade on toast, and at least a pint of tea, headed out with Smudge at his feet.

With plenty of time before he was due to meet Jen at Sally Dent's house, Harry decided to take a somewhat longer stroll before work. He would be driving into town anyway, keen to have his vehicle to hand, so a walk now would do him and Smudge good.

Instead of just heading straight down the hill and into Hawes, he took a right out of his door and followed the narrow lane, pinched on either side by cosy cottages, until he came to a footpath sign pointing over a wall, directing them to Aysgill Force.

The thin path meandered off into the distance in front of Harry, calling him and Smudge on. They followed it, Harry enjoying the quiet, Smudge happily sniffing every tuft of grass as they went. Through fields and over stiles they walked, and soon were following Gayle Beck up into the fells. The path at this point became a little treacherous, and Harry was increasingly aware of the deep gash in the landscape to his left, carved out over millennia by the beck itself, his every footstep taken carefully as he navigated himself over rock and root.

When at last they came to Aysgill Force itself, Harry gazed down into the deep, dark cauldron of rock the waterfall had mined out for itself. Though the falls were little more than a trickle, Harry was still in awe of the place, and was again struck by how the Dales held so many hidden treasures just waiting to be discovered.

Dragging himself away, Harry headed back home, threw himself and Smudge into his RAV, then rolled down into Hawes to Sally Dent's house, which was in a small estate just off the road before the school. Jen was already there, waiting for him.

'Liz get off home okay last night?' he asked.

'Raced off, actually,' Jen said, smiling. 'Apparently, Ben had planned a special night in for them both. Wine, food, and a movie, I think. Sounded romantic.'

'No idea where he gets that from,' Harry said.

'Everyone can be romantic,' Jen said. 'Even you.'

'I just make an arse of myself if I try,' Harry said. 'Shall we crack on?'

Harry walked up to the front door of Sally Dent's house and gave it a sharp knock. When she opened the door, he wasn't sure what he had been expecting, but he knew that it absolutely wasn't Sally charging out towards him with rage in her eyes.

'You've come round here to apologise then, is that it? Because right now that's the least you could do. Not that you will. Not that you care. Unbelievable!'

Sally turned back into her house and slammed the door behind her.

'Well,' Harry said, a little confused.

'I agree,' said Jen.

'Shall we try again?'

Harry lifted a fist to the door, which was yanked open violently.

'Why didn't you tell me on Saturday?' Sally yelled, her eyes wide. 'That's what I want to know. I mean, it's not like this is something everyone knows, is it? But then why would we? Why would anyone know that you have to do it yourself if someone's been murdered on your property?'

Harry said, 'Ms Dent ... Sally ... I'm not sure I understand. Perhaps if we go inside and talk about this in private?'

'You don't understand? Well, you wouldn't, would you? Not unless you've experienced the same thing!'

Harry decided it was best to keep quiet on that point, but gestured into the house and then, without waiting for an invite, stepped in, with Jen behind him.

'Oh, that's right, just come on in, why don't you?'

Hearing the door slam behind them, Harry waited for Sally to show them through to a room they could chat in. She stormed past, shouldering him into the wall, then crashed through another door.

Harry and Jen followed her into a small kitchen diner.

Sally was leaning with her back against the sink, arms folded.

'I've no idea how much it's going to cost, but it's not going to be cheap, whatever it is. And do I look like I've got the money? Really? I make pots, remember? It's not exactly a get-rich-quick scheme, is it? I'm not making pots with one hand and spending my billions with the other!'

Harry took a seat at the dining table, and Jen sat opposite. Sally didn't move, but Harry was impressed with her ability to seethe.

'I haven't got three grand,' Sally said at last, though now her voice was more subdued. 'And that's just the quote. For all I know, it's going to cost more.'

And now Harry knew.

'Forensic cleaning, right?' he said.

'Exactly that,' said Sally. 'I've managed to scrape the money together, but that's me in the shit for months now, isn't it? No emergency fund if things go pear-shaped, if my car breaks down, or the washing machine needs to be fixed.'

Sally dropped her head into her hands for a moment, then looked back up.

'You're not here about that, then?'

'No,' Harry said.

'And there's no one I can write to about it to complain, no fund I can access?'

'You can always write and complain,' said Harry.

Sally laughed.

'Nice dodge of the fund question there,' she said, then looked over to Jen. 'I know you, don't I?'

'Penhill,' said Jen.

'That's it; didn't recognise you with the uniform on.'

'We've bumped into each other a few times. Late nights usually when I'm trying to fit the long runs around the day job.'

'The running helps to tire me out,' said Sally. 'Trouble is, the fitter I get, the longer that seems to take.'

Harry said, 'I really am sorry about the forensics cleanup, but my hands are tied.'

'So, why is it you're here, then?' Sally asked. 'What's

happened? If there's another dead body in my studio, I'm going to be very upset.'

'The night of the meeting,' Harry said, not sure if Sally's tone was jokey or serious. 'I was wondering if you would be able to shed a bit of light on what happened at the pub afterwards.'

Sally's shoulders dropped.

'I knew you'd find out.'

Harry didn't want to lead Sally with his questions, so asked, 'Find out what?'

'I know I should've told you that I slapped Lance,' Sally said. 'He had it coming, though. I told you how he was, what he was like; I couldn't help myself. Kind of just built up in me and I lashed out.'

Harry said, 'You slapped him hard enough to bruise his face, and you knocked his drink out of his hand.'

'I did, didn't I?' said Sally through a small grin. 'Felt good, too, I have to admit.'

'Was it planned?' Harry asked.

Sally clenched her jaw.

'Yes,' she finally said. 'It was. I followed him and I slapped him, and it felt amazing.'

'What about afterwards?' Jen asked.

'I went home, like I said.'

'You didn't wait around and follow him?'

'No,' said Sally. 'I didn't. I know I've no proof of that, but I came straight home, had a few drinks, went to bed.'

Harry noticed Jen staring at him.

'Something the matter?'

'Loo break required,' she said. 'Sally, do you mind if ...?'

'No, go ahead,' said Sally, and directed Jen to the toilet.

With Jen gone, Harry pulled out the letters Jadyn had found in Lance's office.

'Can you have a look at these, please?'

'What are they?' Sally said, taking them from Harry.

'Do you know anything about them?'

Sally read the letters, then handed them back.

'Who would write something like that?' she asked.

'Someone who wanted to get back at Lance,' said Harry. 'The kind of person who had a real problem with him, didn't like what he'd done to them, how he'd treated them.'

Sally folded her arms and laughed.

'I run my own business,' she said. 'I work mad hours doing something I love and somehow manage to keep a roof over my head. I've not the brain space to do anything like that.'

Jen returned and sat down.

'I was just wondering something,' she said, her eyes on Sally. 'I've had a rough few weeks of it, with long days, a heavy training schedule.'

'Tell me about it,' said Sally.

'Thought you'd understand,' Jen smiled. 'Just wondered if you could recommend anything, just to help me get some decent rest. I can manage a few nights here and there, but lately, it's not been good.'

'I've just the thing, actually,' Sally said, and stood up. 'Just a mo' ...'

Sally left the room.

Harry looked over at Jen.

'You do know you shouldn't be taking advantage of a police investigation to help improve your health and fitness, don't you?'

'Of course I do,' said Jen.

'Then what are you doing?'

Sally returned and dropped a small cardboard box in front of Jen.

'You should try these,' she said. 'They're prescription only, though. Took ages to persuade the doctor that I needed them..'

Jen handed the box to Harry, then said, 'Why's that, then?'

Harry read the label on the box, looked at Jen, then turned his eyes to Sally.

'Zipiclone,' he said.

'What about it?'

Harry was tracking back over what he had learned about the

events of Friday evening and the meeting at the Market Hall. He was still unclear about what the final picture would be, but some pieces were maybe slotting into place now.

'It was your drink, wasn't it?' he said.

'What was?'

Harry shook the box of tablets.

'My guess is you crushed a handful of these, and let the powder sit in some vodka at home for a good while, see if you could leach out enough of the drug to have an impact.'

Sally said, 'I don't know what you're talking about.'

But Harry heard a quiver in her voice, a feather of fear tickling the back of her throat.

'Then you strained it off, through a filter paper for a coffee machine I should think, bottled it, then tipped it into your drink at the pub. A quick swilling of the glass and it would all be mixed up.'

'You're making this up.'

Harry shook his head.

'Quite the opposite,' he said. 'I'm taking things I already know and making sense of them. You slapped him, knocked his drink out of his hand, then gave him your own, that double vodka you ordered.'

'It was just a drink.'

'A drink laced with a class C controlled hypnotic medicine,' Harry said. 'You spiked his drink, Sally. Why?'

Harry sat back and waited. The silence in the room became oppressive. And yet still he waited, trusting the years of experience he had in the police and managing situations just like this.

'Okay, alright, I did it. I spiked his drink,' Sally said. 'But I didn't kill him, okay? And you can't think I did.'

Still, Harry said nothing, allowing the pressure of the moment to push Sally on.

'He was a complete arsehole, and he treated me like shit,' she said. 'I wanted to get my own back so that's exactly what I did. I thought it would be funny to see him make a fool of himself.'

'But how would you know?' asked Jen. 'You left the pub before him.'

'Yeah, that's where my plan fell apart,' said Sally. 'I didn't expect everyone else to follow me over there. I was going to ask him for a drink, you see, pretend I wanted to make up or something; with his ego, he'd have lapped it up. But he left the meeting early, so I had to follow, and then before I knew what was happening, everyone else was there. I think I just panicked and ran.'

Harry suddenly felt exhausted. As he had found so often during his life in the police, the circumstances behind so many crimes were sad to the point of being heartbreaking. Lance had treated Sally badly, and she had decided to get back at him. That was understandable because it was human nature to want to lash out, get your own back. Spiking a drink, though? That was serious. And right then, none of them knew the role Sally's actions had played in what had eventually happened to Lance.

'Sally Dent,' Harry said, 'I am arresting you on suspicion of administering a noxious substance without Mr Hamilton's knowledge or consent.'

Shock and dread fell across Sally's face, her eyes wide and staring.

'What? You can't be serious? I'm under arrest? Someone murdered that bastard in my studio, and you're arresting me for making him feel a bit squiffy? You're kidding, right? You have to be!'

'You do not have to say anything,' Harry continued. 'But it may harm your defence if you do not mention when questioned something that you later rely on in court. Anything you do say may be given in evidence.'

'No, you can't arrest me! You can't! I haven't done anything!'

Sally's voice was torn with desperation.

'Jen?' Harry said.

Jen stood up and went to stand at Sally's side.

'Come on,' she said. 'You need to come with us.'

'But I've not done anything! I haven't! I didn't kill him, did I?

That's what you're supposed to be investigating, not this! You can't arrest me! Please!'

Harry joined Jen, standing on the other side of Sally.

'Sally,' he said. 'Please ...?'

Sally pushed herself to her feet.

'I can't believe this,' she said. 'I didn't mean for anything to happen. I promise, I didn't.'

'Is there anything you need?' Jen asked. 'Anything you need to take with you?'

'Please, you can't ...'

Harry stepped back and gave Jen a moment to speak with Sally, then together they gathered a few things in a small bag, and grabbed a jacket.

As Harry and Jen led Sally from her house, she started to cry. By the time she was at the car, tears were streaming down her face, but she wasn't making a sound.

Harry went to put her in the back of his vehicle, but Jen stopped him.

'I'll take her,' she said. 'I know her, so that'll maybe help keep her calm.'

'You're sure?'

'Wouldn't offer otherwise, Boss.'

With Sally in her car, Jen said, 'Sometimes, I really hate this job.' Then she dropped herself into the driver's seat.

'One of the many reasons you're so good at it,' said Harry.

With Jen gone, taking a confused, upset, and terrified Sally Dent down the dale to Harrogate, Harry made his way to the office.

THIRTY-FOUR

Harry found Matt in the office and Smudge went straight over for a bit of fuss.

'Morning,' the DS said. 'Tea?'

Harry didn't answer, just slumped down into a chair, pretty sure a headache was coming on.

'I see you've brought a big cloud of happiness with you,' Matt said.

Harry leaned forward, elbows on his knees, then explained what had just happened with Sally Dent. When he finished, Matt took a while to respond.

'Bloody hell,' he said at last.

'You could say that,' said Harry.

'I could say a lot more, but it wouldn't add anything, would it?' said Matt. 'You okay?'

'I'm fine,' Harry said, lying. 'We'll need to check on Jen in a while, though, just to keep an eye on things.'

'I can do that,' Matt said.

Harry asked, 'Where's everyone else? And have you heard anything from Gordy?'

'Gordy's fine,' said Matt.

'Well, that's something,' said Harry. 'Anna's brother turned himself in. No idea when, but what I do know is that whoever DCI Mason is, he's an arse; didn't see fit to let us know.'

Matt sighed.

'Well, at least it's dealt with,' he said. 'Though I don't envy Anna dealing with the fallout of it. Sounds messy.'

'That it does,' said Harry. 'What about the rest of the team?'

'Jadyn's on with doing a bit more work on that vaping thing,' Matt said. 'Liz was going to head over to speak with Mrs Hamilton, but a call came in from down dale, so she and Jim had to head off; been a crash on those sharp bends at the bottom of Temple Bank.'

Harry knew that name well; it was where Jen had ended up being involved in a hit-and-run herself.

'That just leaves you, then,' said Harry.

'It does,' said Matt. 'First day of a new week, so I'm doing a quick check of everything in the Action Book, then I thought I'd go and see if I can have a word with Leslie myself. I've already given her a call. Managed to catch her, but she said she was busy with her new grandson. I'll try her again in a bit. So, what about yourself, then?'

Harry tapped the side of his head.

'There's too much going on in here right now,' he said. 'I feel like there's a few threads just about visible, but I'm worried if I pull them, everything will fall apart.'

'We've not spoken with Leslie's son, Archie, and his fiancé yet, have we?' Matt asked.

'I was going to leave that to Liz and Jen, seeing as they'd already spoken with the fiancé's parents,' Harry said. 'What was her name again?'

'Ivy,' said Matt. 'Nice name, too. You going to go see them?'

Harry stood up.

'They won't like it, and I hope I don't scare the baby, but yes, seems like that's the best use of my time, doesn't it?'

Matt rose to his feet.

'I may as well come with you, then,' he said. 'Kill two birds with one stone and all that, right?'

'I'd appreciate that,' said Harry. 'You've a little more experience than me with babies.'

'I'm no expert.'

'You're the best I've got.'

'There is that.'

With that agreed, Harry and Matt left the office and were soon on their way over to the Fothergills' farm. They were greeted by a mad rush of puppies, and Mr and Mrs Fothergill at the door.

'Sorry to bother you,' Harry said, deciding it was probably best to start off with an apology. 'I know you're plenty busy enough as it is.'

'We are that,' said Aldwin.

'I'm Detective Chief Inspector Harry Grimm, and this is Detective Sergeant Dinsdale.'

'I know that,' said Aldwin, and looked then at Matt. 'You're in the mountain rescue, aren't you?'

'I am,' Matt said.

'Thought I recognised you. Your lot rescued a few of my sheep from some bog a few years ago. Can't remember which winter it was, but we'd had far too much rain, and some of my daft buggers got out of one of the lower fields and went exploring. No brains, sheep, no brains at all.'

Harry said, 'Can I ask how things are? With the baby, I mean.'

At this, Aldwin beamed and reached out to hug his wife, Karen, then before Harry could do anything about it, hugged him as well.

'We're grandparents!' Aldwin said, as Harry found himself crushed in a bear hug.

'Congratulations,' Harry said, able to speak once Aldwin had let him go, only to turn the hug on Matt. Matt was ready for it, though, and embraced the man warmly.

Karen said, 'Mother and baby are doing well.'

'And the dad?'

'Happy as a pig in shit!' said Aldwin, giving Karen cause to punch him in the arm. 'Well, he is, isn't he?' Aldwin added. 'We all are.'

'A bouncing baby boy,' said Karen. 'Eight and a half pounds. Lovely, he is. Didn't want to come out at first, but when he did, he certainly made sure we all knew about it.'

'He's a pair of lungs on him,' Aldwin said.

'What have they called him?' Harry asked.

'George,' said Karen. 'George Aldwin Fothergill. Lovely, isn't it?'

Harry wasn't about to admit that he didn't really have an opinion on the matter and said, 'It's a good name.'

'You'll be wanting to see him, then?' Aldwin asked.

'The parents mainly,' said Harry, 'but yes, that would be lovely, I'm sure.'

'Come on in, then,' said Karen, and making sure the gang of collie pups didn't follow them, ushered Harry and Matt inside.

Once inside the house, Harry and Matt followed Karen, with Aldwin bringing up the rear.

'They're upstairs,' Aldwin explained. 'This house is bloody enormous, so we've converted some of the upstairs into a separate flat, with a separate bathroom and a little kitchen. It's not perfect, which is why they were so looking forward to moving out.'

On the first floor, Harry and Matt were walked to the end of a long hall, the floor lined with a narrow length of carpet which didn't quite meet the skirting board.

'Through here,' Karen said, and knocked at a scuffed white door now in front of them.

The door was opened by a young man with short dark hair and even darker eyes, the shadows around them betraying all too easily the echoes of the previous disturbed night.

'You've some visitors,' Karen said, and led Harry and Matt through the door.

In the room beyond, Harry found a small room set up to be a lounge and kitchen but done with such care that he rather fancied moving in himself. It was cosy, clean, and seemed to radiate the love Karen and Aldwin had for their daughter's new family. Lying on the sofa was a young woman, and on her chest was a tiny bundle of blankets.

'It's not much, I know,' said Aldwin, 'but I did the best I could with what I've got, which isn't much. Needs decorating, right enough, and I had it all planned out, but then George turned up earlier than we all expected and here we are. Mind you, not sure me decorating would make the place look any better.'

Harry said, 'Not a fan of a paintbrush?'

'I'm not,' said Aldwin.

'Makes two of us, then,' said Harry.

Karen then introduced Harry and Matt.

'We won't take up too much of your time,' Harry said. 'Or we can come back later, whatever suits.'

Archie looked over at Ivy, who looked both exhausted and radiant, Harry thought. Not that she was glowing or anything daft like that, but the smile on her face was bright and full as the midday sun.

'Now's as good a time as any,' Ivy said.

Harry and Matt took a seat. Karen and Aldwin, he noticed, made no effort to leave. Fair enough, he thought, all things considered.

'This is about Lance, isn't it?' Archie said. 'Not sure what use I can be. We weren't exactly close.'

Harry said, 'Are you able to confirm where you were Friday night?'

'Here, where else?' Archie said. 'I saw him that evening, at the meeting in town, then at the pub, but that was it. Like I said, we weren't close; I wasn't about to hang around and have a chat with him over a pint or two, not after what he did.'

'The house, you mean,' Matt said.

'The house,' said Archie. 'I still don't know why he did it. I mean, there's not liking me, and disagreeing with my decisions, and then there's deliberating screwing up my life, isn't there?'

'And you've really no idea why he did it?'

'None,' Archie said.

'Because he was a bastard, that's why,' said Aldwin. 'Spiteful, he was. Never approved of Archie seeing our lass, did he? So, he thought he'd bugger it up. Didn't work though, did it? Look at them; proper little family now, aren't they?'

'Have you spoken to your mum?' Harry asked.

'Briefly,' said Archie. 'She called to tell me what happened, but that's all.'

'When was that?'

'Sometime late Saturday afternoon, I think. Hard to remember exactly, what with little George turning up.'

As if reacting to the mention of his name, George let out a soft gurgling cry, then fell silent again.

'Do you know anything about some letters your dad had been receiving?' Harry asked.

'What do you mean, letters?' Archie asked. 'I've not lived with my parents for years. Couldn't bear it.'

'So, he never mentioned them to you?'

'We didn't speak,' said Archie. 'I'd love to be able to say I hated the man and I'm glad he's gone, but I'll be honest, I don't feel anything. There was never anything between us, not even enough to grow into dislike. He was just someone that my mum, for whatever reason, fell in love with and married, then fell out of love with, just not soon enough. I can't even say that I won't miss him, because there's nothing to not miss, if that makes sense?'

'A little,' said Matt.

Harry glanced over at the DS and knew there was nothing more for either of them to say. But as he made to stand up, Matt spoke up.

'Your mum must be pleased as punch,' he said, looking at Archie.

'You'd think, wouldn't you?' Archie replied.

'How do you mean?' Harry asked.

Matt added, 'I thought we might bump into her, actually. She said she would be here.'

'Well, she isn't,' said Archie. 'I've sent her a text and a photo, and she's replied to that, but she's not come out to see George. Said she was busy and would try and make it later today. Try? What the hell's that about? Her grandson has arrived and she'll try to see him? Madness.'

Harry stood up.

'I think we're done here,' he said, and gave a nod to Matt to follow him out. 'You all look after yourselves now, and congratulations again.'

Ivy said, 'Do you want to see him?'

Harry shook his head.

'No, it's fine, honestly, you stay there, nice and comfy, and we'll—'

Ivy pushed herself up out of the sofa and walked over.

'Here he is,' she said, and turned the little bundle in her arms around so that Harry and Matt could see him.

Before Harry knew what he was doing, he'd reached out a gnarly, scarred finger, and gently stroked little George's cheek.

'If Gordy were here, she'd describe him as bonny,' he said. 'And right now, I can't think of a better description.'

Ivy beamed.

'He is, isn't he?'

A few minutes later, and back outside the Fothergills' farmhouse, Harry and Matt climbed into the RAV, as Aldwin shooed away the collie pups.

'So, now what?' Matt asked, as Harry slowly drove them down the lane.

'I'm not sure,' Harry said. 'I was thinking those letters Jadyn found might have been from Archie, which would be motive enough, I think, for Lance to do what he did with the house.'

'He could be lying.'

'He could be, but I can't see it, can you? And even if they were, did any of what we've just seen strike you as being connected to what happened to Lance? Ignoring the fact that he was here for the whole night and he had a baby on the way, I'm just not seeing him going round to lop off his dad's hands and leave the body at Sally's. Doesn't make sense.'

'None of this does,' said Matt.

Harry, though, wasn't so sure about that. There was something Aldwin had said when they'd gone into the little apartment he and Karen had sorted for Archie and Ivy, and little George, that was bothering him. He just wasn't sure what it was. It was reminding him of his chat with Grace the night before, but why?

'Strange that Leslie wasn't there,' he said.

'Yeah, a bit,' Matt agreed. 'Odd thing to lie about.'

'So, where is she?'

Heading back to Hawes, Harry decided to talk everything through with Matt.

'Here's what we know,' he said. 'Lance went to that meeting on Friday night, then to the pub. The meeting had a good number of attendees who didn't like him.'

'And some of them followed him to the pub.'

'Sally was the first person to turn up,' continued Harry. 'She slapped him, gave him the drink she had drugged, and then left.'

'IT WAS AN EVENTFUL EVENING,' said Matt.

'We know that Jeff Weatherill followed Lance that evening as well,' said Harry.

'And noticed that something was up with him, undoubtedly from that drink Sally had given him.'

As they were talking, Harry was trying to make connections. He knew there had to be one, could sense it, but what the hell was it?

'It doesn't feel planned, does it?' he said. 'What happened to Lance later that night, with what we know, I can't see his violent end being something someone meticulously put together.'

'How do you mean?' Matt asked.

Harry said, 'If you planned to kill Lance by hacking off his hands and letting him bleed to death, and then sit him in a pottery studio, I'm not sure what Sally did would be part of that. There are too many variables. Lance drove into town for the meeting, then instead of driving home, went to the pub and then the fish and chip shop. Only Lance would've known he was going to do any of that.'

'It looks planned, though,' said Matt.

'No, it looks staged,' Harry said, and it was then that a connection fired so brightly in his mind, he almost winced.

'What is it?' asked Matt. 'I know something's up because you're accelerating. What are you thinking?'

'I'm thinking I know how Lance's hands were cut off,' said Harry. 'One of them, anyway. I don't know why, but we might just have to wing this to find out. You busy?'

'Oh, you know me; the days are just packed. But I'm sure I can find a space in my diary for whatever you've got planned. Are you going to tell me what it is, or leave it as a surprise?'

'Oh, everything about this is a surprise,' Harry said.

THIRTY-FIVE

A few minutes later Harry drove them into Hawes, stopping briefly in town to pop into the office, then headed out the way they had just come to park up on the right a couple of hundred metres from the entrance to the auction mart.

Harry took a moment to gather his thoughts, reading through what he had in his notebook. He still didn't know everything, but what had happened with Sally Dent, then their visit to the Fothergills, and the chat in the RAV with Matt had lit a fuse in his head, and that was burning bright now; he wasn't exactly sure what was at the end of it, but there was only one way to find out.

He turned to Matt.

'Ready?'

'When am I ever anything else?'

Harry climbed out of his vehicle, waited for Matt to join him before locking it, then led the way. He spotted a small, red car parked outside the house he was heading towards.

'I recognise that car,' Matt said.

'So do I,' said Harry, pushing through an iron gate, and walking up a flagstone path, Matt by his side, to a door with a stained-glass window.

Harry rang the bell, but didn't have to wait long for the door to be opened.

Leslie Hamilton stood in the doorway, a bright light from the hallway behind her bathing her in an angelic glow. She was wearing an outfit of brown suede, leather boots, a cowboy hat, and was carrying a whip. Around her neck, she was still wearing a scarf, which struck Harry as strange.

'Oh,' she said, her eyes flicking from Harry to Matt and then back to Harry again.

Harry said, 'Hello, Leslie, wondered if you might be here; is Andrew in?'

Leslie seemed frozen to the spot, stunned into silence, so he gave her a second or two to gather herself and answer.

'Didn't see you at the Fothergills' house,' added Matt. 'Strange that, isn't it?'

Leslie did a very good impression of a goldfish.

'Is he in, then?' Harry said. 'Andrew?'

'Of course he is,' Leslie replied, desperately trying to regain some composure. 'This is his house. Is it important?'

'A little,' said Harry.

'You want to come in, then?'

'That would be for the best, I think.'

'But we're busy,' said Leslie. 'The production, it's only two weeks away and we have things to do.'

'We'll be as quick as we can.'

Leslie stared at Harry, then closed the door, which he hadn't been expecting.

'Bit rude,' said Matt.

When the door opened again, Andrew Wilson had replaced Leslie. Harry saw that he was again dressed as Lieutenant Danny Gilmartin.

'Mr Grimm?' Andrew said. 'Can't say I know why you're here, but you can help us with our lines if you want? We're almost there, but any help would be welcome.'

'Sorry for turning up unannounced,' Harry said, ignoring the request for help. He'd never done any acting in his life. Plenty of roleplay, yes, but planning an attack on an enemy position in basic training for the Army, and experiencing trying to arrest someone who really didn't want to be arrested while training for the Police was a little different to reciting lines and pretending he was a thespian. 'But you know how it is sometimes when something just won't wait.'

'And this is one of those times, yes?'

'You could say that. May we come in?'

'Can we not discuss it here?'

'No,' Harry said, unable to disguise his frustration at being delayed at the door. 'We can't.'

Wilson sucked in a frustrated breath through his nose, then exhaled loudly, his nostrils twitching. Then he stepped back and held out a hand to invite Harry inside.

'The study?' Harry asked, but didn't wait for an answer, and made his way through, spotting once again the plug-in air fresheners in the wall, filling the space with a smell he was sure would give him a headache if he was there too long.

The room was as it had been before, a neat space hidden by costumes.

'I don't know how you do it,' Harry said, sitting down in the same chair he had sat in before, Matt taking a seat opposite. 'Running a busy accountancy firm and directing a play. How do you have the time?'

'I don't have the time really,' Wilson said. 'But I make it work somehow. It can't all be work, work, work, can it? We have to do things outside of all that, live a little. You must have a hobby or an interest outside of work?'

Matt laughed at that, though Harry cut it short with a glare.

'No, I don't,' he said, though perhaps running counted. Except that wasn't so much a hobby as a necessity, a vital and painful undertaking to help him be healthy and in shape.

Leslie entered the study, pulled the chair over from behind the desk in the bay window, and smiled at Harry.

Harry wondered about what was really going on in her mind for her to have lost her husband that weekend, and under the worst, most violent of circumstances, but to be more concerned about a play. It was clear that she and her husband hated each other at the end, and had both found comfort in the company of others, but even so, there must have been some feelings there at the beginning, surely? And as she was here, he thought he may as well ask her the first question and get something cleared up before he went any further.

Harry took out his notebook. Matt followed suit.

'I understand you were round here Friday night, Mrs Hamilton, after the pub. Is that correct?'

Leslie's smile vanished.

'Oh, yes, I was,' she said. 'Did I not say? I didn't think it was important.'

'Can I ask what you were doing?'

Leslie stood up and did a twirl, her costume flaring.

'Surely the clue's in what I'm wearing. As I said at the door, the play, it's only two weeks away. We're rather busy.'

'I'm sure. What time did you leave?'

'I just popped in to pick up a pile of costumes. Took them back to give them all a good wash. They get a bit stinky, you see, stale, particularly if they've been in storage for a while.'

Harry remembered Jadyn saying that Leslie had been busy washing clothing when he had visited, so that added up.

He looked at Mr Wilson, who was leaning back in his chair, his hat in his lap, arms folded across his chest. After staring at the man just long enough to make him feel awkward, Harry turned back to Leslie.

'Your husband,' he said. 'Did he have trouble sleeping?'

'What? Lance? Never,' Leslie answered. 'Turn the light off and he'd be out in minutes, snoring away.'

'So, that's a no, then?'

'Very much so. Why do you ask?'

'We've found Zopiclone in his system,' Harry explained.

'They're sleeping tablets,' added Matt. 'The kind you have to get from your doctor. Rather a lot, too.'

'Sleeping tablets? Lance didn't need them,' Leslie said, and clicked her fingers. 'That's how quickly he would go to sleep.' She looked then at Wilson before returning her attention to Harry. 'He must've taken them when he got home.'

'But according to what you told us on Saturday, he didn't go home,' said Matt.

'That leads me to another question,' said Harry. 'How did you know?'

Leslie frowned.

'How did I know what?'

'That Lance hadn't gone home. He'd moved out. Warranted, he'd not exactly gone far, but what made you think he wasn't at home?'

'His car wasn't there.'

'We think that he may well have decided to walk,' said Harry. 'So, if he did, and he had then arrived home, you wouldn't know anyway, would you? And if you'll pardon me for saying so, I didn't get the impression that you'd be all that interested in his where-abouts. I just can't picture you sitting at the window, twitching the curtain, spying on him.'

Leslie opened her mouth, but no words came out.

Harry looked at Wilson. In his mind, slow cogs were turning, gears were engaging, pulling in information from every conversa-tion, every phone call, every meeting, and slotting it into place.

'Mr Wilson,' he said, 'do you enjoy your job?'

'Of course,' Wilson replied. 'As much as I can. Accountancy isn't exactly high adrenaline, but then neither am I.'

'It must be difficult, though, if you have to work with people you don't really like, perhaps don't approve of their practices.'

'It isn't easy, but the bills need to be paid,' Wilson said. 'Though I don't quite understand the question.'

Harry reached into his pocket, then placed on the table three items he had picked up from the office.

'When I was last here, you mentioned that you've just had a bit of decorating done,' he said.

'That's not a crime.'

'All depends on who's decorating,' said Matt.

Harry said, 'Jeff Weatherill was the decorator, yes?'

'How did you know?'

'Detective, remember?' Harry then changed tack once again. 'Leslie, you were here Friday night, picked up some costumes, then headed home, correct?'

'Yes.'

'How did you feel seeing Lance at the meeting, then at the pub, after what he did to you?'

'Did what?'

'Mr Wilson here has already informed me that your husband struck you. Being in the same room as him, so soon after that, well, it must've been very hard for you.'

Leslie stared at Wilson, trying to work out what to say next.

'We had an argument, that's all,' she said. 'Lance told me he'd filed for divorce. I mean, of course he was going to, and I was going to do the same, but I was angry he'd got there first. We argued, and he hit me. Not the first time it's happened, either.'

As Leslie was speaking, Harry noticed Wilson's arms unfold, and his fists clench, before he crossed them again, though more relaxed this time, his right hand resting over his left thigh, close to his belt.

Harry leaned forward to point at the items on the table.

'These letters,' he said, lifting up the copies Jadyn had made. 'Now, Leslie, you were surprised when my constable found these, were you not? In fact, I think you said something along the lines of, *Why didn't he tell me*, correct?'

'I suppose so, yes.'

'Can I ask who you were referring to when you said that?'

'Lance, I suppose,' Leslie said.

Harry rested the letters on the table in full view. He then picked up the letter that had been found in Lance's jacket.

'This,' he said, 'was found in your husband's jacket pocket the night he was murdered. As you can see, it says, *I know it's you. I've always known.* Now, do either of you have any idea what that might mean, or to whom he might be referring?'

Leslie and Andrew stayed quiet.

'You see, what I think,' said Harry, and he glanced at Matt just then to make sure the DS was keeping up, 'is that Lance knew who had written these letters. We believe that on the night he was killed, he was actually planning to give this letter here to the person who had sent him these. Maybe it was to wind them up a little, that kind of thing who knows? More fun than just confronting them, perhaps, maybe even a bit more threatening. But do you know what I think? I think he got it wrong. I think it was someone else entirely who had written these.'

'Where are you going with this?' Leslie asked.

Harry reached for the third item on the table, another sheet of paper folded in half, and opened it.

'This is the list you gave me, Andrew,' he said, using Wilson's first name pointedly enough to get his attention. He placed the list on the table and stared at Wilson, holding his gaze with hard eyes. 'The *handwritten* list you gave me.'

'Well?'

For a moment, no one said a word.

Harry kept his eyes on Wilson, staring hard, and saw Matt lean forward, alert.

Then Wilson jumped to his feet. In his hands was a sword, and he was pointing it directly at Harry's throat.

THIRTY-SIX

'It wasn't my fault,' Wilson said. 'He shouldn't have done what he did!'

Wilson's reaction caught everyone by surprise, and that angered Harry more than anything, as his eyes focused on the sword blade, the pointy end of which was pinching the skin of his throat.

Matt stood up to confront Wilson, but the man swung the sword violently. Matt dodged out of the way just in time, slamming back down into his chair. Then the tip of the blade was back at Harry's throat.

'Don't be a bloody idiot,' he said.

'But it wasn't my fault!' Wilson repeated. 'I didn't mean for any of it to happen!'

'He's right,' Leslie said. 'It wasn't Andrew's fault. It was Lance. All of it. You have to believe us.'

'Frankly, it's hard to believe what anyone's saying when they're trying to persuade you with the dangerous end of a sabre,' said Harry.

He wasn't entirely sure what had just happened. His summations so far had clearly been on the nail, but he hadn't really expected a confession. He'd been in stickier situations, true, but this was the first time he'd been threatened with a sword.

The blade stayed where it was.

Harry saw Matt leaning forward, ready to pounce again, but Harry gave a quick shake of his head and had him restrain himself.

'He just turned up here, shouting and banging on the door and being abusive,' Wilson said. 'He's not a nice man, Mr Grimm, not a nice man at all!'

'That's a moot point now, really, isn't it?' said Harry, and looked at Leslie. 'When Constable Okri showed the letters to you, you said you didn't know why he hadn't told you. Jadyn thought you were talking about your husband, but it wasn't Lance you were talking about, was it? It was Andrew.'

'I came straight round here, once your constable had gone, and asked Andrew what the hell he'd been thinking,' Leslie said. 'I was livid. But I understood in the end. He did it for me, that was all. He meant well by it.'

Harry looked down the blade to Andrew, wondering why the man couldn't have just bought her flowers instead.

'Understood what, Andrew?' Harry asked. 'Why did you send those letters? And just how the hell did you go from sending them to Lance, to having Lance end up in Sally's studio?'

Andrew was quiet, his eyes darting between Harry and Leslie and Matt. The sword in his hand was unsteady, but that didn't make Harry feel any better about where he was in relation to it.

'I'd had enough, that's all,' Andrew said. 'The way he treated people, the way he treated Leslie. It wasn't right. It wasn't. I thought the letters might scare him off a bit. I'm not one for confrontation, you see, Mr Grimm. I'm not a fighting man. But I understand words, so I used them.'

'But he didn't know they were from you, did he?'

Wilson frowned.

'You type all your letters.' said Harry. 'You told me that yourself, remember? You said how even your signature is electronic. He wouldn't recognise your writing at all, would he? Which is why my guess is that Lance thought they were from Archie, and not you at all, and why he then gazumped that house deal Archie had with Ivy. That's the only reason he'd have done what he did, isn't it?'That revelation sent a shockwave through the room, so Harry used it to his advantage and pressed on.

'And that makes me wonder why Lance was here that night at all. I mean, it's pretty far out of his way on his journey home, seeing as he was walking, isn't it? Until now, we assumed he'd got his chips and stumbled off home. But he didn't, did he? Which leads me neatly back to your recent decorating.'Wilson's frown only deepened.

'Decorating? What are you talking about?'

'Lance's car,' said Harry, 'Again, we assumed it was it was someone who hated Lance - I mean there's no shortage of suspects, is there? But just now, as we were on our way here in the car, it suddenly struck me as a tad unnecessary. A tad theatrical, you might even say. Which again, brought me back to you. My guess is you did that. As a diversion. It was clever, I'll give you that.'

Leslie looked shocked.

'What about Lance's car?'

'You knew he'd won it playing poker, didn't you?' said Harry, still focused on Wilson. 'You figured damaging the car with the paint you had left over from your hallway remodel would be a nice little diversion. You knew it was an end-of-the-line colour, guessed we would probably link the paint chucked all over the car to Jeff. Something to muddy the waters of the investigation. Draw the spotlight from you and onto Jeff. Because it was you, wasn't it, Andrew? You murdered Lance and then you trashed his car to throw us off the scent.'

'You've no proof,' sneered Wilson, his confidence undermined, however, by the colour rapidly draining from his face.'The paint is the proof,' Harry said, his voice cutting into Wilson's reply. 'Now, back to Lance turning up at your door.' He turned his eyes on Leslie. 'I saw your car parked outside when we arrived. Lovely little red sports car, isn't it?'

'Yes, it is,' Leslie said.

'Stands out, as well. It would've been easy for Lance to spot, I think. He'd have put two and two together, and perhaps thought it would be fun to come and have a word.'

'He was drunk,' Leslie spat contemptuously. 'He could hardly stand up straight.'

'He wasn't drunk,' explained Harry. 'He was doped up to the eyeballs, poor bloke.' 'Through no fault of his own, I might add. The drug in his system, if you overdose on it, it doesn't just make you sleep-walk; you end up doing things you can't even remember doing when you wake up.'

'Like what?' asked Leslie.

'Like driving a car, for example. Or seeing your soon-to-be ex-wife's car outside the house of your accountant, going inside, and attacking her and her not-so-secret lover.'

Leslie gasped.

'He was hammering at the door!' Wilson said, his voice loud and pinched. 'Screaming Leslie's name. I had to do something, didn't I? You understand that, surely?'

'What did you do?' Harry asked.

'It was self-defence!' Wilson said, blurting the words out, and covering Harry in a spray of spit. 'I didn't mean for it to happen, I promise you!'

Harry noticed that the sword's blade was dropping ever so slowly.

'He was at the door making all that noise,' continued Wilson. 'I went to see what he wanted. He pushed past me, started yelling for Leslie. She was in here, you see, in the study, and he just came in and started pushing her around. It was awful.'

'He was out of control,' said Leslie. 'Raging, but he wasn't making sense. Kept yelling at me that he'd taught Archie a lesson for what he'd done, and that now it was time for me to be taught a lesson, too. I was terrified. Then he grabbed me.' She pointed at her throat. 'Here.'

'Thus the scarf,' said Harry.

'It all happened so fast,' said Wilson, the blade dropping further as he looked across at Leslie. 'I thought he was going to kill her. I grabbed him and pulled him away, but then he came at me and ...'

Andrew's voice died.

'And what, Andrew?' Harry asked.

The sudden silence that descended was suffocating, and to Harry, it seemed as though the costumes hanging on the book-shelves were listening in like inquisitive ghosts.

'I didn't even realise it was in my hand,' Wilson said, his voice breaking, turning into a sob. 'It was just there, and I lashed out at him, that was all. I didn't aim, I didn't mean to do anything, I just wanted to keep him away, to get him to stop.'

'That isn't a dummy sword, is it?' Harry asked.

Andrew shook his head.

'I've had it for years. Bought it from Tennants, that antiques place over in Leyburn. I don't even use it on stage, you know? It's in its scabbard the whole time, so it's not dangerous. Just thought it would be nice hanging on the wall, you see? And then, when we decided to do Calamity Jane, I thought it would be perfect.'

Harry remembered what Sowerby had said about how Lance's hands had been removed, one cleanly, the other sawn off.

The sword fell further, then Wilson sat back down.

'I just wanted him to stop, that's all. I didn't mean ... I didn't mean to do what I did.'

'He bled out in this room, then,' Harry said.

Wilson nodded. Leslie, he noticed, was statue still and white as marble.

'My guess is that those air fresheners plugged in out in the hallway aren't to disguise the smell of paint,' Harry added.

'I sent Leslie home,' Wilson said. 'Told her I would deal with it. Not that I knew what I was going to do. Then I remembered the slap Sally had given him in the pub and I thought, why not?'

'Most people would think, "I know, I'll call the police,"' Matt said, shaking his head.

'I found the key to Sally's studio in Lance's pocket,' said Wilson. 'The idiot had left her label on it, so I thought, you know, if I made the crime scene bizarre enough, added a bit of theatre to it all, then it would never get back to me. It couldn't.'

'Which is why one hand wasn't enough,' Harry said.

'The second one took a while to cut off,' Wilson said. 'I used a kitchen knife, had to chop at the bone.'

Leslie's eyes widened in horror.

'Don't suppose you could tell us where they are?' Matt asked. 'We never found them.'

'Can't say I'm surprised,' Wilson said. 'That was the point really, to get rid of the evidence.'

'How, though?'

'The kiln,' Wilson said. 'Sally had shown me how to use one. Did you know that a kiln runs twice as hot as a cremator? If there's anything left at all, it'll just be ashes now.'

Harry made a note of that.

'Is there anything else?' Harry asked.

'Yes,' Wilson said. 'Leslie had nothing to do with it. It's all me.'

'But you turned up at Sally's pottery studio,' said Harry, looking back at Leslie. 'How did you know?'

'This is Hawes,' Leslie said. 'Everyone knows everything; haven't you learned that, yet?'

'Haven't I just,' Harry replied, somewhat ruefully. 'I knew it couldn't be anything else.'

'But your reaction,' Harry said. 'You were visibly upset. I was there. I saw how you tried to attack Sally Dent.'

Leslie shrugged.

'Best acting I've done in years,' she said.

'But she had nothing to do with it,' Wilson repeated. 'It was all me. I'll swear to that. What do I have to do to make you understand it was all me? Lance attacked her, then he went for me. All I did was try and stop him.'

'With a sword,' Harry said, then looked over to Matt, who

reached into a pocket and pulled out a pair of rubber gloves, slipping them on. 'Would you mind?'

Wilson held out the sword hilt first and Matt took it from his hands, relief in his eyes.

'I'm sorry,' Wilson said. 'I'm just so sorry.'

Harry thought back to what Jen had said earlier at Sally Dent's house. Sometimes, we all hate this job, he thought. He then stood up and, with Matt's help, led them both out of the house, reading them their rights as they went.

THIRTY-SEVEN

The next day, Harry was at the vicarage in Askrigg, sitting with Anna and Gordy. Anna was getting ready to head out, and Gordy was stretched out on the sofa.

'You look well,' he said a little too enthusiastically, sitting down in a comfy chair opposite.

'You may have no use of most of the nerves in your face, but I can still tell you're lying,' smiled Gordy. 'You mean well, though, and I appreciate it.'

'I'm not lying,' Harry protested, but Anna jumped in.

'Quit while you're ahead,' she said, doing up her jacket.

Harry sat back, trying to think of something to say.

Gordy looked gaunt, he thought, as though somewhere in her mind she was watching a high-definition replay of what had happened, all of it in slow motion, each and every moment etched into her mind forever.

Harry knew what that was like, better than most.

'So, your brother, then,' he said, looking over at Anna.

'That's where I'm going now,' Anna said. 'What he's done, what he was trying to do, his state of mind, none of it's easy.'

'He tried to hit you with his car,' Harry said. 'He could've killed you. And he nearly killed Gordy.'

'I know,' Anna replied. 'It's what happens next though. That's what's worrying me.'

'He'll be prosecuted,' said Harry. 'That's what happens next.'

'He needs help, though,' said Anna.

'That's as may be, but it doesn't excuse what he's done, does it? If it did, the prisons would be empty.'

Anna walked over and rested a gentle kiss on Gordy's forehead.

'No moving around while I'm out,' she said. 'Bathroom and kitchen, and that's it. Understood?'

Gordy said, 'She's a bit of a battle axe when she wants to be.' Then she winked at Harry.

Anna left the room and Harry heard the front door open and close.

'Sorry about all this,' Gordy said, gesturing at herself laid out on the sofa, almost as though she would never move again.

'Nothing to apologise for, is there?' Harry said. 'You just need to take a bit of time and get yourself better, that's all. It's not the same on the team without you there.'

Gordy smiled weakly.

'I might need more than rest to feel better after this,' she replied.

'What do you mean?' asked Harry, worry creeping into his words.

'I don't know. This...it feels like more than just a setback. It's made me realise just how short life is, and question what exactly I'm doing with my life.'

'You're a copper. Always have been. I know that better than anyone. We're cut from the same cloth, you and I.'

'That's what worries me,' added Gordy, staring hard at him. 'I mean, no offense Harry, but look at you. And I don't mean the scars on your face. It's the ones on the inside that worry me. And I'm collecting a fair few of my own.' She winced slightly, rearranging herself slightly on the sofa. 'Do you know how many bereaved parents, husbands, wives, sons and daughters I've had to break the worst possible kind of news to these past few years?'

Harry just stared at her, lost for words.

'No? Neither do I. But it wears you down. You know that as well as I do.'

'But that's the job. It's what we do,' countered Harry. 'And things like this,' he added, 'sure, they happen now and then, but we lock them away and move on.' But even as the words left his mouth, he realized how ridiculous he sounded.

'Yeah, right,' snorted Gordy. 'Except they don't go anywhere, do they? Not really. You end up dragging it all with you, and at some point it all gets so heavy that it stops you moving forward and getting on with life. Sound familiar to you?'

Harry said nothing, but he couldn't help thinking back to his chat with Grace at the Fountain.

'Look, you're tired and only just out of hospital,' he continued, somewhat desperately. 'You'll be back at work soon enough and things will look different then.'

Gordy shook her head.

'No, Harry, that's not what I meant.'

Harry felt his gut twist.

'What do you mean? And I'm only asking because if you mean what I think you mean, then you can't mean it, surely? You're not leaving?'

'I don't know, Harry. I've a few things to work out, but I can't promise anything either way at the moment.'

Harry sat stunned, unsure what to say next. As a visit to check up on an injured friend, this wasn't exactly going as Harry had expected, and certainly not as he wanted.

'But you can't leave.'

'Yes, I can.'

'I know you can, but you know damned well what I mean.'

Gordy squeezed Harry's hand.

'I need to live a little,' she said. 'Whatever that means. And so do you, I'm guessing.'

Harry went to speak, but was interrupted by Gordy's phone buzzing.

'You need to get going,' she said.

'I do?'

'Jadyn's waiting outside for you, isn't he?'

'How do you know?'

Gordy lifted up her phone from the sofa.

'Anna texted me. Saw him outside and he asked how long you were going to be and if you could hurry up.'

'He's keen, I'll give him that,' Harry said.

'Sounds urgent.'

'It is,' said Harry. 'Jadyn's apparently smashed open the vast underground network of illegal vapes in Wensleydale.'

'How vast?'

'We're heading off to arrest the son of a newsagent,' Harry said, and Gordy chuckled. 'He's been selling dodgy disposables to teenagers. A kid ended up in hospital.'

'Definitely urgent, then.'

Harry stood up.

'Look after yourself,' he said.

'I aim to,' Gordy replied. 'And you'd best do the same. Open your eyes for once, Harry, and have a look around you. What you've got? It's pretty special.'

'I know.'

Outside, Harry dropped into the passenger seat next to Jadyn, pulled the door shut, and clipped himself in.

'Ready to crack a few skulls?' he asked.

'Like you wouldn't believe, Boss,' Jadyn said.

'Then let's go and pay Nathan a little visit, shall we?'

———

There's no rest for Harry and the team as they're soon in the grip of another chilling investigation in Dark Harvest

———

JOIN THE VIP CLUB!

WOULD you like to find out what happened when Matt went to investigate exactly what was going on with that chainsaw and motorbike? Of course you do! Then download it here and sign up to my VIP Club! You will also receive the exclusive short origin story, 'Homecoming', to find out where it all began, and how Harry decided to join the police. By joining the VIP Club, you'll receive regular updates on the series, plus VIP access to a photo gallery of locations from the books, and the chance to win amazing free stuff in some fantastic competitions.

You can also connect with other fans of DCI Grimm and his team by joining The Official DCI Harry Grimm Reader Group.

Enjoyed this book? Then please tell others!

The best thing about reviews is they help people like you: other readers. So, if you can spare a few seconds and leave a review, that would be fantastic. I love hearing what readers think about my books, so you can also email me the link to your review at dave@davidjgatward.com.

ABOUT DAVID J. GATWARD

David had his first book published when he was 18 and has written extensively for children and young adults. *Dead Man's Hands* is his fifteenth DCI Harry Grimm crime thriller.

Visit David's website to find out more about him and the DCI Harry Grimm books.

facebook.com/davidjgatwardauthor

ALSO BY DAVID J. GATWARD

THE DCI HARRY GRIMM SERIES

Welcome to Yorkshire. Where the beer is warm, the scenery beautiful, and the locals have murder on their minds.

Printed in Great Britain
by Amazon

27431962R10165